CW00661358

The BALLER

— A DOWN AND DIRTY FOOTBALL NOVEL —

VI KEELAND

The Baller

Edited by: Caitlin Alexander
Cover model: Jack Ryan
Cover designer: Sommer Stein, Perfect Pear Creative
Photographer: Simon Barnes
Interior Formatting & Proofreading by Elaine York
www.allusiongraphics.com

THIS ONE IS FOR JAKE.
(JUST DON'T READ IT, OKAY?)

Delilah
CHAPTER 1

My boss was a world-class dick.

Monday afternoon mandatory meetings consisted of three hours of Charles Ulysses Macy *the Third* telling the mostly men in the sports programs division about his latest conquest. I stared blankly out the window as he droned on, wondering if any of his male ancestors had gotten their pillowcases monogrammed with their initials. Imagine how much character some bright red throw pillows would add to a guest room—flaunting the initials the Macy men saw fit to pass down through their lineage—CUM.

I smirked and stood.

"Ms. Maddox?" Mr. CUM called out from the head of the conference table. The table seated twenty, and the chairs were three rows deep. Sixty pairs of eyes turned to look in my direction.

"Yes, Mr. Macy?"

"Did you have something to say?"

"No. I was actually hoping to slip out quietly. There's a game tonight, and I need to get down to wardrobe."

"Well, run along. Don't let a little thing like a team meeting keep you from playing dress-up."

Dick.

There were a few snickers as I headed for the door, but I didn't really care. Most of them were just jealous anyway. Tonight I would cover the New York Steel playing the Cowboys live while they watched the game on TV with a beer in one hand and the other tucked into the waistband of their sweatpants.

More than thirty journalists had interviewed for my new position as World Media Broadcasting's staff football sportscaster. But it was me who was going to talk to the players tonight after the game—not them. That didn't make me very popular around the proverbial water cooler. Even though I'd worked eighty hours a week the last few years to get where I was, the men who worked thirty were the first ones to blame my success on my magical vagina. *Screw them.*

Instead of heading straight to wardrobe, I detoured to my office. Indie wasted no time following me inside. She flicked her ankles and sent her heels sailing into the air before perching on the arm of a guest chair, her bare feet on the seat.

"Thought you could use that." Her eyes pointed to a bar of Irish Spring sitting in the middle of my messy desk.

"Do I smell?"

"It's for the locker room after the game. It's been a while for you. Figured you could use a little *I dropped the soap* doggy-style slam."

"You're worse than Mr. CUM." I packed files of research into my leather briefcase while we chatted. I knew every statistic by heart, but I planned to review it all again on the train anyway. "No soap for me. I have another month on my cleanse."

"Cleanses are for colons, not vaginas."

"It's only been five months, but it's been good for the soul."

Indie snickered. "And for Duracell."

"You should try it. Six months date-free is a great detox."

"I'll stick to juice cleanses, thanks." Indie opened her bag and took out a bottle of hot pink nail polish. She proceeded to begin to paint her toenails, which were already hot pink, right there in my office.

"What are you doing?"

6

She stopped and looked up at me as if I were a moron. "Painting my toes. I put a first coat on this morning, but this color really needs a second. One-coat polish, my ass."

"Do you have to paint your nails in my office?"

"It'll smell up mine."

"But it's okay to smell up mine?"

"You're always smelling shit anyway. Books, food . . . don't think I didn't see you take a whiff of the new tennis ball you took out of the canister when we played a few weeks ago."

"That's different. I *choose* to smell those." It wasn't the time to admit that two days ago I'd ordered L'Oreal Perfumeries nail polish. Why hadn't someone invented scented nail polish sooner?

"You're leaving anyway." She shrugged. "You get to go interview sweaty half-naked men. I should have gone into journalism instead of marketing."

"But you're so good at selling people a line of crap."

"You're right. I am." She sighed. "Hey . . . Easton is back today."

"I know. Two weeks sooner than originally thought."

"Did you know his nickname is Subway?"

I squinted. "No one calls him Subway in the press."

"Ahh. It's not the press's nickname."

I was skeptical, but I bit the hook she'd baited anyway. "Who calls him Subway, then?"

"Women." Indie wiggled her eyebrows. Her bright red lipstick was a shade lighter than her flame-colored hair. The look totally worked for her, although it was hard to focus on anything but her colorful lips set against her pale skin.

"Because he's originally from Brooklyn and rode the subway to visit women?"

"Nope. But that's not a bad guess."

"Enlighten me." I slung my leather bag over my shoulder. "I need to get down to wardrobe and get going."

"It's way more fun to make you guess."

7

I exited my office, and Indie followed me to the elevator, walking on the balls of her feet to avoid smudging her nails. "Because he can ride all day?"

"No. But I bet he can. Did you see that last touchdown dance he did? That man can swivel his narrow hips like a pro stripper."

The elevator dinged, and she followed me in. I pushed two for wardrobe. "Because he packs in the ladies like the morning commute?"

"That one sucked."

"Unless you're going to help me get dressed and follow me to the stadium, I think our game is just about over anyway."

The elevator stopped three floors down. Indie held the doors open, shouting at me as I walked down the long hall toward wardrobe, "Wrong subway. Not the commuting vehicle, the sandwich shops. You know . . . where you can get a *delicious twelve-inch hero.*"

I shook my head, yelling back without turning around. "Good-bye, Indie."

"Wear red, it's your best color. And a cinch belt. Something that shows off your little waist and curvy hips. I'm sure last year's Super Bowl hero will appreciate the extra effort!"

It was my second coverage of the New York Steel, but my first time in the locker room. I stood outside with a dozen other reporters and tried to look as nonchalant as they did. The big blue door was heavily dented, likely the victim of player frustration. Multiple championship wins framed the oversized door, last year's Super Bowl victory sign proudly displayed in the middle under the team's logo.

After a few minutes, a security guard opened the door and motioned everyone to enter. Some reporters held up their badges as they passed; others apparently needed no introduction. Henry, as the worn tag on his guard uniform indicated, greeted those by their first names. A few reporters asked how his daughter was feeling. Apparently, Larissa

8

had recently broken her arm playing basketball. This was a tight-knit group.

I was anxious to get inside, but certainly in no hurry. The crowd thinned quickly, leaving just four of us in the hall. I took a deep breath and marched to the door, trying not to let my fear show. I smiled and held up my badge, pointing to his. *Henry Inez.* "Hi."

"Hi." He nodded.

"Your initials. They spell Hi."

Great job not letting my fear show. I tended to ramble when I was nervous.

Hi looked down at me, his brows furrowed. Then he took my badge, patted his chest as if looking for reading glasses, then sighed and held my card out at a distance to read it. "Got a middle name, Delilah Maddox?"

"Anne."

He grinned. "Dam."

The silly exchange did something to calm me, and I let out a breath I hadn't realized I was holding.

Hi offered me back my badge. "You're Tom's daughter, right?"

I nodded.

"Worked here thirty years. They don't make 'em like him anymore. One of the finest athletes to ever walk into this room. No ego. A true gentleman. I'm sorry for your loss. It was a loss to the entire sport."

"Thank you."

He pointed inside the locker room. "These boys? Nothing but ego. Don't let 'em get to you. Okay, Dam?"

I took my credentials back from him with a nod and a hopeful smile. "I won't."

The first thing that surprised me as I made my way into the inner sanctum was its sheer size. I'd seen enough pictures to know locker rooms were large, but taking it all in from inside, the vast expanse had me instantly awestruck. Wide lockers lined the perimeter; the center was mostly open, with a few seating areas set up. Each seating area had four wide leather chairs and a glass table between them. Everything was just so pristine and organized. Lighting showcased the names above each locker, and players were chatting away with reporters all over the place. The mood was light and easy, most likely due to the score at the end of the game. The Steel had won twenty-eight to nothing. Nobody seemed to notice me—the lone woman standing in the center of the room. Or if they noticed, they didn't seem bothered at all. My stiffened shoulders relaxed a little.

I found Nick, my cameraman, who was already inside, and saw that the Steel's kicker wasn't busy, so I headed over to ask him a few questions. He was still in his uniform, but he removed the rest of his padding as we spoke. It was an easy first interview to get under my belt, and the exchange made me confident.

"Thank you for your time, Aaron," I said when the camera switched off.

"Anytime. And welcome. You replaced Frank Munnard, right?"

"I did."

"Guy was awful. Glad he retired. He got half our names wrong even though they're printed right above our heads." His tilted his chin up to the large lettering above his locker. "And thanks for that last question about coaching my son's football team. He'll be excited I had the opportunity to mention his name on the air."

I smiled, remembering when I was a little girl and my dad mentioned my name on the air. It made me feel like a celebrity. I hadn't thought of it, but those memories may have had a lot to do with why I always made my last interview question a personal one. Watching my father week after week, the statistics talk got old quick. But the small glimpses into a player's personal life always held my attention. It made them seem more like real people and less like hotshot athletes.

Moving on, I scanned the room. One area of the giant rotunda was packed, reporters lined up so deep I couldn't even catch a glimpse of the player. But I knew who they were waiting for without having to look up at the name above the locker.

Brody Easton.

Everywhere the man went the media followed, mostly because he was an arrogant showman who gave them something to report. It didn't hurt that the camera loved his handsome face and body, as did the women who frequently surrounded him in photos.

I hit a few other players, skipping the ones who were in various states of undress. A lot of skin was flashing around, but most of it was bare chest and ass. Almost all of the men turned and faced their lockers as they changed. My eyes might have feasted a second or two on Darryl Smith's tight ass—*damn, that's some muscular rear*—but I quickly caught myself. I needed to act like a professional, especially if I expected the players to do the same.

When the crowd circling Easton finally dwindled, I made my way over. He had a towel wrapped around his waist and no shirt on. *Holy shit.* Maybe this cleanse wasn't so smart after all. It was like going to the supermarket when you hadn't eaten in days. And since I had a penchant for athletes, this supermarket trip was filled with all of my favorite foods. *I need to get my shit together.*

The cameraman in front of me raised his lighting up into position to film, dragging my attention from Brody's titanesque shoulders to the face that had been splashed across so many Monday morning newspapers. His jaw was rugged and chiseled, with just a hint of a five o'clock shadow on his sun-kissed skin. I followed the carved line of his cheekbones up, passing sinfully full lips and an imperious Roman nose before rising to the most incredible eyes I'd ever seen. *Jesus. He's even sexier in person.*

Pale green, almond-shaped eyes sparkled beneath luscious thick, dark lashes. His eyes were captivating in a way that startled me. I shook my head in an attempt to disconnect from the magnetic vision in front of me. Luckily, Nick forced my attention back to reality.

"Easton's been vocal about thinking women shouldn't be allowed in the locker room. Don't count on him being as cordial to you as he is to the good ol' boys." Nick had been filming the team for more than ten years; his warning was from experience rather than rumor.

I also knew about the feud between Brody Easton and Susan Metzinger, a reporter from a rival station. She'd publicly slammed him for using foul language in the locker room, and the incident had turned into a month-long tabloid war. He suggested she didn't belong in the locker room anyway and that none of the *male* reporters seemed to mind. She did a full-page write-up dedicated to Easton quotes in which he used language she found degrading to women. The quotes were pretty much all taken out of context, but the article was accompanied by a half-dozen video stills that caught his eyes looking in the direction of a woman's ass or cleavage. Things only escalated from there. It had happened more than a year ago, but I mentally prepared myself for attitude from the famed quarterback.

"You ready?" Nick slung his bag over his shoulder and lifted his camera. The reporter in front of us wrapped up his interview and shook hands with Easton.

As I'll ever be. "Sure."

I stepped forward and extended my hand. "I'm Delilah Maddox with WMBC Sports News."

A slow grin spread across Easton's face. He surprised me by leaning in and kissing me on the cheek. "Pleasure to meet you."

I wasn't sure if he was baiting me into an argument—expecting me to lash out at him for kissing me when he'd just shaken the last *male* reporter's hand—or if he was trying to use his blatant sexuality to throw me off. Either way, I wasn't playing his game. I cleared my throat and stood straighter, even though my knees felt a little wobbly.

"Do you mind if I ask you some questions?"

"Why else would you be in here?"

I ignored his sarcasm. He was still smiling at me. Actually, it was more like a smirk, and it made me feel like a toy he was about to play with. "You ready, Nick?" My cameraman finished setting up the lighting, then lifted the camera into position and gave me a hand signal.

"Congratulations on the win today, Brody. How is your knee feeling after your first game back?" I lifted my microphone high, knowing Nick was filming in close.

"I feel . . . " He nonchalantly reached to the towel wrapped around his waist and tugged at the corner. The towel fell to the ground. "Great. I feel great. And how about you? It's your first trip into the locker room, isn't it? Do you like what you see so far?" His lips curled up into a full-blown wicked smile.

Before I could catch myself, my eyes dropped to his naked lower half. *Shit*. He was dangling in the wind. I totally got distracted by just *how low* the thing dangled. *Subway*. The nickname was damn well suited. It was probably a full minute before I responded to his question. *A full minute of dead air time. Great.* "Yes. Umm . . . the locker room is . . . ummm . . . nice."

I sounded like a total ditz. *On air*.

The jackass continued interviewing me. "Is it as big as you thought it would be?"

"Ummm . . . it's much bigger than I imagined."

His smile grew even wider.

Ugh.

I needed to get back on track or my first locker room interview would become a laughingstock blooper. Viewers had no idea he was naked from the waist down. "Do you think you were at one hundred percent today?"

His eyebrows jumped. "If you're referring to today's game, definitely. I had one hundred percent out there on the field. There're some other areas where I have a lot of *growth potential*, but my knee felt one hundred percent today."

His pale green eyes darkened, and I watched his long lashes lower. I followed his line of sight, and suddenly I was staring at his naked package. *Again. Damn it.* My eyes darted back up, but I felt my cheeks heating. I had to end this, or I was going to be beet red on air.

"Well, welcome back. And congratulations on today's win."

I waited until Nick lowered his camera and turned off the light. Then I looked right at Brody Easton's smug face. "You're an asshole, you know that?"

His eyes sparkled. "I do."

I heard the chuckles and high fives at my back as I stormed out of the locker room.

CHAPTER 2

"Good morning, Mr. Easton."

"Morning, Shannon. How is she this week?"

"She's been a little down and her sleeping has been a bit off. But your Tuesday visits always seem to cheer her up. She's up and ready for you. I think she's in the day room."

Grouper stopped sweeping the hall as I approached. "Grandson is going to be disappointed."

"And that shit has nothing to do with him not getting a game ball this week. Damn kid's named after a fish."

Grouper chuckled and extended his hand. "You looked like shit out there yesterday."

"You can't sweep for crap," I said, smiling. "I should talk to the administrator about firing your old ass. Place looks like a blind man cleans it. And I threw for two hundred twenty-eight yards . . . that's not looking like shit. That's me being fuck-ass spectacular."

"Marlene'll wash that mouth out with soap, she hears you using that language."

He wasn't kidding. She might be eighty years old, but the little lady still scared the shit out of me. When Willow and I first started dating, I knew it was Marlene who would chop my balls off if I hurt her granddaughter, and not her large husband.

I spent another minute exchanging insults with Grouper before heading into the day room to look for Marlene. I didn't have to look very far. There were only a few people in the room, and the crazy old bat was the only one wearing an evening gown.

"Hot date tonight, Marlene?" She was sitting in her wheelchair; I leaned down and kissed her forehead. It took her a minute, but then her eyes smiled, and I knew today's visit would be better than last week's.

"Well, don't you look handsome?"

"I always look handsome." I wheeled her to a corner of the room and positioned her chair across from me before taking a seat on the couch.

"Shouldn't you be wearing a tuxedo?"

Well, that explains the evening gown. As usual, I went with it. "I had practice this morning. I'm going to change in a little while."

She nodded. "Tell my granddaughter to wear a blue dress. It will bring out her eyes."

Willow's eyes were a cross between sky blue and spring-grass green. If she wore blue, her eyes changed to aquamarine. If she wore green, her eyes shifted to peridot. I had always preferred it when she didn't wear either—I could stare at those eyes all day debating which color I loved more. Unless the color she was wearing was flesh, then it wasn't her eyes that I was as focused on.

"I'll make sure she wears blue."

Marlene got quiet for a few minutes, and I watched her expression, knowing she was going somewhere else. I just never knew where we'd land.

"I think someone stole my teeth."

My eyebrows shot up. "Your teeth are in your mouth, Marlene."

Slowly, her shaky hand reached up and found her pearly white dentures. "Damn it. I've been looking all over for them for nothing."

My visit went like that for at least another hour, back and forth between topics—some thirty years old, some current. I had to be at the stadium at two to watch the game playback. Not wanting a two-thousand-dollar fine for being late to a mandatory offensive-line meeting, I stood to say my goodbyes.

"Do you want me to bring you someplace before I head out?"

"Heidelman's on Thirty-Fourth and Amsterdam. I can go for a Reuben."

"I'll bring you one when I come back next week." I leaned down and kissed her forehead, skipping telling her Heidelman's had closed fifteen years ago.

"And don't let old man Heidelman make the sandwich. That old man is a few Bradys short of a bunch."

I chuckled. "Got it. No old man Heidelman."

"Give Willow a kiss for me."

"Will do. And you make sure to tell Grouper your room needs a better cleaning, okay?"

"Does it? Okay."

Marlene wanted to stay in the day room, but I popped into her empty room on my way out to check things out. As usual, it was pristine. Hell, you could eat off the floor with how Grouper kept the place. But I liked to get Marlene in on the action of busting his balls anyway.

On my way out, the old bastard was washing the glass front doors. I splayed my five fingers wide to intentionally leave a handprint on the spotless door. "You missed a spot."

"Asshole."

"And proud of it."

"Next week, I want two balls."

"Yours shrivel up and fall off or something?"

"Bite me."

"Later, Grouper."

Delilah
CHAPTER 3

"Did you not hear a word I just said?" I shouted at Indie. We were in her car, driving to the Baxter Bowl, a charity event held every year in honor of former player Marcus Baxter. Marcus was a field-goal kicker for the New York Steel who'd been killed by a drunk driver six years ago. The team and league had been sponsoring the charity event ever since. WMBC had purchased three tables this year. It was my first invite, but Indie, as VP of Marketing, had been attending for years.

"I heard you. He's a jerk. He showed you his dick. He embarrassed you."

"And yet you ask me if I dreamt about him last night?"

"Did you?"

"No!" *Maybe.*

She shrugged. "I would have."

"The guy is arrogant and crass."

"Sounds like he's your type."

She has a point. My dating history wasn't the greatest. I tended to be attracted to the wrong type of guy. "Not anymore. After this cleanse is over, I'm only dating men who are nice, well mannered and dependable."

"I'll introduce you to my father's best friend, Hughey."

"Very funny."

"What? He's very nice. I swear. I'm pretty sure that's why his wife divorced him and married her forty-five-year-old ballroom dance instructor. He was too boring...I mean nice."

"I'll keep Hughey in mind."

"So what are you going to do next week if he does it again?"

"Ignore it and continue with the interview. I expected him to be a dick. I didn't expect him to *show me* his dick. He caught me off guard. I'll be ready for him next time."

"I'm ready for him right now. If I was wearing panties, they might be a little wet thinking about that body. Do you think he'll be there tonight?"

"I hope not." A minuscule, dark, masochistic part of my brain looked forward to seeing him. Although there was no way in hell I'd ever admit it.

My table at the Baxter Bowl was filled with an interesting mix of people from WMBC and New York Steel management, including the station owner's charming grandson, Michael Langley, who was also head of broadcasting operations—technically that made him Mr. CUM's boss's boss. We'd been talking for almost an hour, and I was surprised to find we had so much in common. We'd both attended Stanford, although he was a few years my senior. Both of our dads had been professional quarterbacks when they were young, and we both rose at the crack of dawn. The Langley family was legendary in New York sports. Michael's grandfather not only owned WMBC, but was also the majority owner of the New York Steel.

When they'd finished clearing our dinner plates, Michael leaned into me. "Want to dance?"

"Sure. I'd love to."

Out on the dance floor, he led me through one slow dance. He had a firm hand and definitely knew how to lead. And he was pretty easy on the eyes, too. *Matt Damon in glasses.* Well groomed, intelligent, and handsome—my night could be worse.

"I like your hair up." *Sweet too.*

It had taken the stylist almost two hours to tame my unruly mass of dark curls enough to pin it all on top of my head. A few tendrils had already escaped.

"Thank you. You don't smoke, do you? Because I'm pretty sure if I go anywhere near a cigarette, I might catch fire with the amount of spray the stylist had to put in to get it to stay."

Michael smiled. "No worries. I'm smoke-free."

Why isn't *this* the type of guy I usually dated? Following in his father's footsteps, Michael had played college football before a torn ACL ended his career before it even started. With his knowledge of the game and all-American good looks, his transition to sportscaster came easily. Although moving up the chain of command had taken him more behind the scenes the last few years. "Do you have any interviews planned this season? I'd love to watch you filming and learn. Your interviews always came across as if you were having a casual talk in the living room, rather than sitting on a set in front of cameras."

"Thank you. I actually don't have any on the calendar as of now, but you just gave me a reason to change that."

A new song had just started, and I was enjoying his company when a voice behind me said, "Can I cut in?"

My head whipped around, even though I had no doubt whom the gravelly voice belonged to.

Michael was gracious. "I hate to share. But I suppose I have been hogging the most beautiful woman at the event." He let go of my hand and stepped back with a gentlemanly nod. "Thank you for the dance, Delilah."

Again Brody Easton had caught me off guard. Before I knew it, I was dancing with the arrogant jerk. He wrapped his arms around me and pulled my body tight against his. Way tighter than Michael had held me.

"Good to see you again, Lois Lane."

The man had balls; I had to give him that. I looked him straight in the eyes. "Nice to see you with clothes on, Easton."

"Do you prefer me without?"

"I prefer you on the other side of the room."

He chuckled. It was a hearty laugh. "That's what happens sometimes when you decide you want to hang out in the men's locker room."

I tried to pull back, but he tightened his grip and held me in place. I craned my neck. "Let go of me."

"No."

"No?"

"That's right. No."

"I can scream at the top of my lungs."

"I'd like to hear you scream." His tone made it clear he meant he wanted me underneath him while I was doing the screaming.

"You're an asshole. You know that?"

"I do. You asked me that yesterday. For a reporter, you should really try changing up your questions more frequently."

My eyes bulged.

Easton shifted his hand down to the small of my back before twirling us around the dance floor. *Figures the prick can dance.*

"Are you seeing anyone?"

"You can't be serious?"

He ignored my comment. "Would you like to have dinner tonight?"

"We just ate."

"Dessert at my place, then?"

I couldn't help but laugh. "Did you hit your head at the game yesterday?"

"On a diet, huh?"

"Yeah. That's it. I don't want to go to your place for dessert because I'm on a diet."

"Well, that's just a shame." Easton smiled. He was actually pretty quick-witted and funny, but he was still an asshole. The song ended, and the band asked everyone to take a seat while the winners of the silent auction were announced.

"I'd say it was nice seeing you again, but I don't lie."

Easton grinned. He seemed to like my insults. But before I could walk away, he grabbed my hand. "Hey. Be careful with Langley. Met him a few times when he was a field reporter. Guy's a jerk."

"Isn't that ironic coming from you?"

"I am who you see. That guy isn't."

For the rest of the night, I mostly enjoyed myself. Indie introduced me to a load of people I'd never met before, and my conversation with Michael headed from friendly to flirting. A few times, as Michael and I were sitting at the table talking, I looked up to find Easton's eyes on me. The smile that had been on his face was gone, and he looked almost pissed. It made me lean into Michael even closer.

Outside, I waited at the valet stand for Indie's car while she said goodbye to some people from corporate sales. Michael joined me just as his silver Porsche Spyder pulled up.

"Nice car."

"Thanks. I'd love to give you a ride sometime . . . maybe on the way to dinner one night?"

"I'd like that. But my schedule is a little crazy the next few weeks." *Twenty-eight days left on my cleanse.*

"When things calm down, then?" He handed me his cell, and as I was programming in my number, he leaned in. "You smell incredible. I've been meaning to tell you that all night."

"Thank you. It's Rose de Chloe. I just bought it and wasn't sure if it was too floral."

"It's perfect." Instead of taking his phone back from my hand, Michael wrapped his fingers around mine and pulled me in for a hug goodbye. When I looked up, Brody Easton was staring at us. He appeared more than a little angry. So I made Michael's hug last extra-long.

The next week, the Steel was scheduled to play home again, so there was no midweek game traveling. But I was out of town covering the Basketball Hall of Fame inductions. I drove four hours back home late Saturday night to make sure I was at the stadium in time for kickoff the next morning. I watched the game from the sidelines, assisting the play-by-play field broadcaster. After the Steel won again, I headed to the locker room. I didn't dilly-dally this time. Instead, I got right in line to enter when security opened the big blue door.

"What's up, Dam?" Henry held out his hand for me to slap.

"Hi, Hi. I brought you something." I reached into my bag and took out a signed print of Rochelle Teavers, the WNBA's season-high shooter. "I heard some of the reporters say your daughter broke her ankle playing basketball. I covered the Hall of Fame induction this week, and Rochelle was there." My eyes pointed to the glossy photo. "Hope I had her spell Larissa right."

Henry patted his chest and pulled his glasses from the lapel of his uniform. "Well, look at that. This is going to make her old man cool for a change. Thank you very much, Delilah Dam."

"No problem."

I was one of the first few inside the locker room. Another reporter was already setting up to interview Easton, but I intended to get it over with as fast as I could. I walked over with Nick in tow. Brody was talking about his knee, but the minute he noticed me a smile spread across his face. *Shit. He's wearing a towel again.* I was overly prepared for the interview and knew how I'd handle the cocky quarterback if he started to play games again. But that damn smile made me nervous.

When it was my turn, I stepped up with a no-bullshit attitude. "How are we going to play this today, Easton?"

"Did you think of me this week while you were in Boston?"

I lifted one brow. "Keeping tabs on me, are you?"

"Admit you thought of me, and I'll make it easy for you today."

"I'm ready for you and your exhibitionist display. You don't have to go easy. Make it as *hard* as you can." I motioned to Nick to start rolling.

Easton beamed and promptly dropped his towel.

We went live. "So. Congrats on another big win this week. And on your rushing touchdown."

"Thank you."

I held his eyes for a few seconds, then deliberately dropped my gaze—right to his manhood. "It was a *short* run. What, about four inches?"

"Oh no. It was definitely more than four inches. I'd say at least twelve inches."

"I believe the official stat is four inches. Men and their fish stories," I chided.

Easton's smirk got a little less smirky. And it was laced with indignation. I was happy. Clearly, he wasn't. "Tell me, what did you change in the second half? Before halftime, it looked like you were having trouble with your passing game. Wren Jacobs even swatted two of your attempts to pass the ball to Daryl Breezy. Were you just having trouble *getting it up*?"

Easton's eyes narrowed. "No. I wasn't having trouble getting it up. I just needed better protection. Coach made some changes at halftime, which plugged up the gaps we were showing in our offensive line. Once the protection was there, I was able to *slide 'em right in*." Just as I had done, Easton held my gaze for a few seconds, then looked down, taking my eyes with him. My controlled interview went to hell the second I realized he was *getting aroused*.

When I looked back up, he was smiling like a Cheshire cat. Then he took control of *my* interview again. "Bruce Harness did an outstanding job today. That punt block at the start of the second half changed the momentum."

"That block made him break into the top ten of career punt block leaders," I responded.

Easton's smirk disappeared. He looked surprised I knew the statistics for punt blocks off the top of my head.

"That's right. Five more and he could clinch the record for all-time best punt blocker."

"Six more," I corrected him.

"Five."

"Six."

"Five."

"Herman Weaver, nineteen seventy to nineteen eighty. Started with Detroit, ended with the Seahawks. Fourteen blocked punts. Harness has nine. He needs six more to break the record." Easton opened his mouth to speak, then shut it again. I'd regained control of my interview. "One last question?" I turned and saw the line of impatient reporters behind me. "Is your knee ready to face the first-place Chargers next week out in California?"

"Will you be there to cover it?"

"I will."

"Then you can count on me being ready."

Brody

CHAPTER 4

"Go long!"

Grouper's mop clanked to the floor, and he started limp-jogging down the long hallway. Shannon, the nurse in charge of the day shift, walked by, shaking her head. It wasn't the first time she'd seen us doing shit like this . . . we'd been screwing around since Grouper had bite in his step. Hip surgery had slowed the geezer down a few years ago. Now my passes were more of a lob than a bullet.

"He's sixty-nine years old," Shannon called over her shoulder. "You're going to give that sweet old man a heart attack someday." I caught her smiling as she continued on.

When Grouper made it to the far end of the hall, I sent the ball spiraling sixty feet until it fell directly into his hands.

"I still got it." He headed back toward me.

"You never had it. I set that ball into your palms."

"Bullshit. You can't throw for crap. Everyone knows a pass is only as good as the intended receiver."

"Does Little Guppy know how disrespectful his grandpa is to his idol?"

"Pfft. Idol. I'm his damn idol."

The eight-year-old Grouper was a huge football fan and an even bigger Brody Easton fan. For his last birthday, I'd stopped by the kid's party. He was so excited, he actually cried when he saw me. That got me a few weeks of ball-busting material to use on Grouper senior.

I stopped at the nurses' station. "How was her week?"

"It was a good week, actually," Shannon said. "She wants to go shopping. Says she needs new underwear, even though she has a drawer full."

"So have the aide take her shopping."

"You want me to have the aide take her on an outing that will cost you an extra three hundred dollars, plus the cost of the underwear, even though she has forty pairs already."

"Will it make her happy?"

"I suppose."

"Then, yep."

She smiled. "I'll schedule it for this week."

I found Marlene in her room watching a rerun of *The Price Is Right*. The show was playing Bullseye, where you had to add up the total cost of a bunch of different items to come to a certain total.

"Hi, Marlene."

"Shhh."

She had a pad and pencil, and her shaky hand was furiously jotting down prices as they showed each item. Bob Barker held up a gallon of milk and I sneaked a peek at her scribble. *Fifteen cents.* Okay, so I had an idea what year we were in today.

She wasn't happy that her total wasn't even close to the answer. I tried to make her feel better. "They inflate the prices just to make it harder for people."

"I think you're right."

"Of course I am. I'm always right. And damn good looking, too." I opened the paper bag I'd been carrying and unwrapped the white paper, revealing the Reuben she'd wanted last week.

"You went to Heidelman's."

"Yep." Or maybe the Ben's Kosher Deli franchise that took its place ten years ago. It wasn't important.

"I can't wait to dig in. Can you hand me my teeth case?"

"Your teeth are already in your mouth, Marlene."

She took a minute and confirmed I was telling the truth with a tap of her nail against her front tooth. Even though her mind was all over the place, her teeth were almost always a weekly conversation.

"Willow came to see me the other day."

"That's good."

"Yep. She told me what she did."

No idea. "Oh, yeah. What's that? I can't keep track of all the things Willow does anymore."

"The pool. You know. You two should be ashamed of yourself. Next time the police won't be so easy on you."

It never ceased to amaze me how she could remember something from more than ten years ago crystal clear, yet not remember she put her teeth in five minutes ago. It was almost like her memories were fleeing most recent first. I hoped *my* memory of the pool incident never disappeared on me.

It was the first time I saw Willow naked. And the night I realized that the ache in my chest every time the girl I called Wild Willow did something to scare the shit out of me wasn't pain. It was love.

"It was my fault. Willow tried to talk me out of it. She only hopped the fence to get me out. I threw her in the pool."

Marlene looked at me skeptically. Rightly so. No one in her right mind would believe Willow had to be talked into anything that had an edge of recklessness to it. The girl had always danced on the blade of a sword, smiling, while I stood watching, waiting to stop the bleeding when she got cut. It was the most beautiful thing about her. And also the ugliest.

"This is my last warning. If you two get into any more trouble, I'll keep you apart. The two of you act like a couple of screwballs together."

I swiped half of her Reuben and promised to keep out of trouble. The irony was she'd threatened to keep us apart, but in the end, she was the one thing that kept us together.

Delilah
CHAPTER 5

"Whatcha working on?" Indie plopped herself down on the other side of my desk. She lifted her legs and sat Indian-style, even though she was wearing a skirt.

"Nice undies."

"You can't see my underwear."

"Sure I can," I bluffed.

"I'm not wearing any."

"I hope you sat like that in the department-head meeting you just came from."

"Of course I did." Indie leaned forward and swiped a pile of papers off my desk before I could stop her. She thumbed through a few of the articles I'd printed. "Brody Easton, huh?"

"It's research."

"For what? An interview with *Cosmopolitan* magazine? I don't see any sports-related articles here." She spread the papers out with her fingers and fanned herself.

"For this week's game."

"Really?" Indie stopped fanning and plucked a page out of her fan. "What did you learn from this one?"

It was a picture of Brody in his underwear. Tight black boxer briefs.

"I was looking at his knee to see if the picture was taken before or after his surgery."

"You were looking at his dick."

"I was not. The guy *is* a dick."

"Who does it for you."

"He does not."

"Does too."

"Whatever." I rolled my eyes. "You know . . . he definitely has a unique story. First-round draft pick at twenty. Car accident mid second season. He was injured, but nothing too bad. Cut from the team before the start of the third season. Rehab almost two years later, then makes it back to the lineup as a walk-on. Three years later, Super Bowl MVP."

"I remember when he got cut. He was in the news more than when he was starting for the Steel. Drinking and partying. Became a boy toy for a bunch of celebrity women."

"How do you go from being a first-round draft pick to being cut from the team?"

"Drugs and alcohol."

"But he wasn't really known as a party guy until *after* he was cut. I've been digging around, trying to piece together the puzzle of Brody Easton, and I just feel like a few are missing. There isn't anything about him having any issues, and the team didn't cite any when they cut him."

"The league probably didn't want a black eye. Maybe he got hooked on painkillers from his car accident or something."

"He walked away with only a few cuts and bruises. He wasn't badly injured in the accident."

"Was anyone?"

"He was alone in the car, speeding, and lost control."

"Hmm . . . I don't know. But maybe you can ask him during pillow talk." Indie stood up. "When are you back?"

"Monday night."

"Can I keep this?" She held up the photo of Brody in his boxer briefs. It was definitely a keeper.

"By all means. I don't want a picture of that arrogant ass."

"Sure you don't." She blew me a kiss and disappeared.

Delta custom configured planes for professional sports teams. A regular Boeing 757 held more than two hundred, but the aircraft that the league used had seats removed for extra leg space. In the rear of the plane, a few sections of seats faced each other across tables, designed for coaches' meetings during flights.

All fifty-three active players on the Steel roster traveled together two days before the away game, along with seventeen coaches and a few office staff. About a dozen reporters were riding along with the team. Since WMBC was an official team sponsor, I was one of those reporters. And . . . I hated to fly.

Five minutes before boarding, I popped a Xanax and chased it with a full glass of wine. The last thing I remembered before passing out was the pilot saying something about a short delay due to a stubborn flock of birds. *Birds?*

When I woke up, I checked the time on my phone. I'd slept for four hours of the almost six-hour flight to California. My mouth was dry and my eyes even drier.

"Morning, sleepyhead." The voice startled me.

Groggy, I turned my head toward the aisle, confused. "Where . . . where is Alan?" I'd fallen asleep sitting next to Alan Coleman, a reporter for *Sports Chronicles*. Sitting next to me now was none other than Brody Easton. And he was smiling from ear to ear.

"I offered him an exclusive interview on the league's new alcohol rules if he changed seats with me."

"Why would you do that?"

"To sit next to you."

"Did you enjoy watching me sleep?"

"I did. You snore, you know."

"I do not."

"Yes, you do. Want to see the video to prove it?"

My eyes widened. "You videoed me sleeping?"

"No. But you do have a little dried drool." He pointed to the corner of my mouth. "Right here."

I wiped it, even though I wasn't sure if he was serious. "Did you come back here to annoy me?"

"Pretty much." He smiled. It was a real smile; even his green eyes participated. *Damn.*

Just then, the plane hit a bit of turbulence, and whatever calm the Xanax had instilled in me went out the window. I gripped the armrests with both hands.

"Nervous flyer?"

"That's putting it mildly."

"You should take something before you fly."

"I did. But it must have worn off."

"How about a drink to calm your nerves?"

"I shouldn't mix any more alcohol with Xanax." The plane shook again. "I'll have a Merlot."

Brody chuckled as he reached up and hit the button for the flight attendant. The leggy brunette responded quickly. She ignored me and spoke to Brody. "What can I do for you, Mr. Easton?"

"Can you bring us a Merlot and a bottle of water, please?"

"Of course."

The minute it arrived, I gulped almost the entire full glass as if it were medicine. Looking over at Brody, I realized for the first time that he was dressed in a suit. He wore it well. "Nice to see you in pants for a change."

"I can take them off if you'd like."

"I'd need a lot more than one airplane-size bottle of Merlot."

32

Easton quickly reached up and pushed the button for the flight attendant. I actually laughed a little.

"So . . . really . . . why are you sitting here?"

"Have you looked around this plane? There's one hot woman and a hundred hairy men. The question should be, why isn't everyone fighting to sit here?"

"That almost sounded like a compliment, Mr. Easton."

"It was. You're hot as fuck. And I like you."

"Oh really? You have a funny way of showing that you like me. Every time I see you, you try to sabotage my interview."

"Every time I see you, I expose myself to you." He flashed me his trademark smile. "That's how we show girls we like them where I'm from."

"Where are you from, the jungle?"

"Brooklyn."

The offensive-line coach interrupted us. "Brody, I want to make some changes to Red Reverse Four. We just studied the tapes from last week and need to shift the play around a bit."

"You got it, Coach."

Brody took my hand and kissed it. Then he disappeared with the coaches for the rest of the trip. I didn't see him again until game day.

_e_ ——————————————————— _e_

As usual, the sun was shining in San Diego. I really missed California. After college, I thought I'd be back a lot more than I had. But over the years, my fear of flying had escalated, and now the only travel I did by plane was for work. This trip had reminded me that I was letting my fears control me, instead of the other way around.

I stood along the sideline watching the game with Brett Marlin, the on-air, play-by-play reporter. Part of my job as a staff sportscaster was to be Brett's backup eyes. We consulted between live feeds—it was virtually impossible for one person to keep track of twenty-two men on the field at once. Four eyes did a better job.

As expected, the division-rivalry between San Diego and the Steel was intense. The outcome would determine first and second place between the two, and they played as if it were the Super Bowl. The roar of the crowd was so loud that it made it difficult for Brett and I to hear each other in our headsets. I felt the vibrations from feet stamping against the stands in my chest. *God, I love games like this.* With thirty seconds left on the clock before halftime, I stood near the goal line, watching as the Steel moved down the field. On a third and short, Brody dropped back to pass, only to find his receivers all under heavy coverage. Rather than chance an interception, he waited, somehow avoiding the head-on charge of a three-hundred-pound defenseman. Then he lowered his shoulder and charged toward the end zone. His legs never stopped moving until he crossed the line. *Was it just me, or was the sun suddenly getting warmer?*

The crowd went crazy, and I caught myself clapping a little, too. Reporters were supposed to be neutral. As Brody jogged off the field at halftime with the scoring ball in his hand, he surprised me by tossing it to me. I hadn't even realized he had seen me on the sideline.

My mom and I had spent years going to games, sitting in box seats on the fifty-yard line—I loved watching my dad play. Hell, it was growing up going to those games that made me want to be a reporter. I couldn't imagine my life not involving football in some way. But watching Brody out there was different. The way the man moved was sexy and confident. His long strides, thick, powerful thighs, the way he seemed fearless to barrel over people. He was such a dominant force that it was impossible not to be attracted to him. And it wasn't just me. Women actually catcalled almost every time he removed his helmet when he came off the field. During the second half, he scored another running touchdown. When he again tossed the ball my way, some of those adoring lady fans actually booed at me a little.

After the game, I waited outside the locker room, catching up on texts and emails. The first one I opened was from Indie.

Indie: *That skirt is too long. Take that shit up a few inches before you go in the locker room to flirt with Easton.*

I laughed while I typed.

Delilah: *I don't flirt, I interview. It's my JOB.*

Indie: *OMG. He gave you two balls today. Bet he gives you two more tonight!*

Great. The camera had caught Brody Easton tossing me both of his running touchdown balls. I'm sure half the men in the mandatory Monday meetings would have something to say about it.

I swiped over to email and started weeding through the garbage, stopping at one from Michael Langley.

Just wanted to tell you how much I enjoyed spending time with you at the fundraiser last week and that I was thinking about you. I look forward to your month slowing down so I can take you to dinner. And I'm working on adding some interviews to my schedule. Best, M.

Such a sweet guy. Maybe I could end my cleanse a little early.

I kept my nose in my phone, catching up on work, until security opened the locker room for reporters.

Inside the guest team locker room, I interviewed a wide receiver and then headed over to Jennings Astor, a defensive lineman who'd had a key sack in the fourth quarter. Easton, as usual, had a long line. His locker was diagonally across from Jennings, and I could see he was finishing up his current interview. The next person in line was Sandra Halston, a reporter covering the home team. I was curious to watch the interaction between the two.

While Sandra was setting up to begin, the arrogant ass's eyes caught mine.

He grinned wide.

I ignored him. Clarification: I *pretended* to ignore him.

From across the room, I studied Easton's body language. He hadn't dropped the towel for the gorgeous blonde reporter. In fact, he seemed to be treating her exactly as he treated the male reporters. No sexy smirk or sparkle in his eye as he made sexual innuendos. And he wasn't showing off his Subway either. I wondered if Sandra had already gotten her fill of hazing. I really wanted to know if he had ever done the same thing to her, but I wasn't sure why it was important to me.

After wrapping up all the interviews I needed, I headed over to Easton. I wasn't nervous anymore. Instead, I think I was a little . . . excited.

While Nick set up the camera and lights, I said, "Thank you for the . . . balls today."

Easton grinned. "No problem."

"You did that just so I had to say thank you for the balls today, didn't you?"

"Nope. But that was a total bonus. I did it so you'd take them home and every time you looked at them, you would think about me."

"I know the perfect place for them."

"In your bedroom?"

"In the basement, it's creepy down there. Fitting."

As usual, he ignored my insult. "Do you have them in your bag?"

"I do."

He turned around, reached into his locker, and pulled out a Sharpie. "Let me have 'em. I'll sign them for you."

As he signed the second ball, Nick announced that he was ready to film. I shoved the balls into my equipment bag and attempted to tame my wild hair. "You ready?"

"For you? Always."

I shook my head and shot off my first question. I expected him to drop his towel, but he surprised me by staying covered. In fact, he remained in his towel for the entire interview and answered every question without any sexual innuendos. Maybe my hazing was over.

After the camera shut off, I couldn't resist. "Thank you for staying somewhat dressed today."

"It was really *hard* to do."

36

I chuckled as I packed away my microphone and notepad. "So, is it over? The hazing, I mean. I noticed you didn't get naked with Sandra either today. Is that your thing, you treat the new female reporters to full-frontal nudity to embarrass them the first few weeks?"

"Seeing me naked was a treat. I knew it."

"Your head is so big, I'm surprised you can get a helmet on it."

He grinned. "Big head. Big helmet."

"How has no one filed a sexual harassment complaint against you with the league yet?"

He shrugged. "I don't do this with anyone else."

My eyes narrowed. "You mean Sandra has never experienced the towel routine during an interview?"

"Nope."

"Well, aren't I the lucky one?"

"You are. Have dinner with me?"

"No."

"No?" I sort of loved that he was shocked to be turned down.

"That's right. No."

"Why?"

"I don't date players."

"You went out with that kicker from the Saints last year."

"I said I don't date *players*, not I don't date athletes."

For once, Brody Easton didn't have a witty comeback. I walked away, then stopped and turned back. "By the way, researching my dating history? Creepy. Your balls are definitely going down to the basement."

I took the earliest commercial flight on Monday morning, rather than the late-afternoon team flight home. Mr. CUM didn't care that I was halfway across the country; he still expected me to be at his mandatory Monday meetings.

When I arrived at JFK, a corporate town car picked me up at the airport, and I headed directly to the office. We made it less than a mile before we were stopped dead in traffic. I reached into the equipment duffle bag I'd carried on the plane to take out my notepad. A slash of black marker caught my eye. Brody Easton's name was scribbled on the ball, but something was written above it.

I'd really like to fuck you. 212-538-0321

I shook my head. Then I reached down for the other ball. I flipped it over and found:

Stop shaking your head. You know you want to.

I was a little turned on. And a lot pathetic.

Delilah

CHAPTER 6

"The Steel just announced a news conference on Tuesday at ten. Rumor is, Tyrell Oden has a more serious injury than originally anticipated, and they're going to announce a mid-season trade."

Luckily, the writer next to me kicked me under the table to get my attention.

"Sorry. Can you repeat that?"

Mr. CUM huffed.

I felt the need to make an excuse. "I was going over some interview questions in my head."

"Your head should be in this meeting. And eyes on me."

I nodded, and he proceeded to tell me about the news conference, presumably for a second time.

"Already registered," I said.

"Good." He sighed. "Now that we have Ms. Maddox's mind back on the news, why don't we chat about Brody Easton."

Ummm. That *was* where my mind had been. I just couldn't seem to shake the jackass from my thoughts. "Okay."

"Phil Stapleton wants a sit-down with Easton for his weekly show. You seem to have established some sort of rapport with him. I saw him toss a ball your way after a touchdown yesterday."

Two balls. Ones that were in a duffle bag in my office and read, *I'd really like to fuck you*, to be exact. And I was pitifully hard-up in the romance department, because the thought of him wanting me had me shifting in my chair.

"I've interviewed him a few times, yes. Although I'm not sure you'd label our interactions good rapport."

Mr. CUM waved a dismissive hand. "Next week, invite him for a sit-down with Phil. We want him on *Sixty with Stapleton*."

It was a widely known fact that Brody Easton did not do more than required TV locker room interviews and news conferences. Newspaper articles were even limited to those where he had final approval of the words. He'd declined every in-depth, one-on-one televised interview since he'd earned himself a spot back on the team. "He doesn't do sit-down interviews."

"It would be a big score for us. We're lagging in ratings this year, you know."

I gritted my teeth. I knew what he was insinuating. Although the truth of the matter was, we were behind in ratings because of irrelevant content. Many of the old-timers stuck to interviews of the players they were friendly with and reported mostly on notable past sporting events. Viewers wanted fresh stories. "I'll see what I can do."

I sat through another hour of the wasteful meeting and then headed back to my office. Indie was sitting in my chair, tossing a football in the air. The *I'd really like to fuck you* football. And she was smiling from ear to ear.

"Anything you want to talk about?"

"Shut up."

"Guess the cleanse is about to end. Or did it already?"

"I don't think so."

"Why? He's ridiculously hot, and he's obviously into you."

"That man isn't *into* me. He wants *in to* me."

"Same thing."

"No. There's a major difference."

"You know, it's the new millennium. You can have sex without love and commitment."

"Yes. I know. I've dated."

"You date guys for a few months, find something wrong with them and then take a six-month hiatus from penises. Wouldn't it be easier to just have sex and not date? Then you wouldn't need the six-month celibacy recovery period. You could just fuck your brains out year-round."

"That logic made a lot more sense in your head before it came out your mouth, didn't it?" I pulled a file from my cabinet and began to thumb through it.

"So you're going to sleep with Easton?"

"Did you really miss the sarcasm in my voice? The guy only wants to get laid. He'd be gone the morning after I gave in."

"Did he ask you out?"

"I suppose. He asked me out to dinner before delivering that eloquent invitation on the ball."

"See, he's into you."

As much as I hated to admit it, I sort of wanted him to be. There was no denying that I was attracted to him physically. What woman in her right mind wouldn't be? But I just wasn't a one-night-stand type of person. I imagined the day after—going from feeling wanted to being forgotten—was a little bit like bungee jumping and slipping loose from the rope. An exhilarating high as you took the plunge, only to free-fall when you realized nothing was holding you any longer. It was just you—all alone. And you couldn't even remember what made you jump in the first place.

That night, exhausted from travel, I climbed into bed early. Although my body was drained, my mind seemed to be spinning. Thoughts of Brody Easton and the way he looked at me gave me a feeling of excitement I had forgotten existed—a visceral reaction that was pointless to try to tame. Not once since Drew did I have that flutter.

Drew.

I reached over to my bedside nightstand and picked up the small, oval-framed picture taken in middle school. Even though it was always there, I hadn't really looked at it in years. Drew was wearing his football uniform, and the eye black under his sweet brown eyes was smeared from wiping sweat during the game. I smiled, thinking back to how a look from those eyes gave me butterflies growing up.

Lying in bed in the dark, I tried to make sense of my fascination with Brody. But in the end, I decided maybe I simply had a thing for football players. After all, my father was a football player. I'm sure Freud would have had a thing or two to say about that.

❧ ──────────────── ❧

I sat in the back row at Wednesday's scheduled press conference. The dais held five men. From left to right sat the director of team operations; head coach Bill Ryan; Chargers wide receiver Colin Anderson; the Steel's offensive-line coach; and to the far right, Brody Easton. As rumored, Coach Ryan confirmed that Tyrell Oden, one of the team's key offensive-line players, had received a season-ending injury. They also confirmed a rare mid-season trade to replace him. Colin Anderson was to join the Steel this week.

A friend of mine had tipped me off about the trade yesterday, and it had given me time to do a little digging. Although it had never made it onto the media's radar, Colin and Brody apparently had a tumultuous history. They'd attended the same college. Brody's last year before being drafted, they were even on the same offensive line. Apparently, the two didn't get along and there'd been multiple off-the-field fights. I doubted any of the reporters knew about it since I'd only found out because I happened to have a friend in common with Colin. Division One schools kept internal conflicts very quiet. They didn't want to taint a prospective draftee as a troublemaker.

After the announcements, Coach Ryan opened up the floor for questions. Brody caught my eye and winked. Like an idiot, I smiled back. His flirtations were so overtly over-the-top, it was impossible not to find them at least a tiny bit amusing.

Every hand in the room went up. The coach called on a well-known reporter in the front row. I watched Brody scribble something on a piece of paper and slide it down to the coach.

Before the next question, Coach Ryan glanced down at the paper, then scanned the room. He hadn't even found me in the crowd when he said my name. I stood to ask my question anyway.

"My question is for Mr. Easton." Brody looked momentarily pleased. "Are you concerned about the chemistry between yourself and your new receiver?"

Brody folded his arms across his chest and leaned back in his chair. "What were his stats last year, Ms. Maddox?"

"Hundred and eleven catches, fourteen-point-three average yards, eleven touchdowns. Second best in the league."

"You have your answer. Do you have any other questions, Ms. Maddox?"

A few men snickered. But I wanted an actual answer. "The question wasn't how capable of an athlete he is. We all know he's quite talented. My question—perhaps I should repeat it—was are you concerned about the *chemistry* between you and Colin Anderson?"

Brody's jaw tightened. "I'm not planning on dating him."

More snickers.

"I didn't think so. But considering the two of you didn't get along in college, might there be a concern for you?"

His answer was curt. "No. As long as he does his job, I'm not concerned."

"Thank you." I sat and the room began to buzz with chatter.

Brody stared at me with a gleam in his eye for the remainder of the interview. It made me question if I had just poked a lion. Colin, on the other hand, was sporting an evil grin, and it appeared he was enjoying our interaction.

I didn't mill around socializing after the conference ended. I had a hot date with a month's worth of laundry that I'd stood up on multiple occasions. I was texting Indie while walking down the long hallway toward the exit when a hand at my elbow startled me.

"Nice find. Did you have to call my entire dorm to dig up that little piece of information you just unleashed in there?"

"I'm sure if I interviewed your entire dorm, my ears would be bleeding."

"You realize that every journalist will be watching every interaction between that asswipe and me now?"

"Sorry."

"No, you're not."

I stopped walking. Brody was still holding my arm.

I turned to him and shrugged. "Okay. So maybe I'm not. So what?"

He squinted at me.

"Oh. By the way. My station wants me to ask you to do a sit-down interview with Phil Stapleton for the *Sixty with Stapleton* show."

"You're going to ask me for a favor after you just screwed me in there?"

I tilted my head and gave a sugary-sweet smile. "You sabotaged my first locker room interview and then asked me out."

Easton's eyebrows shot up. "So you're getting even with me?"

We reached the front doors of the stadium, and Brody opened one and followed me out. "Are you going to follow me all the way home?"

"Is that an invitation?" He shot me a damn cocky smile.

I shook my head and kept walking. Neither of us said a word until we'd crossed the parking lot and arrived at my car. I unlocked the door and got in. Easton stood outside, holding the door open. "I'll tell you what. I'll do the sit-down for *Sixty with Stapleton*."

"You will?"

"Under two conditions."

"And they are?"

"You do the interview. Not that old jackass Stapleton. He has guest interviewers all the time. They want me, you'll be the guest interviewer."

"Are you serious?"

"Yep."

"Wow. I'm sure Stapleton won't be happy about it. But Mr. Cu—my boss will."

"Then it's settled."

My eyes narrowed. "Why are you being nice to me now, when I just unleashed what will probably turn into a media shitstorm on you?"

"I like you."

I shook my head. "I'll talk to my boss and then call your agent to set it up."

"Sounds good. Can I borrow your cell? Coach is probably wondering where I disappeared to."

I handed him my phone. He dialed a number, hung up and handed the phone back to me without bringing it to his ear.

He read the confusion on my face. "You didn't ask me what condition number two was."

I'd gotten so excited he was going to give me an interview, I'd forgotten he'd said there were *two* conditions. "What's the second condition?"

"You have dinner with me."

"Dinner?"

"That's right."

"Does dinner mean sleeping with you?"

"Hopefully when it's over. But if you want to switch things up a bit and get to the fucking first, I'm happy to oblige."

"No thanks."

"Relax. I'm joking. Dinner means dinner. You know, I take you out to some overpriced restaurant where we share a meal and I tell you how great I am."

"Gee. How can I turn that invitation down?"

He winked. "That's what I thought. I am sort of irresistible."

"If you don't say so yourself."

I was pulling out of the parking lot and still wondering what the hell I'd just agreed to, when my phone buzzed.

Brody: Wednesday night. I'll pick you up at your office at 6. Wear something sexy.

Delilah
CHAPTER 7

"What the hell are you wearing?" Indie arrived just as I returned to my office from the ladies' room on Wednesday evening.

"A new outfit. For my date tonight."

"You're dressed like a sixty-year-old grandmother of nine about to go to church."

I totally was. Some of it I'd actually had to purchase just for the occasion. The Goodwill store on Seventy-Second Street was perfect—a bag full of granny goods for under twenty bucks. I caught my reflection in the glass window. Oversized navy corduroy blazer. Navy elastic waist polyester pants (pretty damn comfortable). Cream-cotton-and-doily-lace button-up blouse, buttoned up to the top, of course. A string of fake pearls. Hair pulled back in a tight bun. Worn penny loafers. (Okay, so those might have been mine.)

I patted my bun and rolled on some bland, mauve lipstick, purposefully swiping some on my front tooth. "You don't like my outfit?"

"Seriously? You look a little insane."

I smoothed my jacket down and picked up the giant dowdy brown church-lady purse. "What? You don't think I look sexy?"

"Are you wearing bloomers under there?"

I flipped off the light switch in my office. "And a nursing bra." I actually had a G-string and a demi cup bra on, but the appalled look on Indie's face was worth the little white lie.

She followed me out of my office. Luckily, the building was already mostly empty, or I might have gotten some strange looks. I really did look a bit nuts.

"Did you get that crap from wardrobe?" Indie asked.

"Nope. I bought it for my date."

"You bought that getup?"

"Sure did."

"I think you've been under too much stress lately." She kissed me on the cheek before jumping on the up elevator to head back to her office. "Breakfast in your office at eight. I can't wait to hear all about this date."

Ten minutes later, I exited the glass turn-style door of WMBC and saw a fancy car double-parked right at the curb. Brody got out and walked around the car to open the passenger door. As his eyes swept me up and down, his brows drew together. Then he blinked repeatedly. "Hi."

I gave him a goofy ear-to-ear smile. "Hi. Where are we going?"

"Um . . . to the . . . um . . . the restaurant at the Regency."

It was everything I could do to not crack up. He had no idea if my outfit was serious or a joke. Although he earned a point for being polite enough not to say anything. I couldn't resist screwing with him a little more after we settled into the car.

"You look nice." He was wearing a hunter-green cashmere sweater that fit him well, snug across his broad shoulders, but not too tight, and simple black slacks.

He glanced at me and back at the road. "Thank you." I wasn't sure if I liked him more or less because he didn't lie and feed me a compliment back about my outfit.

"You look different with your hair up. I like it."

"You do?"

"Yeah. It's sexy librarian."

"Sexy librarian, huh?"

"I've always had a thing for librarians. You know . . . unpin her tight hair, let it loose down her back. And then make her moan between the stacks."

"How romantic." I shifted in my seat at the visual he painted.

"I don't think women want romance as much as they think they do."

I cackled. "You don't know women very well."

"Oh, but I think I do. I think most women, especially women who work hard and have a lot on their mind, prefer a man to come home, lift her off her feet and take her against the wall rather than hand her some bullshit flowers and pussyfoot around with sweet gestures all night."

"We like bullshit flowers and sweet gestures." *Though I could use a good wall banging.*

"Then you haven't been fucked properly against a wall."

"Let me guess. You could demonstrate?"

"We could skip dinner."

"Big of you. But our deal was dinner for an interview."

He shrugged. "Suit yourself."

We arrived at the Regency, and the valet who opened the car door for me knew Brody by name. "Usual time in the morning, Mr. Easton?"

"Actually. I'll probably be using the car again tonight. Why don't you keep it close by?"

"Sure thing, Mr. Easton."

Brody walked around the car. His hand went to the small of my back.

"Probably?"

"A man has to hold on to his dreams." He winked.

As we walked through the lobby, more employees greeted him by name. He was a household name, but they spoke to him with the familiarity of a frequent visitor. "Do you come here often? Dinner at a hotel? How convenient for dessert."

"I live here."

"You live at the Regency?"

"During the season, I do. The field is less than an hour from here, even with traffic."

"Where do you live in the offseason?"

"I have a cabin upstate. I stay there mostly."

"A cabin? In the woods?"

"Yes. I've been working on it for a few years now in the offseason. I figure it should be done in about . . . I don't know . . . twenty or thirty years." He chuckled.

"Sounds like you work fast."

He steered me down the hall toward the restaurant and leaned into me as he spoke. His voice was raspy. "Actually, I like to take my time." The timbre of his voice made my toes curl in my *sensible shoes*.

A part of me suddenly wished I hadn't dressed up like a schoolmarm.

We settled into our table at the beautiful Silver Ivy restaurant, and a waitress came over to take our drink order. She batted her long eyelashes at Brody and gave me the once-over, no doubt jealous of my outfit. "What can I do for you this evening, Mr. Easton?"

Really? Yuck.

"Hey, Siselee." He looked at me. "Do you like red wine?"

"I consider it one of the five major food groups."

He ordered a bottle of wine I'd never heard of. The waitress opened it tableside, poured me a glass and set the bottle in the bucket beside the table.

"Aren't you having any?" The question was directed at Brody, but Siselee answered before he could.

"He only drinks on Tuesday nights." She lifted her chin, proud of herself for knowing the answer.

"Training," Brody offered as means of explanation.

We relaxed into easy conversation, our natural flow leading to sports. Arguing over the greats of all time, we sampled each other's dinners without a lull in our banter. The topic of conversation eventually moved to Brody's new wide receiver.

"I throw, he catches. We don't need to be buddies."

"You need to have trust in each other. My dad always said his receiver was like his wife—he needed a partner he could trust to make the right decisions."

"I have to trust his abilities. Not his morality."

"So is that what the issue is? His morals?"

Brody leaned back in his seat and folded his arms. "Is this an interview? This shit going to be on the air tomorrow?"

"No. Sorry. Habit. I grew up arguing about football. I actually sort of like doing it, if I'm being honest."

"Guess I do, too. What else do you like doing?"

"I don't have much spare time these days, really. Between the traveling and all the research and stats I have to keep up with, there's not much time for anything but work and sleep lately. I haven't had a day off in two months."

"What would you be doing if you were off for a day?"

"Hmm. I love museums and bike riding. But if I had a full day off, I'd probably spend it in bed, watching movies."

"What kind of movies?"

"B horror flicks. The gorier, the better."

"Really?"

"Really." I tipped my glass of wine toward him before bringing it to my lips. "What about you? What would you do with a day of no practice or games?" I knew from growing up with a quarterback dad that a day like that was a rarity during football season. Even on "recovery" days after a game, quarterbacks had films to watch from the last game to prepare for the next one.

"I'd be in bed, too."

"What would you be watching?"

"Your face while I sink inside of you."

I was in the middle of a long sip of my wine and choked. At least the sputtering and coughing gave me an excuse for my face turning beet red.

"You okay?"

It took me a minute, and my voice was a little hoarse when I spoke, but I finally regained my composure. "Why do you say things like that?"

He shrugged. "Because it's true. If I could do anything I wanted on a day off, I'd do . . . you."

"You have a dirty mouth."

"This dirty mouth wants to do dirty things to you."

I had that feeling of teetering on the top of a roller coaster, about to go down a steep hill . . . only that anxious and excited feeling wasn't in my stomach, it was in my panties. And they were growing damp.

Brody lifted the wine bottle from the bucket and refilled my glass. "Tell me something embarrassing about you."

"Embarrassing?"

"Yeah. Maybe it will help me stop thinking about doing dirty things to you."

"Hmm...let me think."

He leaned in. "Hurry. You're sorta hot when you think."

Shaking my head, I shared the first embarrassing story I could think of, even though it was an old one. "When I was sixteen, I told my parents I was going to sleep at my friend's house, but I really went camping with a big group of people. We bought beer and sat around a campfire all night drinking. At some point, after we'd all had too much to drink, we decided to roast marshmallows. I was about as experienced with camping as I was drinking, which is to say I was drunk and didn't belong near a fire. We collected sticks and popped marshmallows on the end. My stick was only about six inches long."

Brody interrupted, grinning. "My stick's bigger."

I rolled my eyes, but continued with my story. "Anyway. I was sitting way too close to the fire with my short stick trying to brown my marshmallow, and my hair caught on fire. I was lucky I didn't get burned badly, but it singed the entire half of my head. I had to walk around with my head shaved for my entire sophomore year. And I was grounded for a month."

We both had a good laugh at my expense. "You know the funniest part of that story?" Brody asked.

"What?"

"I still want to do dirty things to you."

The waitress came to the table and cleared our plates. Brody asked for a few minutes to decide on dessert, which gave me a much-needed minute to regroup. I folded my hands in front of me on the table. "So this is it? This is my courtship? A dinner, which you basically made me come to in order to get an interview for my job, and now I'm supposed to have sex with you?"

"By the tone of your voice, I guess I shouldn't answer yes to that question?"

The waitress returned before I could respond. "Would you like dessert?"

Brody pointed to the menu. "Bring us one of everything, please."

She justifiably looked confused. "You want one of every dessert?"

He looked at me. "That's right. She needs more courtship. Bring us one of everything."

I couldn't help but laugh.

"See," he said when Siselee had gone. "I'm entertaining, too. I'm making you laugh. And you think I'm hot. This is a great courtship. I don't know what you're talking about."

"Excuse me? I never said I thought you were hot."

"You don't have to. I feel it. It's in the air when we're near each other. You're as attracted to me as I am to you."

"You're nuts."

"Admit it."

"Honestly, it wouldn't even matter if I did—"

"You do—"

"Whatever. I don't do casual sex."

"Why not?"

"Because sex has to be more than just . . . sex."

"Why?" His eyebrows drew down. He really didn't comprehend my answer.

"I need an emotional connection with the person to have sex with them."

"You mean like a relationship?"

"Yes. A relationship. I'm not talking about marriage. But dating. Getting to know each other outside of the bedroom."

He blew out a rush of air. "I can't do that. I need to keep things simple."

I forced a smile, hating that I felt a little disappointed. "See, we're better as friends."

"I don't have any girl friends. Well, ones that I haven't, you know."

"Well, then this will be a first for you."

"I guess it will be." He extended his hand to me to shake on our newfound friendship, but he didn't let go. Instead, he leaned in, keeping my hand wrapped in his when he spoke. "I'm disappointed. I was really looking forward to seeing your clothes on my bedroom floor."

"Even these clothes?" I arched an eyebrow.

The waitress wheeled our dessert cart over, forcing us apart. I hated to admit it, but I missed his touch when he let go of my hand. All those sweets would be filling in for something else.

Things returned to normal after that. Well, normal for us. We argued some more. He said some more inappropriate things, and we ate one bite each from thirteen different desserts. I was glad I had on my fancy new elastic-waist pants.

"I'm stuffed." I leaned back in my chair.

"You can sure eat for a little thing."

"That's not something you should ever point out to a woman."

"I can if she's only a friend, right?"

Neither of us made an attempt to end the evening, and it wasn't until we were the only people left in the restaurant that I realized how late it was. "Wow. We've been sitting here for almost four hours."

"Doesn't seem like it."

"I know. Tonight wasn't anything like I expected."

"What did you expect?"

"I don't know. I guess I just didn't expect to get to know you, really."

"You expected me to be just a pretty face, didn't you?"

I laughed off his comment, but that sort of *was* what I had expected. An evening of sexual references and talking shop about football. Don't get me wrong, we had plenty of that, but there was also *more*. I couldn't remember the last time a first date had went that well. *Shit. This isn't a date.*

An hour later, we pulled up at my building. He parked, turned off the car and came around to open my door. "No doorman?"

"He leaves at eleven."

"I'm walking you inside."

The lobby was quiet and, as usual, only one elevator in my high-rise complex was working. I pushed the button, mentally debating if I should invite him up or not.

No. Inviting him up would be misleading.

But I really don't want him to leave.

"So . . . I'll call your agent to set up the interview for this weekend."

"Call me. Not my agent."

"Okay."

The elevator dinged, and I suddenly felt awkward. "Do you want to come up for some coffee?"

He shook his head slowly.

"Okay, then. Well. Thank you for dinner." I stepped into the elevator.

"You're welcome."

The impatient doors began to close. Brody stopped them, holding them open as he leaned in and kissed me on the cheek. His mouth lingered, and he leaned in a little farther to whisper in my ear. "I don't trust myself alone with you. I need a little space between us, or our friendship isn't going to end well."

He leaned back, and we stared at each other for a moment. My heart was racing, my pulse was beating like I'd just run a marathon, and every hair on the back of my neck was standing up from the electricity running between us.

He lifted the arm that was holding the door, and as it closed he said, "Sweet dreams, friend."

I knew they would be. Because I was certain who would be starring in them that evening.

Delilah
CHAPTER 8

"Guess you put out last night?" Indie spun herself around in my ergonomically correct swivel chair. I dropped my bags on the floor and glanced at the beautiful arrangement of flowers sitting in the middle of my desk.

"Where did those come from?"

She lifted the small florist's card in her hand. "Cityscape Florists. Delivered them just before you walked in."

"I need to run to the ladies' room. Why don't you make yourself at home? Oh, wait. You already have." I stashed my purse in a drawer, tossed my cell on the desk and eyed the brown paper bag that I assumed contained the breakfast Indie had brought us. "I hope it's something greasy . . . I need it this morning."

When I returned to my office, Indie was talking on my cell phone. "Here she comes now. The flowers are beautiful, by the way." She extended my cell with a cheeky grin.

"Hello."

"Morning." Brody's voice was laced with morning huskiness. "What kind of flowers were delivered?"

I looked at the arrangement. "Roses. They're beautiful. Thank you."

"Unoriginal."

"Pardon?"

"What asswipe sends a woman like you ordinary roses?"

"You mean . . . they're not from you?"

"No. And the guy who sent them had his secretary send that crap and didn't give it any thought. Probably has an account at the florist and a standard order. Guy's a dick."

"You don't even know who they're from. *I* don't even know who they're from. Yet you know he's a dick?"

"I do."

"Because the flowers are roses?"

"Yep. Dick. I'm sure of it."

I chuckled. "Your assessment is amusing. I'll be sure to keep that in mind when I actually get to read the card and find out who the sweet gesture is from."

"Sweet gesture." He guffawed. "That's not what you really want, and you know it."

After eight hours of tossing and turning in my bed last night, I was beginning to think he was right. As much as I hated to admit it, I'd thought about Brody an awful lot after he left last night. Replaying our conversation over and over about why I couldn't have sex without a relationship, I'd begun to doubt myself. Maybe there was nothing wrong with having sex with a man I was attracted to. Why did I need to tie in some sort of commitment to enjoy the physical benefits of a sexual relationship? I was twenty-six years old—there was nothing wrong with sex just being about sex if that was what I wanted.

"Did you call for a reason other than to tell me what I want, Mr. Easton?"

He groaned.

"What?"

"I like the way 'Mr. Easton' sounds coming from your mouth." He groaned again.

"What?"

"Now I'm thinking of your mouth."

I laughed. "You're not very good at this friend thing, are you?"

"Told you that you'd be the first. It's harder than I thought."

"I bet it is."

"Are you flirting back with me, friend?"

"You have my head spinning. I have no idea what I'm doing. I'm not even sure what you called for yet."

"Shit. Okay. Yeah. Right. I want the interview done in my hotel suite."

"Your hotel suite?"

"Don't sound so worried. You'll have a crew with you. I can't attack you in front of them."

"That's true."

"I'll have to wait until they leave."

I was still standing next to my desk, so I hitched a thumb at Indie to tell her to get out of my chair. "What day?"

"Saturday. Late afternoon. Our game is home on Sunday, so we have practice until two."

"How about five?"

"Works for me."

"Thank you. I can't tell you how much I appreciate you doing this. My boss is going to be thrilled. And he's pretty much always miserable, so that's saying something."

"Glad I can help."

"I'll messenger over advance questions by tomorrow night."

"Actually, why don't you bring them, and we can do a dry run."

"At your hotel?"

"Afraid you can't control yourself?"

"Of course not." *Maybe.*

"Seven. I'll order dinner up."

"Okay."

"Oh, and Delilah?"

"Yes?"

"You can leave your grandmother's clothes at home. It's not going to stop me from wanting to fuck you up against the wall."

59

The phone disconnected, leaving me with my mouth hanging open. When I finally regained my wits, I held my hand out to Indie, palm up. She placed the small florist's card in it.

Delilah. These don't smell half as good as you. Michael Langley.

"Who are they from?"

"I shouldn't even tell you after you just did that on the phone."

"What? I assumed they were from Brody. You went out with him last night, and he was calling first thing this morning."

"Well, you assumed wrong."

"Bet Brody was jealous."

"I don't think so."

Indie plucked the card from my hand. She read it and scrunched up her nose. "Michael Langley."

"What? He's a nice guy. We talked at the fundraiser. We have a lot in common."

"You know what he's missing?"

"What?"

"He's not *Brody Easton*."

"I think *you* should go out with Brody Easton."

"I would. But I follow girl code."

"Girl code?"

"You don't sleep with men your best friend wants to do the dirty with."

"I do not want to do the dirty with him."

"Do too."

There was no point in arguing with her. "Did you at least bring me something good for breakfast?"

"Two eggs over easy, bacon and cheese."

"Thank God."

"If you had slept with Easton, you wouldn't need crappy food this morning. You'd be wanting yogurt or some other stupid healthy food."

"So sleeping with Easton is actually healthy, then? Is that what you're trying to tell me?"

"Absolutely."

e ———————————————————— e

Later in the afternoon, I searched the company directory for Michael Langley's telephone number. His secretary answered on the second ring.

"Michael Langley's office."

"Hi. This is Delilah Maddox. Is Michael available?"

"Oh, hi Delilah. No. Actually, he's out at a meeting this afternoon. Can I take a message?"

"Sure. Can you . . . " Brody's comment replayed in my head. "Actually, I was calling to thank him for sending some flowers. But I probably should actually be thanking you. I'm sure he had you send the beautiful arrangement that came today."

"I can't take all the credit. He did tell me what to put on the card." She chuckled, innocently acknowledging something that shouldn't have mattered. Yet, it did for some reason.

"Well, thank you, and please let him know I called to thank him as well."

"I'll let him know."

I sat in my office, staring out into space for a while after I hung up. A knock at the door startled me.

"Delilah Maddox?"

"Yes?" The deliveryman held a large white box wrapped with a giant blue-and-yellow bow. *Long-stem roses now?*

"These are for you."

He placed the box on my desk and left. I slipped off the bow, taking note that the colors were the Steel team colors. Unwrapping the white tissue paper inside, I expected to find a dozen long-stem roses. Instead, the box was filled with long *sticks*—tree branches—a dozen or so, tied by a bow that matched the one on the outside. The card that accompanied the delivery was in Brody's handwriting. I recognized it from the message he'd left me on the footballs.

In case you want to make s'mores.

Thinking of you. ~Brody

(P.S. The thoughts are dirty)

Delilah
CHAPTER 9

I felt like I was going on a first date. I glanced at the clock almost as many times as I changed my outfit Thursday evening. The thing was . . . it wasn't a date. It was a business meeting. With a guy I'd already flat-out declined an invitation for sex from. A guy I couldn't stop wondering what it would be like to have sex with. What exactly was the right wardrobe for such an event?

Giving in to my wild hair, I left it down, unruly curls tumbling halfway down my back. I ransacked my closet, searching for something that was business-smart, yet attractive without being overtly sexy. Settling for a black pencil skirt and a red form-fitting button-up shirt, I added a few chunky bracelets, slipped on a pair of strappy sandals that wrapped around my ankles and took one last look in the full-length mirror in my bedroom. The weather was still warm enough for bare legs, and the high heel of my open shoe extended my already long legs, making them look even longer. I liked what I saw. Who knew I could pull off smart with a touch of sexy? Now if only I could pull off pretending I wasn't attracted to the arrogant ass.

Right at five, I lifted my hand to knock on the penthouse suite, and the door swung open, leaving my knuckles rapping on air. A beautiful young brunette greeted me wearing a very cropped shirt and second-skin leggings. Half of her tiny waist was on display, and her voice was cheerleaderish peppy. "Hey," she yelled over her shoulder, bouncing on her heels, "your appointment is here, Brody. I'll see you tomorrow." Still smiling, she stepped aside for me to enter and left me with, "I wore him out pretty good, hope it doesn't mess up whatever you plan to do with him."

Confused, I hesitated just inside the door as it closed behind me. Brody walked into the room, looking freshly showered in low-hanging sweats and no shirt. His hair was wet and slicked back. *Damn.*

"Hey." His eyes made a slow sweep of my body, and he stopped in his tracks a few feet away from me. "Wow. You look—"

My body grew warmer from the heat in his eyes. He unabashedly took his time before lifting his eyes to meet mine. "So, how does this work? Friends can't tell friends how they look?"

"Of course they can. Friends can give compliments."

His eyes gleamed. "Good. You look good enough to eat."

God, it really has been too long. My body tightened, and I had to swallow my breath to keep a small gasp from slipping out. Pink rose on my cheeks at the picture he'd just planted in my brain. I could visualize myself looking down at those broad shoulders as he *ate me*. Somehow I knew it wouldn't be slow and tender licking and sucking. No, this man would *devour* me whole.

"I didn't hear you come in. I needed a quick shower after Brittany. That woman might be small, but she's demanding as shit. Worked me over good today."

Abruptly, the switch flipped off. *Nothing like talking about his sexcapades with another woman to cool off my raging libido.* "Wonderful. I'm glad you've taken care of your needs. Perhaps we can skip the games and go straight to work this evening, then?" My tone came out a bit snide.

Brody's eyebrows knitted. He walked toward me, not stopping until he was invading my personal space. I was still just inside the suite, and the door was only a foot or two behind me. The urge to take a step or two back was great, but I held my ground.

"No games. There's nothing more I'd like to do than take you up against that door right now. And the fact that you just got jealous of Brittany, *my physical therapist*, proves that I'm not off-base. You want me inside of you as much as I want to bury myself. You just haven't admitted it to yourself . . . " He craned his neck down so we were nose to nose. "Yet. But you will."

I swallowed. For a change, I was at a loss for words. Eventually, he groaned and took a step back. Running a hand raggedly through his hair, he said, "We need to do this somewhere else. I don't trust myself in this hotel suite alone with you."

I thought he was joking, but a few minutes later he came out dressed with a baseball cap and sweatshirt on.

"Where are we going?"

"Someplace where I can't try to take advantage of you."

Rather than have the valet get his car, he opted for a cab. "Amsterdam and 112th Street, please."

"Morningside Heights? That's where you can't take advantage of me?"

"Yep."

My eyes were glued to the vividly painted ceiling as we walked inside. "This place is incredible. I've passed it a hundred times before, but never come inside."

Brody and I walked through St. John the Divine. He steered me down a long aisle on the left side of the church and waved to two priests sitting in a row, talking. At the end of the aisle, he opened a door and ushered me in first.

"Where are we going?"

"To the roof."

"The roof?"

"Yeah. I come here sometimes. A friend of mine used to work here. He had a pigeon coop on the roof. When I was a kid, I would stop in and hang out with him all the time. It's quiet. Most people go to the top of the Empire State Building or Top of the Rock to get a view. You can see the city just as good from upstairs."

"And you're allowed up there?"

"Nah. You might get arrested. I'll be able to run when the cops come, but you're going to be slow as crap in those sexy shoes."

"What?"

"I'm kidding. It's open to the public during tours. But I know most of the people who work here, so they let me come up whenever. Carl worked here for fifty years before he retired. I grew up next to him and his wife, Marlene."

Brody wasn't exaggerating. The view from the roof was pretty spectacular. Nestled between two of the church peaks was a cozy little seating area that looked out on the entire city.

"So what happened to the pigeon coops after Carl retired?" There was no sign of a cage—or a pigeon, for that matter.

"He kept up with it for a while. After he died, Marlene donated everything to the West Side Pigeon Club. There are a lot of pigeon people in this city."

We stood along the brick rooftop rail, and Brody pointed out some buildings. He was pretty knowledgeable about the area and architecture.

"What was your major in college?" I asked.

"You mean you don't have that memorized?"

"I'm better with statistics than actual words."

"Engineering."

"That's right. Pretty difficult major while playing football at a Big Ten."

"See. I'm not just a pretty face. Got some brains, too."

I rolled my eyes. "So, is this where you take all your dates? It's definitely not what I would've expected."

"If this were a real date, we definitely wouldn't be in the one place where I can't maul you or tell you what I'm thinking of doing to your body."

"So this is my safe place?"

Brody motioned for me to sit on the stone bench and then sat next to me. "It might be your only one."

"Okay, then." I cleared my throat and reached into my bag for my notebook. "Why don't we get started? I'll go easy on you."

He smirked. "I wouldn't be going easy on you if this was my show."

I shook my head. "How do you feel about the changes in coaching and management that are planned for next year?" Coach Ryan had been the Steel's coach since Brody began his career. He'd cut Brody from the team, but also hired him back and gave him a second chance. Due to his wife's health issues, Ryan was retiring at the end of the season.

Brody blew out a breath. "Not looking forward to it. Coach is tough, but fair, and built the team to what it is today. I respect him and wish he was sticking around. But I respect him even more for putting his family first."

"Any idea who they have in mind for his replacement?"

"Nope. But I'm hoping the decision is made before Coach retires. The sooner, the better. It'll make for a smoother transition to have the two coaches work together for a while. Bob Langley has been solid with coaching picks. Just hope it continues.

"That brings me nicely to my next question. It's rumored that Bob Langley might sell a—"

"Were the roses from Langley?"

"Why would the owner of your team send me roses, I've never met the man?" I knew exactly whom he meant. He was referring to Bob's son, Michael.

"The dipshit son you work with, not Bob."

"I don't think that's any of your business."

"Maybe not. But I'm asking the question."

I held his stare. "Yes."

"Guy's a—"

"We're at a church," I reminded him.

"Are you seeing him?"

"He asked me to dinner, if you must know."

"You'll go out to dinner with him, but not me?"

"His dinner invitation is to get to know me, not to get inside of me."

"That's where you're wrong. I'm just more upfront about it than he is."

"How did my pre-interview turn into *you* asking *me* questions?"

Brody leaned back and folded his arms over his chest. "Question for question."

"Excuse me?"

"For every question you ask, I get to ask one."

"That's ridiculous."

"Not if you want the interview."

"Let me guess. All of your questions will be personal?"

"Only when yours are."

"Fine," I huffed. I'd just steer clear of personal questions. Perusing the list I had prepared, I skipped the first one that was clearly more personal than professional. "The offensive line seems to have become a second-half team. Sixty-eight percent of the scoring has been done in the second half, and the Steel have come from behind in the second half in four out of five of their wins. What happens in the locker room at halftime that makes the team rally together better?"

Brody looked pleased with my question. He spent almost a full five minutes talking about the halftime changes that Coach Ryan made during previous games. Unlike many quarterbacks, he didn't take credit for the improvements that caused his team to win. Instead, he chalked things up to strong coaching.

"My turn," Brody said when I finished scribbling notes.

"I'm almost afraid to hear it. But go ahead."

"If you had to marry one man from *Gilligan's Island*, which one would you choose?"

I laughed. "That's your question?"

"It is." He had a boyish grin on his face.

"That's easy. The Professor."

"Good answer."

"Was there really any other logical answer?"

"You could have picked Mr. Howell. He's rich and old."

My next question was about the expanded definition of the defenseless player penalty. Then it was Brody's turn again. "Name of your first pet?"

"I actually never had a pet."

"Everybody's had a pet at one time or another. Dog, cat, rabbit, snake, lizard, hamster, turtle...something?"

I shook my head. "Nope. We traveled a lot on weekends to see my dad's games, so we never had any pets because no one was around to take care of them."

"You know I have the urge to buy you a dog now, right? A giant one, maybe a Newfie or a Great Dane."

"Don't you dare."

We sat on the roof of that church for almost two more hours. Brody's odd line of questioning found some unusual commonalities between the two of us. Both of our mothers' middle names were Yvonne, neither of us liked chocolate, and we both grew up in apartments with street addresses numbered three-three-three. I'd skipped over one particular question, knowing I'd have to answer a personal one of my own. It was the only one left. "Last question."

"Shoot."

"Available or taken?" I explained the question, trying not to be personally invested in his answer. "Every woman will want to know the answer."

He looked me in the eyes when he answered. "Neither."

I wasn't prepared for that answer, so I had no follow-up question. I nodded and proceeded to pack my notes. Sitting upright, I readied myself. "Go ahead. Ask your personal question."

Brody stood and offered his hand to help me up. "I'll reserve mine for later."

————————————————————

We walked two blocks up the street to a diner. Brody had said he was going to order in food for us in his suite, so I hadn't eaten all day. My stomach growled as we sat.

"What was that?" Brody teased.

"Shut up. You told me you'd feed me and then took me to church instead. My stomach is allowed to complain."

The waitress did a double-take when she came for our order. "Aren't you . . . aren't you . . . Brody Easton?"

"I am."

"Oh my god!" she shrieked. "I'm a huge fan. But my eleven-year-old son. He's a quarterback at his middle school. He thinks you're the greatest."

"Thank you. How is his team doing this season?"

"They've lost every game. But my Joey, he never gets defeated. Kid takes after me in height. He can barely see over the line anymore. But he has more heart than boys twice his size."

"That's good. He's still got time to grow. But you either have your heart in the sport, or you don't. He's halfway there."

"He's never going to believe I met you."

"Well, how about if we take a picture together and send it to him?"

The waitress's eyes bulged with excitement, but her face quickly fell. "I don't have a phone anymore. Bill gets too high with two lines, and my son really wanted one. Plus, I'm always here, and I like to be able to reach him when I need to."

"How about we use my phone and send it to Joey then?"

"Oh my god. You'd do that? He would totally flip."

I piped in, "I'll take it. You two get together." The waitress beamed as Brody stood and put his arm around her, leaning in. After I snapped off a few photos and checked that they turned out okay, I gave her my phone, and she sent the picture to her son with a cute note. As she started to hand the phone back to me, Brody stopped her.

"Actually. Would you mind taking a picture of us together?"

"Sure."

I looked at Brody questioningly. He gave me a sly grin and came around to my side of the table, squatting down so we were at eye level.

"You ready?" the waitress asked.

Brody leaned in and whispered in my ear, "I'd much rather be eating you than anything on the menu here." He pulled his head back to catch a glimpse of my expression. "Ready," he called back to the waitress, who captured a photo of Brody's eyes twinkling as they looked over at my hooded ones.

We ordered, and I did my best to pretend I wasn't affected. "Tell me something about you," Brody said, resting his arm casually along the back of the booth.

"Like what?"

"I don't know. Anything. Tell me something about you that annoys people."

"You ask odd questions."

"Good thing I don't have your job then."

I chuckled. "True." Sipping my soda, I gave his question some thought. "I talk during movies."

"So? Everyone talks during a movie at some point."

"No. I *talk* during movies. Mostly it happens when I like the movie. I get excited and need to retell everything that's happening on the screen to the person next to me."

Brody looked amused. "So better to take you to a movie you don't like, then?"

"Well . . . if I don't like the movie, then I tend to get bored and daydream a bit and I lose track of what's going on. Then I ask loads of question instead of retelling you the movie."

"If you know you do it, and it annoys people, why don't you stop doing it?"

"I can't help myself. So what do you do that annoys people?"

"I say what I think."

"You sure do."

"Does it annoy you?"

"At first it did. I guess I'm starting to expect it now."

"I'm like fungus, I grow on you."

"Charming."

The hours disappeared while we talked. Especially when we argued about football. It was almost midnight by the time we were ready to leave the diner. The waitress brought the bill, and Brody refused to let me pay, even though I'd argued it was technically a business dinner, and the station would pick up the tab. He didn't say anything, but I caught that he left the waitress a tip of at least a few hundred dollars. The fact that he didn't want me to notice what he'd done made the gesture that much more meaningful.

He hailed a cab, and light late-night traffic had us pulling up in front of my building in less than fifteen minutes. Brody told the cabbie to give him a few minutes and walked me into my building.

"Thank you for taking the time to let me pre-interview you. It'll actually make me a lot more comfortable on Saturday now that we've done that."

"You're very welcome."

I pushed the button to call the elevator. "And thank you again for dinner."

Brody nodded. "You know . . . I still have that one personal question left."

I had actually forgotten. "Saving the best one for last?"

"You could say that. Yes."

The flutter in my stomach knew what was coming. In a sweet gesture, he brushed the hair from my face and tucked it behind my ear. His hand caressed my cheek and then tipped my chin slightly so I was looking straight into his eyes when he spoke. "What's it going to take to get you underneath me, Delilah?"

I swallowed. He wasn't teasing to get my attention this time. No, he was dead serious and watching me intently, waiting for an answer.

"I like you. You're full of yourself and direct. But despite all that, I actually really enjoy spending time with you. I'm just not looking for a physical-only relationship. I need more than that."

"Like what?"

"I don't know. Dating. Going out together. Exclusivity. I need to spend time with someone, other than just in his bed. Like talking to them during a movie." I forced a smile. "It's just who I am."

The normally slow elevator appeared quickly for a change. The doors slid open behind me, and I waited for Brody to say something. But he only nodded.

"See you Saturday?" I asked.

"Saturday." He nodded.

The doors slid closed and carried me up to the fourteenth floor. But it felt like a little piece of my heart had been left behind.

Delilah
CHAPTER 10

Only two days had passed since I'd seen Brody, yet I still couldn't get him out of my mind. Apparently, I wasn't the only one.

"Cute." Indie gave an unenthused wave to the guy at the other end of the bar who tipped his drink in our direction. She sighed as she brought her martini glass to her mouth. "But he's no Brody Easton."

"Can we not go there again? Your interest is bordering on stalkerish."

"Well, I guess there's always that guy." She tilted her glass in the direction of an older guy who seriously resembled Dr. Hannibal Lecter from *The Silence of the Lambs.* He was standing alone in a corner, leering in our direction, and when he caught us looking, his rickety-toothed smile grew ridiculously wide. I would have felt safer if Hannibal had had the leather mask wrapped around his face. "I'm sure he'd be happy to break the seal on your revirginized vagina . . . before he eats half your face off."

"Think I'll pass. I do have other opportunities, you know. Michael Langley texted me today."

"Oh yeah. And did you agree to go out with him yet?"

"I was busy. I didn't have time to text him back yet."

"You're stalling because you want Brody, and you know it."

"Am not."

"Are too."

"You're not busy now." She motioned for the bartender, pointing to her empty glass. "Go ahead. I'll wait. Text him and tell him you'll go out with him, then. If you're not holding out for Brody Easton, then there's nothing stopping you. Your cleanse is just about over anyway."

"I will."

"I'm waiting." Indie tapped her fingers on the bar. Needing to prove her wrong, I took out my phone and thumbed off a quick response to Michael.

"Happy?" I turned my phone in her direction so she could see the word *sent* on my screen. She snatched it from my hand and read my response.

Thank you. Yet another crazy week. I promise to catch up with you again next week.

"That is not telling him you'll go out with him. That's pushing him off again for another week."

"But I *am* busy. How would you have liked me to respond?"

She tapped on my keypad and turned the phone in my direction. Luckily, she hadn't pressed Send. Her text read. *On second thought. I don't think I can wait another week. Dinner on Saturday night?*

"I'm not that forward." I grasped for my phone. She pulled it back, out of my reach.

With a huge smile, she said, "You are now." She hit Send.

My eyes bulged. "I can not believe you just did that!"

Ignoring me, she ordered us two shots when the bartender returned with her third martini. I wasn't much of a drinker. Two glasses of wine was the limit on our regular Friday night happy hour. If I was being honest, I came for the company and the free finger food—half of the single people in bars in New York did the same thing. None of us wanted to cook in our tiny kitchens if we didn't have to.

I was still pouting when my phone buzzed on the bar. Michael's name flashed on the screen. Turning to Indie, I lifted the shot she'd ordered me and drank. Then I drank hers, too. After shaking off the willies the alcohol left behind, I summoned the courage to read Michael's response.

I was beginning to think you were blowing me off. Your text made my otherwise rotten day bright again. Eight on Saturday?

Maybe Indie was right. I *was* stalling because of a lingering attraction to a certain quarterback. One that deep down I knew I shouldn't even be tempted to explore. There really was no reason not to start dating again.

I sighed. "Okay. Maybe you were right."

"Come again?"

I spoke louder. "I said, maybe you were right."

"Oh, I heard you the first time. I just loved to hear you admit it."

Indie and I sat at the bar until almost eleven. I was beyond tipsy when she hailed a cab for us, foregoing our usual subway trek home. The driver dropped her first, and I sat in traffic staring out the window in an alcohol-induced daze. A bus pulled up next to me and caught my attention. An old ad was peeling from the side. It had the New York Steel logo along with a picture of Brody's handsome face and read, *Easton is back.* It must have been a few years old.

The alcohol had me making rash decisions. Without thinking, I thumbed off a text.

Delilah: Just saw your picture on the side of a bus. Do you like having your face on public transportation?

He responded thirty seconds later.

Brody: I like having my face anywhere that makes you think about me. But I'd rather have my face between your legs.

Who said things like that? And why the hell did I like it? Seriously, the lower half of my body began to tingle.

Delilah: You have a real way with words, friend.

Brody: I have a real way with my tongue. When are you going to give in and let me show you?

Delilah: Tempting. But I think I'll stick to men who are interested in more than just my orifices.

Brody: I'm getting hard just because you used the word orifices.

I chuckled out loud. The cabbie looked at me in the rearview mirror, and I held up my phone in explanation. He didn't give a crap.

Delilah: Good night, Brody.

The man could make me laugh and ignite at the same time. It was a combination that my entire body quite liked.

Brody: See you in your dreams.

He most certainly would be.

e ——————————————————— *e*

Saturday afternoon, I was a wreck. I had the rare one-on-one interview with Brody at five, followed by a date with Michael at eight. As I headed to the Regency, I wanted to kill Indie for setting up my dinner for this evening.

"Nervous?" Nick glanced at me and then back to the road. We were carrying more equipment than we normally would for a locker room interview, so he had picked me up in the station's van.

"Does it show?"

"You've been spinning that pen around in your hand since you got in."

I clutched the pen in my fist to stop myself. I was definitely a nervous fidgeter and had no idea I was even doing it. "Sorry."

"Doesn't bother me any. But I'm surprised. To me, heading into the locker room would be more nerve-racking than this sit-down. You always seem so calm, waiting to go in after the games."

"I must just be better at hiding it then. Plus. I have a date tonight after the interview. It's been a while. I was on a self-imposed six-month hiatus from dating."

"Well, that explains it, then. What time is your date?"

"Eight."

"Plenty of time. We'll be out of there by seven."

We arrived at Brody's hotel a few minutes early, and he opened the door fresh from the shower. His hair was slicked back, and droplets of water beaded on his ridiculously toned chest. God, I wanted to lick them off.

Brody caught me gaping. A knowing grin spread across his gorgeous face. I wanted to smack if off. *Or kiss it off.*

"Come on in. Figured Delilah could help me pick out something to wear while you set up." He shook Nick's hand and then leaned in and kissed me on the cheek. "You look beautiful."

Nick and Brody spoke about where to set up and spent a few minutes talking sports. The man was definitely a charmer—to both men and women. It just came naturally to him. It was part of what made him larger than life on camera. He exuded confidence and charisma. Eventually, he turned his attention to me. "You ready to dress me?"

I rolled my eyes. As Brody led the way to his bedroom, Nick yelled, "Don't take as long as you take to pick your own clothes out, or you'll miss half your date."

I walked straight into Brody when he stopped in his tracks. "Date?"

Swallowing, I felt like I'd done something wrong. "Yes, I have a date tonight after our interview."

"What time?"

"Eight."

He surprised me by not discussing it any further. We walked through the bedroom into the large walk-in closet. "What do you think? Suit or something more casual?"

"I think casual. A sweater and slacks maybe."

"Go for it." He extended his arm toward the built-in shelves holding piles of neatly folded sweaters.

Fingering through them, I noticed every piece of clothing was folded exactly the same. "I guess you have someone who puts away your laundry for you."

He walked up close behind me. Very close. I felt the heat from his body. *His shirtless, magnificent body.*

"I do. If I didn't, you'd be sorting through a mess of clothes on the floor."

Trying to pretend his nearness didn't affect me, I focused on the task of picking out his outfit. Reaching up, I grabbed a navy cashmere sweater. "How about this?" I turned to show him my selection and smacked straight into the brick wall of his chest. He hadn't budged. It was a big closet, yet there was little room between the shelves behind me and the man in front of me.

He shrugged. "If you like it, I'll wear it."

"You're easy."

"Wish I could say the same about you."

"Something tells me if I was, you'd have already lost interest."

"Is that what you think? That I only like the chase?"

I looked him straight in the eyes. "I do. Yes. I think you enjoy the chase. I'm guessing it's a novelty to you these days. That you're normally the chased, not the chaser."

He took a step closer to me; I backed up and hit the shelving behind me. Placing one forearm against the wall on either side of my head, he effectively caged me in. I should have wanted to flee from the feeling, but instead I had the sudden urge to press my body against his. Thankfully, a little self-control still existed in my brain.

He lowered his face to mine. "Who's your date with tonight?"

"None of your business."

He leaned in a little closer, so our lips were just inches apart. "Do you feel what you're feeling right now when you're near him?"

No. "Maybe."

"Bullshit. Tell me I can kiss you." He lowered his head and gently ran his nose along my throat. My body was buzzing like a college boy on frat initiation night.

"No." The word came out barely above a whisper. My voice was thick and strained, clear evidence that he was getting to me.

He continued trailing his nose along my skin. The sensual touch left a stream of goose bumps in its wake. When he reached my ear, his voice was edgy and laced with need. "Tell me I can kiss you. I smell your body getting turned on. Tell me."

My knees were trembling, and my mouth opened to finally give in. *I want him to kiss me so badly.*

Luckily, Nick's voice broke the moment. "Brody, can I run a chord from—whoa . . . sorry. I didn't mean to interrupt."

Brody responded without moving. "Do whatever you need to, Nick."

"Yeah. All right, man," Nick said. His footsteps rapidly receded.

It was only a few seconds of distraction. But it gave me a chance to snap out of my lust-induced haze. "This is really unprofessional of me." I ducked under his arm and practically ran out of the closet.

I spent a few minutes composing myself in the bathroom before joining Nick in the living room. He was almost through setting up. "Sorry about that. I didn't realize your date tonight was with Brody."

My mouth opened, but the response came from the man who entered the room behind me. "It's not. But it fucking should be."

I turned, finding Brody wearing the navy cashmere sweater I'd picked out and a pair of well fitting slacks. The deep blue color brought out the intensity in his eyes. Eyes that were boring into me.

"Coach needs to talk to me. I have to jump on a call for a while. Why don't you two make yourselves at home? I'll order some snacks from room service before I get started."

"No problem. Thanks, Brody," Nick said.

Then he was gone.

For almost *two full hours*.

Eventually, I ventured into the back to look for him. It was quiet, no indication that he was still on the phone. I knocked lightly on the bedroom door, but there was no response. So I knocked again. When there was still nothing but silence, I creaked the bedroom door open. Brody was lying in the middle of his king-size bed. *Sound asleep.*

"Brody?"

His eyes opened with a flutter. "It's the woman from my dreams."

My hands went to my hips. "What do you think you're doing?"

"I guess I fell asleep."

"Before or after your fake coach's phone call?"

He swung his legs over the side of the bed and sat up. Running his hands through his hair, he said, "You ready to get started?"

"I've been ready for more than two hours."

"Sorry. I guess you'll have to cancel your date for tonight."

Brody was grinning, and I smiled back. But mine wasn't a friendly smile. It was more like a *Bend over, I'm about to stick my foot right up your ass* smile. "That's okay. We can just skip dinner and go straight to whatever he has planned for after."

Brody's smile fell. Mine grew bigger.

Ten minutes later, we were finally sitting and ready to begin the interview.

The first few questions were stiff. My annoyance was bleeding through, and his responses were curt. Things started to change around the fourth question, when we got into a heated debate about statistics. More than an hour and a half of tape rolled, even though we only had to fill a twenty-two-minute segment, after factoring in commercials, for the half-hour feature.

We were up to the last question: "Available or taken?" His answer had been "neither" during the pre-interview, which I thought was a pretty interesting and accurate description of his dating life. He wasn't taken, but he also wasn't available.

Only this time, when I asked the question, his response caught me off guard.

"Taken."

He could see the confusion on my face, but I quickly jumped back into reporter mode. "Really? Is this new?"

"It is."

"How new?"

"So new, she doesn't even know about it yet."

"Pardon?"

"I plan to tell her about our new relationship right after this interview."

"Tell her? Not ask her?"

"Yep. We've been playing cat-and-mouse for a while. There's been something going on for weeks. But I've been avoiding it because I'm not the best at relationships."

"And now that's changed?"

"It has. She makes me nuts. But I also can't stop thinking about her. So it's time to make it official and take myself off the market to see how things go."

I had no idea how to respond to that, so I wrapped things up. Turning to the camera, I delivered my closing. "You heard it here first, ladies. Brody Easton has taken himself off the market. I'm sure there are legions of women devastated by the news. But WMBC wishes the Super Bowl MVP good luck in the game tomorrow and with his new relationship. This reporter guesses one might be easier for him to manage than the other."

Nick turned off the camera. While he packed up the lighting, he said, "Great interview. Edit is going to have a hard time finding things to cut to get the final twenty-two in the can."

"Thanks, Nick."

Brody and I helped pack up the rest of the equipment. It was after nine by the time we were done. Nick glanced at his phone. "Want me to drop you at your date? You're already late."

"Thanks, but I sent him a text earlier and postponed."

Nick nodded. "Drop you at home?"

"I'll drop her," Brody said. "Let me help you lug this shit to the van."

I picked up a bag. Brody took it from my hand. "Stay. I got it. I'll be right back."

While he was gone, I rearranged the living room furniture back to how it had been before the interview. Brody came in just as I was finishing setting the throw pillows back on the couch.

"You should get some monogrammed throw pillows for the couch," I said. "Make it seem less like a hotel and more homey."

"When did you postpone the date?"

I held one pillow against my chest. "After I came out of the closet."

"Not after I made you late?"

I shook my head. The way I'd felt when I walked out of that closet, I knew going on a date with Michael would have been wrong. Whether I was acting upon them or not, I had feelings for another man. It was wrong to begin a relationship with someone when my thoughts were really with someone else.

"You're postponing it indefinitely."

"Am I?"

He nodded and walked around the couch. Reaching for my hand, he looked into my eyes. "I can do exclusive. Hell, the thought of you with anyone else makes me fucking insane. I insist on exclusive. And dating. I'm game for whatever you want to do. The relationship part, I'm probably going to need you to bear with me on. It's been a long time since I've had one. I'll probably fuck up and piss you off a lot, but I'd like to try."

Wow. I wasn't about to mention that I'd been ready to give in to his sex-only arrangement. I guess I'd won the battle of the holdout. *By about thirty seconds.* "Okay."

"Okay?"

"Yes. I'd like to try, too. You're an arrogant ass. But there's something about you I like."

He picked up my other hand and brought it to his lips, dropping a sweet kiss on the top. "Awesome. Dinner, then fucking? Or fucking, then dinner?

"Gee. How is a girl to decide with such titillating choices?"

"Flip a coin. Heads—you give me. Tails—I take yours. It's a total win-win for you." He winked. "By the way, I really like when you work 'tit' into our conversation, dirty girl."

I laughed. "How about we start with an actual date?"

"Let's go."

"Not so fast."

Brody looked like I'd kicked his puppy. "What?"

"If we're going to do this, let's start it right. You have a game tomorrow. I want a real date. How about next weekend?"

"No way."

"Impatient much?"

"Patience is bitter. It's the fruit that's sweet."

"Did you just quote Aristotle?"

"Maybe." He yanked the hand he was holding, pulling me against him hard. "Dinner. Wednesday night. I'll pick you up at seven."

"Okay."

"Now kiss me already, goddamn it."

I didn't have time to respond. In a heartbeat, his lips were on mine. His arms wrapped possessively around me, pulling me snugly against him. My knees went weak. My heart was pounding in my chest, and I would have sworn there was a mass of butterflies flapping their wings in the pit of my stomach. With a groan that echoed through our mouths and vibrated down my entire body, he licked my lips and nudged my mouth open. His tongue aggressively pursued mine and then took everything I gave. The desperation and intensity of the kiss was like nothing I'd ever felt before. My hands dug into his hair as he grabbed a handful of mine and tugged my head back further to where he wanted me. I whimpered, feeling desire flow from him and wrap around me. I moaned when I felt his hard-on pushing up against my stomach.

Holy shit.

We stayed like that for a long time. Grabbing and groping. Pulling and needing. When he finally released my mouth, he sucked on my bottom lip and released a hungry groan. "Overnight bag. Bring a bag Wednesday. Because there's no way I'm letting you go again."

Brody

CHAPTER 11

"You know, when I was a kid they had real football players. They wore leather helmets and didn't have *bi*-weeks. What kind of a sissy athlete needs a week off in the middle of the season?"

"When you were a kid, they kept score by chiseling X marks into stone." I tossed a jersey to Grouper. Next week was a designated throwback week, when the team wore replica uniforms from years back. I'd ordered an extra for Grouper III. "Tell Guppy I signed it with a washable marker this time. Don't want his mother getting another smelly-boy call from the school."

Grouper held it up and sighed nostalgically. "I remember this uniform. This was from the non-pussy-player period."

"Bite me, old man."

Marlene was sitting on the edge of her bed, a floral swim cap on her head. She was scribbling some notes on her notepad while the closing credits of *The Price Is Right* rolled on the TV screen behind her. *Guess I'm late today.*

"Going swimming, Marlene?" I leaned in and kissed her cheek.

She looked up at me blankly. "Are you the bus driver?"

"No. I'm Brody. Remember?"

She still looked confused.

"I used to live next door."

Recognition registered. "Willow's Brody." She looked around me. "Is she with you today?"

"Not today, Marlene."

"She didn't want to come?"

I hated when she asked me these questions. Sometimes it was easier when she didn't remember who I was. "She's working on an art project up at my cabin. You know how she can get when she's working."

That seemed to pacify her. So I changed the subject to one of her favorites. "How did you do today on your show?"

She looked down at her notepad. "I would have won the whole shebang. The woman who was in the finale, Kathryn, her name was, only had one oar in the water."

"They can't all be like you. Or it wouldn't be much of a game, would it?"

"That Barker's microphone is too skinny. I don't know what he's trying to prove."

I chuckled. "Yeah. I'm not sure on that one either."

Marlene took the remote off her nightstand and flicked the TV off.

"What time is swimming? I didn't realize they changed the schedule."

"Eleven."

I looked down at my watch. It was five after twelve.

Marlene and I shot the shit for a while, and eventually Shannon walked in, carrying a small clear plastic shot glass containing a few pills. She handed them to Marlene with a cup of water.

"Are they running late for swimming?" I asked.

"Nope. Swimming isn't until Wednesday at two."

I glanced sideways at Marlene's swim cap, then back to Shannon.

She shrugged. "She got upset when I tried to take it off of her this morning. I told her swimming wasn't until tomorrow. She told me I had shit for brains. Right, Marlene?"

Marlene nodded and handed her back the empty pill cup. She spoke as if she were verifying the time. "That's right. Shit for brains, that one."

Shannon gave me a thumbs-up and a wink as she left the room.

An hour later, Marlene let me help her remove the rubber swim cap. The damn thing was so tight, it left a red indent across her forehead where the edge cut off her circulation.

"I'm going to get going. Late practice this afternoon."

She nodded. "You kiss that granddaughter of mine and tell her not to work too hard."

"I will."

Delilah
CHAPTER 12

After I'd returned from a two-hour session in the editing room, the receptionist walked into my office carrying a tall glass vase full not of flowers but of *water*. The puzzled look on her face matched mine. Until I saw that the vase wasn't actually empty. A single blue beta fish was swimming around, and the floor was lined with a layer of blue and yellow colored gravel. She handed me the small florist's card, glanced at the other vase on my desk—the one full of sticks—and walked out, shaking her head.

I unsealed the card. *I named him Brody. You're welcome.*

I smiled, remembering our conversation about me never having a pet before. For a man who'd told me women didn't really want bullshit flowers and sweet gestures—what they really wanted was a good banging against the wall—I was pretty sure he was giving me both today.

Later that afternoon, I was viewing a replay of my interview with Brody on my laptop. The sound of his gritty voice and the confidence he exuded was a little like foreplay for our date tonight. I was anxious, excited and nervous all at once. Closing my eyes as he spoke, I leaned back in my chair and visualized him standing before me, that commanding voice telling me to undress.

Unbutton your shirt.

Take off that bra.

God, even imagining it stirred a feminine place in me.

Lift that skirt.

Higher, Delilah.

You know what I'm going to do to you...

A knock on my office door startled me, and I jumped out of my seat. *Shit.*

"Hey. Sorry, didn't mean to scare you. I thought you saw me."

"Michael. Hi. Guess I was lost in my work." I had texted at the last minute to cancel our date the other night, and he'd been very understanding. I hadn't exactly lied when I told him an interview was running a few hours later than planned and asked for a rain check. Last night, he'd texted me to cash in the rain check I'd promised—and not knowing how to respond, I just never responded.

"Just stopped in to say hello. See how you were doing."

"I'm good. Busy. Sorry I didn't text back yet. My schedule has just been so crazy lately."

His eyes zoned in on the roses he sent displayed on the file cabinet behind me, then he took note of the vase full of sticks on the corner of the front of my desk. He looked justifiably puzzled. They added something to my otherwise drab office—perhaps a splash of crazy. Yet he didn't question the oddity.

"Would you be up for grabbing a bite for dinner tonight?"

"I actually have plans for tonight. Sorry."

"Work again?"

Michael was watching me, waiting for a response. It felt odd to tell him that I was going on a date. Probably because of my gnawing guilt that the date was with the guy I'd canceled on him the other night because of. So I lied. "Yes. I need to reshoot part of an interview I did."

A look of relief passed over Michael's face. "Man, being the boss around here doesn't earn any perks, does it?"

"I guess not." I tried to laugh it off.

"One night next week, then?"

I nodded, leaving things very noncommittal. Thankfully, my phone rang.

"Excuse me a minute." I was relieved to get out of the conversation and answer my office line. "Delilah Maddox."

Brody's sexy voice growled through the phone. "Did you bring an overnight bag to work?"

I looked up at Michael; he was still standing in my doorway. "I did."

"You actually don't need anything in it. I'll pick you up in an hour. You'll get your date. Then I'm going to give you my own version of those sweet gestures you like so much."

I cleared my throat. "Okay. That sounds good."

"Is someone standing there?"

"Yes, that's right."

"Are you wearing a skirt?"

"Yes."

"Take off your panties before I pick you up."

"Umm . . ."

"An hour, Delilah. No panties. I'm salivating at the thought of tasting you."

The phone disconnected, and I was left sitting there like an idiot, my body buzzing and my mouth hanging open.

"Are you okay?" Michael looked concerned.

"Yes." I blinked myself back to the moment. "Sorry about that."

"I'll let you get back to work. Call you next week?"

"That sounds great. Sure."

Maybe by then, I'd grow a backbone.

In the ten minutes I stood in the bathroom stall, I'd taken my underwear off and put it back on three times. The outer door opened again, and two women whose voices I didn't recognize walked in, chatting. *This was ridiculous.*

I decided to rise to the challenge. I balled the black lacy thong I was wearing in my palm, then stuffed it into the zippered compartment of my purse. Stepping out, it felt liberating. I washed my hands and headed to the exit of my office complex.

Through the glass front doors, I saw Brody leaning against his car. He was swinging the keys around casually and watching the people come and go from the building. I was an equal mix of excited and nervous as I stepped onto the sidewalk. When he caught sight of me, his face curved into a delicious grin. He folded his arms across his chest and watched me intently as I walked toward the car. The street was filled with people walking in all directions, yet he didn't seem to notice a single one of them. It was the craziest thing—the way he was looking at me, watching every move I made with desire on his face—was actually turning me on a little. My body became aroused without a single touch. I was suddenly starving, but it definitely wasn't for dinner.

He extended a hand to me as I neared, then abruptly tugged it hard, pulling me against him. Surprising me, he proceeded to kiss me—right there on the street. *And what a kiss.*

My brain was short-circuited when he finally released my mouth. "Damn." His hands slid down and locked around my waist, keeping me flush against him. "We could skip the date."

Even though my body wanted nothing more than to do exactly that, I said, "I can't make it that easy for you now, can I?"

"You've done nothing but make me hard since the day I met you." He pulled me even tighter against him—I literally felt his sincerity. Pushing against my stomach.

"So where are we going?"

"Dinner and a museum."

"Museum?"

"You said you loved them the other day."

"For a guy who doesn't believe in bullshit flowers and sweet gestures, you're pretty damn good at them."

Even though we went to a small restaurant that was off the celebrity grid, between the time the valet took the car and when we were seated at a quiet table in the corner, two people stopped us.

"Sorry about that."

"It's fine. I'm used to it. Only I don't remember the wives of the men who stopped my dad looking at him the way that last guy's wife was ogling you."

"I met your dad once."

"You did?"

"Yep. Training camp my first year on the team. He took me aside, and we talked for about a half hour. He used to come the first day of every season."

"What did you talk about?"

"He told me if I ever went near his daughter, he'd crush my nuts in a vise."

My eyes widened. "Really?"

"Nah, I'm just screwing with you."

I laughed. I did that a lot around Brody. He had an uncanny ability to change my mood in an instant. One minute I would be laughing, the next I could be practically panting from the extreme sexual tension.

After we had ordered wine and appetizers, another excited fan interrupted our conversation and asked for an autograph. It was mid football season, and I was having dinner with the starting quarterback of the number-two-ranked team.

"Does it bother you? Fame?"

"Not usually. I generally don't do anything in public that I care about being interrupted. Believe it or not, I don't go out too much."

"I've seen you photographed with plenty of women."

"Most of that was from events. Obligations for sponsors or the team. I actually can't remember the last time I had a date like this. Without it being something I was required to attend."

"Why is that? I'm guessing it isn't from lack of opportunity."

"I like to keep my focus on the game."

"So you've never had a serious relationship?"

Brody leaned back into his chair and glanced around the restaurant. "I've had a relationship, yes."

"Just one?"

"Just one." A muscle in his jaw flexed. Clearly this conversation made him uncomfortable. But I wanted to know more about him.

"What happened?"

"It ended."

"I gathered that much, considering we're sitting here, and you've been trying to get me to sleep with you for weeks."

Brody's eyebrows shot up. "Why does it always feel like I'm being interviewed when we're together?"

"Probably because you don't volunteer much information."

The waitress stopped by our table. "Can I take these plates for you?"

Brody nodded. "That would be great."

When she disappeared, he tried to change the subject. "So, journalism?"

I wasn't letting him off the hook so easily. I sipped my wine and ignored his blatant attempt. "So you have had a relationship before?"

"Yes."

"How long ago did it end?"

"I don't know, Delilah. I haven't kept a calendar. Four years ago, maybe."

"So only casual dating since then?"

"Yes."

"Interesting."

"Not really. Is it my turn to ask the questions yet?"

"By all means." I waved my hand as if I were giving him the floor.

He scratched his chin for a moment. "If you knew you were going to be stranded on an island for a month and could only bring three things, what would you bring with you?"

I laughed. "You could have just brought up football or politics to change the subject."

94

"I could have, but I really want to know if you'd pick a vibrator as one of your three items."

"You think if I was going to be stranded on an island and I could only bring three things, I'd bring a vibrator?"

"Guess I'm kind of hoping you would."

"Don't think that would be on my short list."

"What would be?"

"I don't know. Off the top of my head? Matches, water and a fishing net."

"Smart choices. I'm disappointed. But at least you won't starve."

"Your questions are bizarre, you know that, right?"

"Maybe. But your answer just told me a lot about you. Like I just learned you're practical. You know you can get yourself off with your hand, so you won't waste one of your three things on an unnecessary toy." He tapped his finger to his temple and grinned. "Good thinking."

"Let me ask you something. If we eventually have sex—"

Brody interrupted. "If?"

"When. *When,* you know..."

"I fuck you..."

"Yes, that. Will you stop talking about sex so much afterward?"

He leaned forward. "Not a fucking chance. I'm gonna bet that once I'm inside of you, it's only going to get worse."

"Okay then." *God, it's warm in here.* I needed to change the subject, or this date was going to end very soon. Taking a cue from Brody, I asked, "If you could have your pick of any Disney princess, which one would it be?"

Brody smiled. "Nice. Let me think about that one."

He was quiet for a moment, then surprised me. He was taking my question seriously. "Definitely not Sleeping Beauty. She lies around sleeping all day, waiting for some shmuck wearing tights to come kiss her."

"That's not exactly how I would have summed her up. But, okay . . . continue."

He rubbed his chin. "Snow White's voice would annoy the shit out of me. Plus, I'm six-two, and she's into short guys." He paused. "I'm not sure I know any other princesses. Wait. No. That chick from *Aladdin* is hot. Or the *Little Mermaid*. But can a mermaid spread her legs? And is she even a princess?"

The rest of the evening continued the same way. We asked each other ridiculous questions, and the answers actually revealed a lot about each other. I started to think maybe I should throw one oddball question into my interviews from now on. After Brody had paid the bill, we waited outside for the valet to bring his car around. There was a crowd of people talking, and I noticed he steered us away from them and turned his back so as not to call attention to himself.

"Favorite position?" he asked.

Easy. "Quarterback, of course. I'm a daddy's girl."

He leaned in, whispering in my ear. "I meant favorite position naked."

"Oh." *Oh!*

He was actually waiting for a response. "I'm not sure. Never really gave it any thought." I swallowed. "What about you?"

He took my hands in his and brought them together behind my back. Capturing both my wrists in one of his large hands, his other lifted to my face and brushed a lock of hair from my cheek. "On top. Doesn't even matter how. I've just had an ache to be on top of you since the day we met. As much as I'd love to watch you ride me, I think on top is what I'll like best with you. And probably missionary. Because for some reason, there's nothing more I want to do than watch your face as I sink deep inside of you."

It wasn't the most romantic thing anyone had ever said to me, yet I felt it everywhere, even in my chest. "Jesus, Brody."

He brushed his lips against mine. "Our museum trip is going to be a quick one."

The tenderness of his touch, combined with the rawness of his words, left me with a yearning I'd never experienced before. I leaned in, our mouths again lightly joining, and let my words vibrate against our lips. "Let's skip the museum."

————————————

When we pulled up to the hotel that was his football-season home, Brody waved off the valet and jogged around to the passenger side of the car. He extended his hand to help me out.

"In for the night, Mr. Easton?"

He laced our fingers together and pulled me toward the door, responding over his shoulder without stopping. "I may never come back out."

My breath quickened as the elevator neared the top floor. We weren't alone in the car, yet the only thing I could smell or hear was Brody. I watched his chest rise and fall in the reflection on the shiny silver doors, and my breaths began to match his. He was standing behind me, and I could feel his every breath. I didn't try to fit my breathing into his pattern, my body just naturally joined in with his. It wasn't going to be the only rhythm that came to us innately; there was no doubt of that. Raw sexual chemistry had been running like a current between us since the first day we met.

The sound of the lock closing behind me echoed through the hotel suite. I walked a few feet inside of the room but didn't turn around. Brody was behind me. He wasn't touching, yet I could feel him near. He tossed his keys onto a table; they rattled loudly. My body was so fired up, so filled with anticipation, that the sound actually made me gasp a little.

The suite was dark. It seemed to intensify what I heard, what I smelled, what I felt. Brody's hand gripped my hip from behind as he moved in closer. He swept my hair to one side with his other hand. When his head dipped down, and he ran his nose along the pulse line of my throat, I let out a small moan, lifting my arms over my head and wrapping them around his neck. Thoughts of what was about to happen made me weak in the knees.

"There are so many things I want to do to you." Brody's voice was low and gritty, filled with all of the want and desire I was feeling myself.

"Like what?"

He kept his mouth at my ear while his hands caressed my body. Slowly, he ran his fingers down my side—from my hip over the curve of my waist, then around to my front, cupping both my breasts in his hands. He squeezed firmly. "I want to suck on your tits. Hard. Nibble on your nipples until you can't take it anymore."

"What else?" Any shyness I had was gone. The man made me desperate.

"Then I think I'll eat you out. I want you to sit on my face while I do that. So you can control where you want me to suck, how hard you want to ride my tongue."

"Oh God."

"Then, when you're good and wet . . . when you're soaked for me and I can smell that you want me, I'm going to hold your hands over your head and fuck you. I won't be able to go easy the first time. We'll save that for the morning when the sunlight streams in on your naked body, and I can watch the way your face changes with every stroke, listen to the way your breath changes as I bury myself deep inside of you."

Brody's hands left my breasts and ran down the front of my body. He sucked on my earlobe and gripped my sides, pulling me against him. His erection was straining through his pants and pushing all the way up to my lower back.

"This ass. I'd like to have that, too. Maybe not tonight. But someday soon. I want to be inside every part of this body. Try everything with you. Own every piece of this body."

I pushed back, rubbing my ass harder against him.

He groaned.

"That first day I met you in the locker room? I was hard the entire afternoon after you left. Not even a cold shower with a bunch of hairy football players nearby could calm me down. I came home and jerked myself off to a visual of your face on my eyelids."

He spun me around, wisely holding onto me when he did. I was lightheaded from all the blood rushing to other parts of my body. Then he devoured my mouth, kissing me in a way I'd never been kissed before. Dominant, yet not forceful. Composed, yet needing. There was no question he was in control of my body. Our tongues tangled, lips meshed and bodies melted into each other. Separating for only as long as it took, he lifted my shirt off.

Lowering his head, he pushed down my bra cup with his thumb and drew a nipple into his hungry mouth. I closed my eyes as his tongue swirled and sucked. He alternated between breasts, licking and nibbling until I was panting.

When he ran his hand under my skirt, he groaned at finding I wasn't wearing any underwear. "Fuck. You took them off." He slid one finger inside me. I was already wet and ready. He groaned and added a second finger. "I really wanted to take my time with you the first time. But I need to be inside you right now. I'll make it up to you later. I promise."

He wasn't kidding. A minute later, I heard the tear of a condom wrapper, and I was up against the wall. "Tell me this is okay. I want to take you against the wall. Hard."

"It's more than okay."

"Thank fuck." He bunched my skirt up and lifted me into the air. "Wrap your legs around me."

I did, and he walked us to the wall and pinned my back up against it. He positioned himself and then lifted me up slightly, bringing me down onto his cock. I gripped his shoulders, a moan billowing from my lips as he sunk inside of me. Then he stilled. "You okay?"

"Very."

He reclaimed my mouth and began to ease in and out of me. My body wrapped around him like a fist and each gentle stroke massaged up and down, zapping more and more nerves to life. I didn't remember anything feeling that good before, especially not the first time.

After he sufficiently unraveled my tight body, he began to move faster. Harder. Longer, deeper, stronger strokes. One hand gripped my ass tightly. His rhythm ramped to a pounding, and we both groaned as he seated himself deep and began to gyrate his hips around, grinding the base of his cock against my clit.

Letting go, my muscles began to spasm around him. "Brody."

He amped up his pace even more. "Fuucck." As he drove into me relentlessly, my body finally gave in, pulsing in orgasm all around him. When my body went limp, he sped up his pace for a few thrusts, then rooted himself deep within me, allowing his own release.

Many hours and more orgasms later, my head lay on Brody's chest as I listened to his heartbeat. Filled with new hope, I fell asleep feeling oddly calm. Maybe it was euphoria from the best sex of my life, maybe it was the way I felt safe and protected as Brody wrapped me tightly in his arms. Whatever it was, the feeling wouldn't last long.

Brody

CHAPTER 13

It was late by the time I finally got to Marlene's place. It took me nearly two hours to drag my ass out of bed once Delilah left for work. And I'd made her late, too—but I couldn't resist one more go around when I saw her in that little black skirt she was wearing. She was dressed so prim and proper, with her high-heeled pumps and her hair pinned up on top of her head. My hard-on was raging to bend the librarian over the bedframe. She left with her clothes slightly disheveled, her hair hanging loose and a just-fucked smile on her flush face. It was a good look for her. A *really* good look.

I'd be paying for a night of pretty strenuous cardio later. Midweek practices were always the hardest. It was going to be a killer after last night and barely any sleep. But I didn't give a shit. I hadn't felt this good in a damn long time. Four years, to be exact.

Grouper was cleaning the floor in the dining room when I passed by on the way to see Marlene. Without a ball to float his way, some improvisation was needed. The lunch service was done for the afternoon, but the staff was still putting away the leftovers, so I grabbed three small milks from a crate that one of Grouper's maintenance guys was lifting and yelled, "Go long. Or you're going to be cleaning up a puddle of cow piss."

Grouper grumbled something but took off running toward the other end of the food hall. I sailed the first two mini milk cartons into his hands. Just as he was about to catch the third one, Shannon yelled to me and distracted Grouper. The third milk went through his open hands and hit him in the shoulder, right before falling to the ground and exploding all over the place.

"You can't throw for shit."

"Super Bowl MVP, old man. Super Bowl MVP."

Shannon's face warned me my afternoon was not going to be as uplifting as my morning.

"What's up, Shannon?"

"She's having a bad day, Brody." Her voice cracked as she reached out and touched my forearm. The nurses at Marlene's home were incredible. They'd seen so much heartbreak with these old people; it took a lot for them to get choked up.

"Physically or mentally?"

"Mentally. She remembers some things about Willow. Things she hasn't remembered in a long time."

Marlene was distraught and crying when I entered her room. I sat down on the side of her bed and took her hand. "What's going on, Marlene?" I couldn't judge what her memory was haunting her with, and I didn't want to make it any worse than it needed to be.

"It's Willow."

Over the past four years I had learned to talk about Willow. It hadn't been easy at first, but time had dulled the pain that hearing her name had made me feel in the beginning.

"What about Willow?"

"She called me last night. Said she was going to come see me next week for my birthday. Then the police came this morning."

I looked to Shannon, who shook her head. "Someone did call her phone last night." She lifted Marlene's chart and flipped the pages. "The night nurse wrote it down. We suspect it was a telemarketer. Maybe the person happened to have had the name Willow?"

Marlene began to sob.

Shannon whispered, "She's been doing that off and on for hours. Keeps rambling on about the police and a body in the river."

Blocking Willow from my daily life was one thing, but the memories were still buried inside of me. Our memories. The good ones outnumbered the bad, even if the bad ones overshadowed the good.

"It's okay, Marlene. It's going to be okay."

I was reassuring her the same way I had four years ago in the hospital waiting room. The same internal battle haunted me. Only now, Marlene's dementia wasn't early-onset. The days when she remembered the details of her granddaughter's life were few and far between. There was less reason to tell her the whole truth now than there had been back then.

"Blue. She was so blue, Brody."

The vision that had taken me almost a year to stop seeing every time I closed my eyes came barreling back. Willow being wheeled into the emergency room. By the time the river incident happened, she was already frail. My Willow was long gone, replaced by a three-bag-a-day heroin junkie who would disappear for weeks at a time. Her occasional visits were usually to steal what we were no longer willing to give her.

Marlene's cry broke into a sob. I wrapped my arms around her. The night they pulled Willow from the East River wasn't a night I ever wanted to reenact. Unfortunately, this was our second go around on the highlight reel of Marlene's life. If only the memories people lost were just the bad ones.

"They don't think she's going to make it, Brody."

"I know. It's okay, Marlene. It's okay."

Bits and pieces of that night continued to flush out for the next hour. "Eighty degrees. They said her body temperature was eighty degrees."

"They're trying to warm her up. They're doing everything they can, Marlene."

I went along for the ride. There was no reason to make things worse. Like last time, I comforted her until the episode passed. There was no reason to break her heart all over again, to catch her up on all the bad things just so she could live through hell again . . . and likely not remember it the next day.

The sedative the nurse gave Marlene finally kicked in and she calmed down, eventually falling asleep.

"You got one of those injections for me?" I joked when Shannon came in to check on us.

"You have practice today?"

"I do."

She smiled ruefully. "Then no. But if you'd like to speak to Dr. Pallen, she's making rounds. I can page her to come in and talk to you."

"Thanks, Shannon. But I'm good. How long will that thing knock her out for?"

"She'll probably be out for most of the day." She put her hand on my shoulder as I sat watching Marlene sleep. "Don't worry, Brody. We'll keep a good eye on her. We'll call you if anything happens or if she wakes up upset again."

"I'll stop back after practice tonight."

"I'll make sure the night nurses know she can have a visitor after hours."

"Thanks."

⸾ ————————————— ⸾

To say I got my ass kicked during practice would be putting it too mildly. Between the physical toll of staying up all night and my head being a fucking mess from the shit that had gone down with Marlene, it was no surprise that I found myself tossed around like a sack of hay. At one point, the practice squad actually started to go easy on me. Which just pissed off Coach even more than my slacking.

After practice, my knee was blown up like a balloon from all the twisting it did every time I got my ass knocked down. The team physical therapist ordered me a fifteen-minute soak in the ice bathtub. As if the morning's stroll down memory lane hadn't fucked with me enough, a soak in freezing water was just what I needed to remind me all over again of Willow's ice-cold body being pulled from the Hudson.

Delilah
CHAPTER 14

Brody texted every day after our night together. And we'd spoken on the phone twice. I'd grown up only catching glimpses of my dad during football season, so I wasn't surprised he was busy. But that didn't stop me from feeling disappointed. The sex had been nothing short of spectacular. Yet it was the hours we'd spent in bed talking that had me feeling something that I hadn't felt in years. *Hope.* That's what our night together gave me. I'd almost forgotten what it felt like. As I boarded the plane to Texas for the Steel's away game, I was reminded why I'd given up hope after Drew. Because getting your hopes crushed *sucked.*

I headed to my assigned seat in row twenty-six as the captain came over the loudspeaker and asked everyone to take their seats quickly. We'd been cleared for departure early, and with a storm front moving in he didn't want to lose our place in the takeoff queue. *Great. A freaking storm. Just what I want to hear.* The traffic on the way to the airport had been so heavy, I hadn't had time to grab a drink and get my Xanax down until five minutes ago. I was going to be a disaster for takeoff.

As I arrived at my row, Brody looked up and caught my eye from his seat a few rows back. Feeling awkward, I smiled and rushed to stow my bag. I was checking my seatbelt for the third time when Brody's voice startled me.

"Connors," he addressed the reporter sitting next to me. "Row thirty-one." He thumbed toward the back of the plane.

The reporter looked up at Brody, then at me. "We're about to take off."

"Yeah, that's why you should hurry up."

"All my stuff is in the overhead."

"I'll bring it to you once we're in the air. There's a bottle of Merlot waiting and an empty seat next to you."

He huffed, but Connors made the switch. Brody settled in beside me.

"Guess you didn't notice the empty seat next to me."

I actually hadn't. "I was preoccupied with getting seated. And trying not to focus on the fact that we're going to be in the air, and my Xanax has another twenty minutes before it kicks in."

Just then, the plane began to taxi away from the gate. It was barely a bump, and we were moving at a snail's pace, yet my hands gripped the arms of the seat.

Brody peeled back my white-knuckled fingers and laced them with his. "I got you."

"When we're careening from the sky five hundred miles an hour toward the Earth, will you have me then?"

His eyebrows shot up. My insides were starting to freak out, and I couldn't control it. I felt my heart racing inside my chest. Brody turned around in his chair and spoke to the reporter behind us. "Five rows back. Thirty-one A. Pass that bottle of Merlot up."

I downed a glass before we took off. It wasn't really helping. Especially not when the captain came on again to give us an update, letting us all know we were third in line for takeoff, and we should be on our way in five minutes.

"You know, I earn a good living with that hand." Brody's eyes narrowed on our joined hands. Mine was squeezing all the color from his, except where my nails were nearly piercing his skin.

"Sorry."

"I'm teasing. Squeeze away." He leaned toward me. "I like the feel of your nails digging into me. I miss the way they scratch at my back when you're close and I slow down."

"Really? You're going to go there when I'm busy trying to have a panic attack?"

He chuckled. "You need a distraction."

"Well, how about talking to me about the weather. Or sports? Did you know the Eagles' punter holds the record for the most consecutive games for a player since 1971? Or that there are currently eight players named Smith in the league, which is the record for—" I was rambling. Mid-sentence, Brody decided to shut me up. His mouth descended upon mine, kissing me in that way that made me weak in the knees. Aggressive, controlling, it felt like he couldn't get enough.

I was entirely lost in the kiss and didn't even notice that the plane had taken off until we came up for air. "See. Takeoff is awesome if you just sit back and enjoy the ride."

"I'll have to try that more often. Wonder who will be sitting next to me on the way home?"

"Not even funny." The way he looked at me quelled the growing feeling of uneasiness that had crept up the last few days. It was football season. I, of all people, should know that was where his focus needed to be.

We caught up for a while until my Xanax began to kick in, and I eventually leaned my head on his shoulder and dozed off. When I woke up, we were already landing.

"I wasn't sure you were breathing there for a while."

I stretched in my seat. "I was really out."

"I know. I tried to wake you to join the mile-high club, but you didn't budge. Got as far as slipping off your panties, but after that you were like dead wood."

"You did not."

He shrugged and smirked. Then went back to studying his playbook.

I smoothed out my wrinkly skirt and while I was at it, I discreetly checked for panties.

Brody didn't look up from his book when he spoke. "Knew you'd check."

Two buses transported us from the airport to the hotel. Rather than the normal lobby check-in, we were escorted to a conference room where a half-dozen hotel staff walked around with a checklist and gave out key cards.

Of course, Brody didn't need to give his name. "Good afternoon, Mr. Easton. Welcome to Sonetta Hotel. I'm Gail. If there is anything out of the ordinary that you need, both mine and the manager's cell phone numbers are on the back of this business card, and here are two keys to your suite." She scribbled something down on her clipboard and turned it toward Brody, handing him a pen to sign.

"Thank you."

Gail turned her attention to me. "Are you with the team or press?"

"She's with me," Brody responded.

The clerk nodded and looked like she was about to move on in the room full of players, so I piped in. "I'm also a guest here. I need to check in."

Brody narrowed his eyes at me, then spoke to Gail, "She doesn't need a room."

"Yes. I do."

"You're not planning on being in my bed tonight?"

Gail looked as uncomfortable as I did with this conversation. "I didn't say that. But if you embarrass me anymore in front of this nice lady, no, I won't be in your bed tonight."

I turned to Gail. "Maddox, two Ds."

Brody didn't say another word until Gail was done checking me in. Then he extended his hand, offering her the keycards back. "I'd like to check out."

"Excuse me?"

"I'd like to check out. I don't need the room. I'm staying in hers." He nodded toward me.

"Um." Poor Gail looked confused. "Your room is a suite, Mr. Easton. Ms. Maddox's is a standard room."

"Does hers have a bed?"

"It does."

"I'd like to check out."

My room was on the sixth floor. Just as Gail had said, it was standard. A bed, dresser, small mini fridge, TV and bathroom. Brody stored our suitcases in the closet while I went to freshen up. I felt like I'd just woken up from a full night of sleep, rather than a medicinally induced nap. When I came out, Brody was lying in the center of the bed, his hands clasped leisurely behind his head.

"You didn't want to stay with me?" It was the first time I'd ever heard his confidence waver. There was something endearing about it. I hiked up my skirt and climbed onto the bed, straddling his hips.

"I have to put my expense reports in each week, and I didn't want anyone to ask where my hotel bill is."

"Why would they care if you didn't put in a bill? You'd be saving them money."

"My boss already gives me a hard time. He was against my being promoted; it was his boss who picked me for the job."

"Why didn't he want to give you the job?"

"Because he's a sexist jerk who thinks women don't belong in the locker room. Sound familiar?"

"I just gave you a hard time because I thought you were hot as shit."

"I was trying to do my job."

"I know. I'm a selfish bastard. I didn't really think about that. I just wanted to screw with you, and I got carried away."

"And what about Susan Metzinger? You were so vocal that she shouldn't be allowed in the locker room."

"Susan Metzinger shouldn't be."

"And why not?" I hoisted my women's lib flag proudly.

"She came into the locker room and grabbed my junk. I wasn't interested."

"Really?"

"Yep. Gleason from WMBC caught the whole thing on film. He was interviewing Smith at the locker next to me." He paused. "One of the seven Smiths."

"Why didn't you expose her? She ran you through the wringer in the media."

"I guess I felt bad for rejecting her."

"So you really don't have anything against women in the locker room?"

"I have something against you in the locker room." He pulled me from sitting to lying on top of him.

"Why?"

"Because the only dick I want you seeing these days is mine."

"That's an oddly sweet statement."

"I'm an oddly sweet kinda guy. Now shut up and kiss me."

My bottom was still sitting on his hips, but I was bent at the waist, my chest pressed to his. My lips rested lightly against his. "I'm on top, you know. You told me this wouldn't be your favorite position with me."

"Better make sure I was right."

Brody had a team meeting, and I had some work to do. When he came back, we ordered a ridiculous amount of room service and spent the rest of the night in bed. Since I'd had a nap, I wasn't tired. And since Brody only required four to six hours of sleep, even though he did ten times the exercise of most in-shape humans on any given day, he wasn't tired yet either.

After a few more go-arounds exploring each other's bodies, we were back to our own unique form of getting to know each other. That was, I asked normal questions, and Brody shot off ridiculous ones. For the most part, it kept things light. Until he stumbled unknowingly onto the part of my life that I didn't talk about.

I was tracing figure eights on his bare chest when he came out with yet another oddball question. "If you could interview anyone from your life, living or dead, who would it be?"

I didn't think about my answer, but perhaps I should have. "Drew Martin." My finger stopped drawing. The second the words came out I wished I could take them back.

"Why do I know that name?"

"He was in the draft the year after you. Second round. Kicker."

Brody shifted us so we were both lying on our sides. I would have preferred to keep my head on his chest, where he couldn't look at my face.

"Should I be jealous?" He said it half joking.

"I don't think so." I swallowed. The words never got any easier to say. "He's dead."

"Was he a relative of yours?"

I shook my head.

"He's from your life?"

I nodded.

"Do you want to talk about it?"

"Not really."

He surprised me when he pulled me to him and kissed the top of my forehead. "Okay. We'll talk about it when you're ready."

CHAPTER 15

The Steel had a game on Sunday and then were playing on Thursday night again. Since it was a short recovery week, the team was heading back home right after the game, rather than leaving on Monday morning. That meant there wouldn't be locker room interviews after the game Sunday. Field reporters could attempt to grab a key player or two as they walked off the field, but regular access to the entire team was limited to an after-practice open locker room.

Reporters could enter at five tonight. I worked from my laptop at the hotel in the morning, managed to drag my ass to the gym for a forty-five-minute run, and got to the field where the Steel were practicing by three. I climbed the bleachers and sat watching the special teams unit run through drills.

It had been a really long time since I'd sat on the cold metal on a chilly fall day to watch a practice. Even though a huge part of my life had been spent on the bleachers of a football field, it was almost as if my life was in two acts, and the curtain had come down on part one. Yet here I was back again. It was almost surreal.

Talking about Drew last night and watching the team my father captained for so many years weighed heavy on my heart. When Drew and I had first started dating, he was a hardcore soccer player. He'd never even tried football. I remembered the first time I brought Drew around to meet Dad. We were in tenth grade, and he was half starstruck to meet the great Tom Maddox.

Dad told him to have a seat and spent the better part of two hours selling him on the benefits of being a football kicker rather than a soccer player. That fall, Drew tried out for the varsity football team and became the starting kicker.

A loud whistle brought my attention back to the field. Brody had been talking to Coach Ryan on the sideline while the special teams unit finished up on the field, but the practice squads were changing places now. The offensive linemen jogged onto the field while the other players jogged off. I couldn't hear anything, but I watched intently as Brody took his place behind the center and pointed to various things. Players made adjustments and moved around at his command.

The man was no different off the field than he was on. He was aggressive, confident, aware of everything going on around him and completely in charge. I felt like a high school cheerleader, but I was also a little turned on watching Brody in action so closely. I'd missed this part of my life. I loved the game itself. But watching someone I cared about play out on that field did something to me. The catches, the leaps, the sheer athleticism of twenty-two men joining together to form one unit and compete. There was something just so innately beautiful about it.

Even though I'd never stopped being involved with football, something reawakened in me while I watched from the bleachers that afternoon. I wasn't sure if it was my love of the sport or hope that I could one day again combine my love for the sport with a man on the field.

The locker room had a very different vibe after practice than it did after a game. It was more relaxed and laid-back; even coaches were laughing. Nick had flown in that morning, so I found him, and we got an interview with a rookie wide receiver who was starting this weekend, then moved on to bigger fish. Brody was surrounded by his usual long line, so I looked around for another player to grab in the meantime.

Curiosity had me on the second longest line for more than one reason. Colin Anderson was about to play his first game with the Steel, and no one had yet discovered the reason behind the college feud with Brody.

Colin was changing at a locker four over from Brody, but the one player who was utilizing the space between them had already disappeared into the shower. Nick and I waited a solid twenty minutes before we were next to interview Colin. In my peripheral vision, I caught Brody eyeing where I was. He looked at me, glared at Colin, then turned his attention back to me until our eyes met.

When it was our turn, I introduced myself as I normally would. "Hi, Colin, I'm Delilah Maddox with—"

"Brody Easton." He gave me a sly smile and then looked over at Brody, who was doing his own interview, but the two men locked gazes for a brief second.

"Actually, I'm with WMBC Sports News." I attempted to change the subject. "Could I ask you a few questions for our Sunday pregame report?"

"Anything for you."

Just what I need. "Ready, Nick?" I had a bad feeling and wanted this over before I'd even started.

Luckily Nick never took long, and we were rolling thirty seconds later. "Congratulations on your trade, Colin. Are you excited to play your first game with the team on Sunday?"

"I am. I've only been here a few weeks, but it feels good. I think I've found my home with the Steel."

Even though I was dying to ask what had happened with him and Brody back in college, I didn't. Something told me that Colin was looking for a reason to screw with Brody, and I wasn't going to be the spark to ignite that old fire.

The interview went off without a hitch. Colin was actually charming and very professional. After it was over, Nick lowered his equipment, and I tossed my microphone into my bag. "Thank you for your time, Colin. Best of luck Sunday."

He caught me off guard when he leaned in and kissed my cheek. "The pleasure was all mine." As I started to walk away, he stopped me. "I'm in Suite 801. I don't mind sharing if you're down with it. It'll be like the old days for Brody and me."

What the hell?

"Come on, Delilah," Nick said. "Locker room is only open for another ten minutes. We need to get Easton in the can."

My head was spinning while we waited to interview Brody. Was that what the feud had been about? The two of them had been sharing women in college? I wasn't naïve; there was a certain group of women who would do anything to be with a player. They didn't even have to be professional yet. In fact, the football groupies were even more prevalent in college. Young bodies, raging hormones and the stardom that came with televised Big Ten football. Brody's confidence with women hadn't come from sitting in his dorm room studying. I knew there was ample opportunity for players; I even knew he was a player. I just didn't need that reminder shoved in my face about the man I was sleeping with—a man I had started to fall for.

I was glad there were a few people ahead of us; it gave me time to cool off and remind myself that being inside this locker room was for my career, not for my personal life. I needed to act like a professional.

When our turn came to interview Brody, I put on my best game face. "Long line for you today. I promise to make it quick."

"What did he say to you?"

"Who?" I knew damn well who.

"Anderson."

"He answered my interview questions."

"And after he *kissed* you. What the fuck did he whisper in your ear?"

I had been hoping he hadn't caught that. "It was nothing."

"Delilah," he growled.

"Can we discuss this later? I'd rather have this talk in private."

Brody turned to Nick and stared at him. Nick had been fiddling with his camera, but he caught on quick.

"You want me to give you a few minutes?"

I said no at the exact same time that Brody said yes. Poor Nick looked torn.

"Give us a minute, will ya, Nick?" Brody was asking, but the sternness in his voice made it not really a question.

Nick stepped away. "What did he say, Delilah?"

"It's not important."

"To me it is. Was he hitting on you? I can handle that if that's what you're worried about. I'll have a talk with him another time, but I won't cause a scene if that's all it was."

I looked in his eyes. He was sincere. "Yes. He was just flirting. Told me he didn't mind sharing. That sharing with you would be *just like the old college days.*"

I expected Brody to be angry. I also expected him to keep to his word not to cause a scene. Shit, was I wrong.

In a matter of seconds, all hell broke loose. Brody slammed Colin up against a locker. Reporters were yelling, players hurdled benches to get to the two men, and coaches were ripping bodies out of their way to get to their star players.

Brody threw a punch, someone grabbed Colin and jerked him to the right, and Brody landed a fist into a locker so hard, the metal was dented by a massive fist print. Both men attempted to get at each other, but there were so many people holding them back, no actual blows were exchanged.

When the two of them were separated, Coach Ryan blew a loud whistle and yelled for everyone except the team to vacate the locker room. Reporters were wrangled like cattle to the exit.

"What the hell is between those two?" Nick asked me when we were out in the hall.

I had no idea, but I was about to find out.

Delilah
CHAPTER 16

It was after midnight when the hotel room door creaked open. When Brody hadn't come back after a few hours, I'd assumed he wasn't staying in my room tonight. And that was just fine with me. After the way he'd reacted, I had no desire to be around him.

Obviously, the two men had history. But he wasn't the only one who would suffer the consequences from today. Behaving the way he did validated to men like Mr. CUM that women didn't belong in the locker room. Not to mention that I really didn't need any more attention on my personal life. My job was to report stories, not *be* the story. Yet, as I tossed and turned, unable to fall asleep, I wondered if he was okay.

The room was pitch dark. I considered pretending to be asleep. Morning would likely bring more clarity. Not much good usually came from getting upset at midnight.

Brody didn't turn on any lights. He made his way to the other side of the room, and I heard him unzip his pants and toss them on the chair in the corner. He didn't turn on the light in the bathroom until the door was closed. A few minutes later, the bed dipped, and he slipped in beside me. My eyes were shut, but I could feel him looking at me.

"Her name was Willow." His voice was barely a whisper, and there was a sadness to it that made me forget I was pissed at him in an instant.

Even though the room was virtually dark, I could see his eyes. They were filled with an anguish that caused a physical ache in my pounding chest. I cupped his cheek, and he closed his eyes for a few moments. When he reopened them, he continued. "I was thirteen when she moved in next door to me. She and her mother moved in with her grandmother. She was beautiful. And wild. I wasn't a saint, that was sure as shit, but Willow . . . she just had a streak in her."

He paused for a long time. I wanted to say something, but I couldn't find the right words. It was obvious that wherever this story would lead, it wasn't going to end well. So I waited until he was ready.

"Her mother was a drug addict. She didn't stick around very long. She'd disappear for months at a time, and every once in a while she'd reappear long enough to rob her mother blind and screw up Willow all over again."

"I'm sorry."

"We did normal, wild teenager things, like pool hopping in the community pool, taking the train to jump off the rocks into the Harlem River where the waterway meets Spuyten Duyvil Creek, or stealing a bottle from her grandmother's liquor cabinet and riding the subways while passing it back and forth in a brown paper bag. Teenage shit. But Willow was always pushing for more. It seemed to get worse every time her mother would reappear. We lived in apartment buildings next to each other in Brooklyn. They were close together, but not attached. There was maybe three, three-and-a-half feet between our flat rooftops. When her mother would reappear, Willow would come to my apartment, jumping from roof to roof. She'd straddle the jump, not thinking twice about the thirty-foot drop to concrete below her. She'd go from being wild to dangerous."

There was a hollow feeling in the pit of my stomach listening to him talk about Willow. For so many reasons. I'd met Drew around the same age as he'd met Willow. I knew how my story ended, and now I knew his wasn't going to be pretty either.

"I could spend hours telling you the shit we went through together over the years. But I'd rather fast forward and give you the Cliffs Notes version so you can understand why I lost it today."

"Okay."

"By the time we were seniors in high school, Willow had followed in her mother's footsteps. She'd found drugs and quickly went from experimenting to chasing a high on a daily basis." Brody let out a humorless laugh. "You should see the looks you get riding the subway at two a.m. with an eighteen-year-old you just pulled out of a crack house and a seventy-year-old woman in a bathrobe and curlers. There were nights when I'd have to toss Willow over my shoulder because she couldn't walk, and poor Marlene would be right next to me."

Brody paused again, and his next words hit me hard. "I hated her so damn much, but I couldn't make myself stop loving her."

I laced my fingers together with his and squeezed.

"I was recruited by some of the best colleges in the country, but I wanted to stay local. Senior year, I'd narrowed it down to Syracuse and University of Georgia. My dad was pushing for me to be a Bulldog and we all knew why, although we didn't talk about it. When Willow disappeared for six weeks right before I had to commit to a school, I was so pissed off at her, I committed to Georgia. After I left, I kept in touch with Marlene and kept tabs on Willow, but I started to move on."

"That's understandable. It sounds like you'd already done so much."

"The summer between my freshman and sophomore year, I came home. Marlene had had a mild heart attack, and it seemed to have woken Willow up. She was clean and even had a part-time job at a music store that she loved. We spent a lot of time together, and I hated to go back to school when August rolled around. I felt like I had the girl back I'd fallen in love with, and I was afraid she'd disappear again when I left. Marlene sensed I was considering not going back, so she decided she and Willow were going to fly down for homecoming weekend to see me play. That way I was going to see her again in only three weeks."

Brody paused again. "I promise. I'm finally getting to the point of dumping all this shit on you."

"Take your time. We're in no rush."

He nodded. "Anyway, two days after I got back to school and we started practicing again, Willow stopped answering her phone. That was never a good sign. I talked to Marlene, and she said Willow hadn't come home all weekend. We were practicing six hours a day, NFL scouts were starting to come to practices, and all I wanted to do was go back home. But I couldn't. Eventually, Willow surfaced again, most likely because she had run out of money, and the next three weeks she played on her grandmother's weaknesses. I hadn't actually expected her to show up for homecoming, but somehow Marlene got her on the plane. She meant well. She thought getting her away from her dealers and back near me might help. But scoring on a college campus is a heck of a lot easier than some people might think. After homecoming, Willow disappeared, and Marlene and I spent a week looking for her, but the drug addicts I threatened to help me find her were more scared of losing their source than they were of me beating the shit out of them. People with nothing aren't easy to find."

I was afraid to ask how she eventually turned up, but since we hadn't gotten to Colin yet, I knew the worst was yet to come. "I don't even know what to say."

"You don't have to say anything. I do. I owe you an explanation and an apology. If you'll have me when I'm done explaining, I hope to give you a long, multiple apology." Even in the middle of an obviously painful story, Brody was . . . Brody. It made me smile, for the first time since the bleachers this afternoon.

"Well, then get on with the story so we can get to the apology," I teased. At that moment, we needed a little levity.

"Colin was a freshman at Georgia. We'd met the first day of August practice, and I didn't like him right away. He had a gigantic chip on his shoulder and constantly talked about women like they were sexual objects. Not to mention he had a short fuse that was easily lit. Guy's still an asshole."

Whereas before Brody sounded like he was close to breaking, speaking of Colin changed his tone. "Anyway, one night, some of the guys in my frat dragged me to a party. It was off campus, and I really wasn't in the mood to begin with. When we got there, it wasn't the standard keg-and-plastic-cup college drunk fest. The place was a hellhole, and there were some pretty seedy looking people smoking crap from a glass pipe that smelled like burned plastic. Colin was already there with some of the other freshmen from the team. He was bragging about some girl he was going to get with. She was getting high with his buddy, and he could tell she was down for it—*it was shaping up to be a good party*. The way he was talking about the woman made me sick. I voiced that if the woman was too high to know what the hell she was doing, *it was shaping up to sound like fucking rape to me*."

"I knew it had to be something bad for you to react that way today."

"That's not the half of it."

It was getting worse by the moment. My original assumption that two men had fought over sharing some cheerleader was starting to feel like wishful thinking.

"I had driven to the party, and some of the guys wanted to stay for a while, so I wound up staying longer than I wanted to. More and more people were showing up, and I didn't like the looks of most of them. I wanted to get the hell out of there before the cops arrived. Eventually, I told the guys I was going to the bathroom and then leaving. They could come or find their own way back to campus. There were people all over the place, so at first, it didn't seem strange that two guys were waiting outside of a closed door next to the bathroom. While I was waiting my turn, I asked what they were doing, and one of the guys said their friend was inside with some hot crackhead."

"No—"

"I don't know why, but I still didn't put two and two together. I went to the bathroom, came out and saw the two guys still standing there. Halfway down the stairs, I heard one say to the other, 'What's the chick's name Colin's got in there?' The other asshole responded, 'I don't know. Rose, Violet, Meadow? Some sort of flowery shit.'"

My hand went to my chest. "Oh God."

"I'll save you the details, but Willow was in *no* condition to make a decision to be with anyone. She could barely speak. I had to carry her out of there."

"That's rape."

"It almost was, if you ask me. Luckily, it never got that far. Colin claimed they were fooling around, and then he realized how out of it she really was and tried to help her up. *With his pants fucking open,* he was trying to help her."

"Did anything ever happen to him?"

"Other than my fist breaking his nose, no. I went to the police. But it was pretty much my word against his. Willow didn't remember anything and had disappeared again by the time they finished their investigation. The whole thing was sealed, and I had to throw him the ball for another two years. I thought I was finally rid of the asshole, until the Steel's midseason trade."

"And then he used me to screw with you by making that comment about sharing."

"I'm sorry he said anything to you."

"It's not your fault."

"Maybe. But I'm sorry about the way I acted. And about not coming right to you after the coach reamed me a new asshole."

"Did you get suspended?"

"I won't know until tomorrow. A fine is definite, but I'm hoping that's all I get. Coach was a lot calmer when I left."

"Where did you go after you talked to him?"

"I just needed some time to clear my head. Get my shit together before I came to you. I don't want the past to be part of my future anymore."

"I appreciate that. I really do."

"Do you forgive me?"

There was so much more I wanted to know. The least of which was whatever became of Willow. Was she still a part of his life? But looking into Brody's eyes at that moment, I saw what telling the story had done to him. He really needed a break. "I don't think I forgive you yet."

"No?"

"Maybe I will after I get those multiple apologies you promised."

Brody reached down and grabbed a handful of my ass, squeezing. "There's nothing else I would like to do than fuck you full of sorry."

What became of Willow could certainly wait until tomorrow.

Delilah
CHAPTER 17

We slept in the next morning, having spent until the sun began to rise working hard on those apologies. Warm water beaded over my achy muscles as I reached out with both hands and braced myself against the shower wall. Closing my eyes, I replayed the way Brody had looked as he'd come undone last night. I wasn't sure if it was emotions still running high from our talk or not, but the sex had felt special, more intimate. Less like sex and more like making love. The thought made my heart squeeze. The last person I'd felt that with was Drew. I knew it was ridiculous, but a part of me felt guilty for the feelings growing inside of me. Brody had said last night that he wanted to keep the past behind him—I did, too. But in order for me to do that, I needed to tell him that a part of my heart would always be with another man.

I was halfway to my eleven a.m. appointment to interview one of the assistant coaches of the Texas Lions when I got a call that they needed to push back the time until two. Brody had already left for practice, so rather than return to my empty hotel room, I decided to stop for a second, much-needed cup of coffee. The inside of Starbucks smelled of pumpkin and everything fall, which seemed odd considering it was almost eighty outside.

"I'll have a Pumpkin Spice Latte. I was coming in for a plain old coffee, but the smell got me."

The tiny barista's words were spoken rapid-fire, "Tell me about it. I've had three already today." *Gee, I'd never have guessed.*

"What's your name?" She pointed her sharpie to a tall cup.

"Delilah."

"That's a pretty name."

My eyes drifted to her nametag. *Puma*

She caught me noticing. "Yep. It's my real name. My parents were hippies."

I tried to sound sincere. "It's nice. Unique."

"At least they gave me a cool middle name—Ophelia. That sort of sounds like Delilah. And my married name is nice and simple—Oar."

I smiled and moved to the other end of the counter to wait for *Poo* to make my latte.

Settling into an oversized leather chair in the corner, I sipped my Pumpkin Spice Latte and flipped open my MacBook to catch up on the morning news. My tongue prickled as the hot pseudo coffee burnt the tip. *Damn it.*

When I logged into WMBC's live news webfeed, my eyes did a double take. There, on the front page of an Associated Press sports article, was a picture of Brody and me coming out of the elevator the other day. It was a shot taken from an angle, but you could clearly see his hand on my ass. Then I read the headline. *WMBC Reporter Love Triangle.* Underneath, there were a few pictures of the locker room would-be brawl. One showed Colin up against a locker with Brody's forearm pressed against his neck. Colin's face wore the same slimy smirk he'd given me when he was taunting Brody.

Shit. How would anyone take me seriously after this?

My phone began to buzz. *My office.* I took a deep breath and answered, "Delilah Maddox."

"Did you have underwear on? I blew the shot up on my laptop, and I see absolutely no panty lines."

Indie. Thank God. I let out a huge breath.

"Am I the laughingstock of the office?"

"No idea. I shut my office door as soon as I saw it come across my feed. I might have spent a few minutes ogling Brody's chest before I moved on to your ass."

"You're supposed to be my eyes and ears."

"After looking at that picture, I'd much rather be your tits and ass."

I caught Indie up on everything that had transpired, keeping the details of the actual feud behind Brody and Colin to myself. I didn't want to betray Brody's confidence—he'd told the story to the woman he was seeing, not the reporter vying for a story. It was best leaving it at "the two men had history."

"Is he flying back or waiting around for you until you're done Sunday?"

"We're both scheduled to fly back with the team after the game."

"I didn't think he'd be allowed to fly with the team."

"Why not?"

"Eh. What the hell do I know? The other article said suspended players couldn't have contact with any team members or attend the game. I figured they'd make him hitch another way home."

"Brody doesn't think he'll get a suspension, probably just a fine."

"Uh . . . I guess you didn't get past looking at your ass on the screen. Brody was suspended. Came across about an hour ago."

I hung up quickly and scoured the rest of the morning feed until I came across the other article Indie was referring to. *Easton Headed Back East.* The article said he'd been fined and suspended for one game for violating the team's new personal-conduct policy. Colin Anderson, on the other hand, had only been fined.

Shit.

Double shit.

Brody was going to be devastated he was suspended, and I didn't even bring my own employer the scoop on a story *I* was involved in.

e ———————————————————— e

I'd tried calling and texting Brody all afternoon, but he never responded. As soon as my interview wrapped, I headed straight back to the hotel.

"Hey. What are you doing?" Brody was sitting in a chair, the room quiet, a glass full of clear liquid in his hand.

"Proving everyone right." He gulped back the remainder of his drink.

I sat on the edge of the bed across from him. "I'm sorry. I heard. I tried to reach you, but your phone must be off."

"It is. Permanently." He eyed the phone on the table next to him. The screen was smashed. I didn't need to ask how it happened.

"Is it appealable?"

"I'm not going to appeal it."

"Why? Especially if Colin only got a slap on the wrist?"

"Because it will just drag me back into a bad place. I don't need that shit."

"I don't understand."

"After I got drafted into the NFL, I started to move on with my life. Until Willow reappeared again. I lost focus. Crashed my car speeding one night heading to find her when she went on a binge. I started missing practice and workouts, couldn't concentrate on the game. My performance took a nosedive, and Coach benched me to teach me a lesson. I eventually lost my spot on the team by getting sucked into Willow's life again."

"I get it."

"You do?"

"Yeah. I do. After Drew died, I couldn't let go. My grades dropped. I stopped going to classes. Eventually, I took a semester off. Little by little it got easier, but all it took was the slightest memory, and I would be right back there."

"I figured he was important to you."

"He was my fiancé. We got engaged right after high school but wanted to wait until after the draft. He was riding a quad one Saturday and hit something. It flipped over, and he broke his neck. Died instantly."

Brody blew out a long breath and reached for me. "Come here." I sat on his lap. "You're pretty fucking incredible, you know that?"

"Is that the liquor talking, or you?"

"You said liquor and all I heard was 'lick her.' I have a flight back to New York tonight. But now I have a hard-on and need a taste before I go."

"You realize you just went from brooding to perverted in under five minutes."

"Told ya. I'm moving on." He started to unbutton my blouse.

"What time is your flight?"

"About an hour after I come inside of you twice. Whatever time that is."

Brody

CHAPTER 18

Even in the offseason, I stuck to my Tuesday schedule for visiting Marlene. The Sunday staff at Broadhollow Manor had never seen me before. I signed in and introduced myself.

"We spoke on the phone a few times this week. I'm Karen. I do weeknights and Sundays. It's nice to meet you, Mr. Easton."

"Brody, please."

She nodded. "Brody."

"How is she today?"

"Still the same. Whatever it was that made her so upset last week seems to have been forgotten. She's more like her normal self again."

"You mean like telling a nurse she should wear less lipstick so people concentrate on her figure more and on her face less?"

Karen covered her smiling mouth. "I heard about that one. She's a hoot."

"Says the lady who can pull off bright red, shiny lips."

The nurse blushed.

"Is she in her room?"

"I think she's still in the activity room. One of our staff was playing checkers with her when I passed by before."

I was not expecting that staff member to be Grouper. He wasn't dressed in his usual uniform either. He had on a long-sleeve checkered shirt with a sweater vest over it.

"Well, if it ain't Mr. Rogers. What are you doing here?" I walked to Marlene and kissed her cheek. "You're not trying to hit on my woman, are you?"

Grouper waved me off and grumbled something.

"It's Sunday," Marlene said. "We play checkers and watch TV. But there's no football on today."

"I was in the neighborhood, so thought I'd stop in and check on things." Grouper tried to play off his visit as casual.

"He turns on my television every week before we play. I don't really like football, but we play checkers, too, so I don't say anything."

"Is that so? The old bastard even comes in on his day off, huh?"

"That's not nice. He's not a bastard. He's just old and moves sort of slow. And a little hard of hearing, too."

I grinned at Grouper. The only thing I was looking forward to in aging was being able to say whatever the hell was on my mind and getting away with it.

Grouper gave me the evil eye. "It's quiet in here this Sunday without any games to watch."

I should have known I was going to hear shit from him about getting suspended. "I'm not happy *there's no game* today either."

"You *should be* unhappy. Waste of perfectly good talent to not be playing a game today."

An hour later, I was sitting across from Marlene, and Grouper was looking on as the two of us played checkers. Five minutes into the game, half of her black pieces were kings, and she'd stolen half my reds. She pulled a double jump I didn't see coming. "What the hell? You're a checkers shark?"

Grouper chuckled. "You were sitting there thinking I was letting her win, weren't you?"

"Actually, I was thinking you weren't capable of beating her. That's why I joined in. Give Marlene a little challenge." I actually *had* thought Grouper was letting her win.

"Only one who ever gave me a run for my money was my Willow." Marlene slid her piece into my home base. "King me." Grouper and I looked at each other. Both of us were silently waiting to see what would come next. The last time she'd thought about Willow hadn't gone well.

"Go easy on me, lady. Or see what happens the next time you want a pastrami on rye from Heidelman's."

She waved off my comment. "Tell Willow to bring the wooden checkers set from the bottom cabinet of the china closet in the dining room." It blew my mind how she could remember where she kept a game board, but couldn't recall her only granddaughter hadn't been here to see her in three years."

"You got it."

"She said she's been busy but is coming to see me on my birthday."

"Oh yeah."

"And tell her to stop by Zen Garden. They have the best wonton soup."

Grouper piped in, "The salt in that stuff isn't good for you."

Yeah. *No worries there.* I was pretty sure Willow wasn't coming.

Delilah
CHAPTER 19

My normally jittery nerves were anxious as I boarded the flight back to New York on Monday afternoon. The team and most of the reporters had headed back after the game last night, but I'd had to stay for an interview with a local college running back who was thought to be the number-one draft pick next season. Brody had acted fine when I spoke to him earlier, but I imagined the team's loss yesterday weighed heavily on his shoulders. The second-string quarterback had thrown four interceptions, any one of which cost the team the loss.

The captain's voice came overhead to tell us bad weather to the east had takeoffs backed up, and we were returning to the gate, although we wouldn't be disembarking the plane. We should sit back and enjoy a complimentary beverage. *Sure. Easy for you to say.* These tin cans obviously didn't have the same effect on him. Why did every flight I was on lately have to mention bad weather or some other potentially catastrophic scenario?

Once we parked and the seatbelt sign turned off, I made a quick trip to the ladies' room, then dug in my bag for my cell to tell Brody I was running late. The screen illuminated, then immediately flashed a lightning bolt with a drained battery and proceeded to power down. "Damn it."

"You need help with something?" My seatmate was probably in his late sixties. I thought about asking him to use his phone, but I had no idea what Brody's number even was. I'd never actually dialed it before.

I held up my phone. "My phone died, and I don't know the person's number. I'm supposed to meet him at my apartment, and I'm guessing we're going to be late since they just shut off the engine."

"Ah. Cell phone withdrawal. The effects can be just as daunting as heroin, they say."

"You don't have one?"

"Nope."

"Is someone picking you up at the airport when we land?""

"Yes. My wife."

"Does she have a phone?"

He shook his head, mildly amused.

"How will she know we're delayed?"

"I supposed she'll pick up the phone and call the airline, as she has for the last forty years. I take it whomever you are meeting won't do that?"

"Definitely not." I smiled and tucked my bag back under the seat. "So how do you pass the time without Candy Crush, then?"

"Candy what?"

For the next half hour, I explained the intricacies of a game that didn't sound as riveting as it was while being played. My new friend returned the favor by explaining the art of cognac. When the flight attendant came to offer us a drink, he requested only two cups. Then he pulled out a bottle from his bag, and we proceeded to sample the liquor. It tasted like crap, but one small glass mixed with my flight medication, and I was out like a light.

When we finally landed, more than three hours late, it was exactly the time Brody would be picking me up at my place. Knowing traffic would be a nightmare, I stopped in the bathroom near the gate and plugged in my phone while I used the toilet and fixed myself up. The phone illuminated again after a few minutes, enough for me to shoot off a text to Brody.

Delilah: Just landed. Phone died before we took off. Are you already at my place?

Brody: Just pulled into the parking garage.

Delilah: Sorry. Will probably take me an hour to get home. Give it two minutes, then ring 3E. Patrick has a key to my place. I'll text him now and tell him to give it to you.

Brody: Why does Patrick have a key to your place?

I wanted to get the hell out of the bathroom. We could discuss the logistics later.

Delilah: To unlock the door. Why does anyone have a key?

I smirked, knowing he wouldn't love that answer, and then shot off a quick text to Patrick before I unplugged and headed home.

e ———————————————— e

Traffic was surprisingly light, and I made it home in less than half the time it ordinarily took. It was odd that I was returning after a football trip, and Brody was at my house waiting for me. The roles were typically reversed.

"Hello?" The kitchen light was on, but everything else was dark. Looking down the hallway to the bedroom, I saw the bathroom was lit.

"I'm in here."

The door was open. I stopped in my tracks as I entered. The visual was one of the funniest things I'd ever seen.

"What are you doing?"

"Exactly what it looks like I'm doing."

"You're . . . you're taking a bubble bath?" Brody was sunk down into my tub, his head lolling back against the tile wall. The full length of his tall body didn't quite fit—his legs were sticking out and over the

135

rim. Bubbles overflowed from the tub and onto the floor. The entire room smelled like scented bath soap.

"No tub at my place. I like to soak. Feels good on my muscles."

"And you usually soak in bubble bath?" I could barely contain my laughter.

"I don't have any of this crap. The directions on the pink shit . . . " He pointed to a large plastic bottle that had been full when I left but was now half empty. " . . . said it was good for soothing muscles."

"You only need to use a capful."

"I was really sore."

"You look . . . ridiculous in there."

"What? You don't find the bubbles sexy? If I saw you in a bathtub, I'd think it was fucking hot."

"It's just sort of . . . girly."

He reached under the bubbles and took himself into his hand, the head of his semi-erect penis peeking out from the water. "Does this look girly to you?" He stroked himself leisurely.

I stopped seeing the bubbles. All I could see was his strong hand around his thick shaft, slowly rubbing up and down. The vision was positively erotic. I'd never watched a man masturbate up close before. My eyes were glued as he stroked.

"Do you pleasure yourself in here sometimes, Delilah?"

I swallowed and nodded.

"I want to watch you. See you slip your fingers inside that wet pussy and make yourself come—my cock is getting hard just thinking about it." The speed of his pumps accelerated. I tore my eyes away and gazed up at his face; his jaw was set and tense. When our eyes caught, he swallowed, his Adam's apple bobbing up and down on his stubbled throat while his pale green eyes darkened with lust. All it took was his look—I didn't need to be touched—and my body was humming with need. When he spoke again, his voice was low, but gruff and commanding. "Take your shirt off."

I followed every instruction he gave me, my clothes disappearing slowly, one piece at a time, until I was standing before him wearing only my underwear and shoes.

He stared at my black lace thong. "Take it off. I want to see every inch of you." His hand fisted around his cock as he stroked faster. "Are you wet for me already, Delilah?"

Hooking my fingers into the sides of the lace, I shimmied my panties down my legs. My answer was a whisper in the quiet room. "I am." I stepped out of the pooled black lace and reached down to remove the last of my clothing—black high heels with a strap that wrapped around my ankle.

"Leave them on." I stopped unfastening and looked up at him. "You need the height."

He stood from the tub. His body was gorgeous, a mass of carved muscle and smoothly tanned skin. The full length of his thick erection pressed against his hard stomach. Unconsciously, I licked my lips.

"I want to bend you over the sink, take you from behind."

God, yes.

"And I want you to watch yourself in the mirror. I'm going to fuck you hard until you come. Then I'm going to push deep inside of you and fill your pussy with every ounce of my cum."

"Jesus, Brody." My knees were half weak as he walked to me. Turning my body to face the mirror, he swept my hair to the side and pressed his lips to my neck from behind. His chest was wet, but warm and hard against my body. The full length of him pushed up against the top of my ass.

"Spread your legs for me."

I did.

"Wider."

Slowly, he rubbed his body up and down me from behind, his cock nudging at my ass as he reached around to rub my clit. "So fucking wet for me."

It felt so good, my eyes drifted closed as I lifted my arms and wrapped them around his neck. When he slipped two fingers inside of me, a throaty moan fell from my lips.

His other hand turned my chin to the side, giving him access to my mouth. Crushing his lips to mine, his kiss was wild and shamelessly hungry. I loved that he wasn't gentle, his actions expressing emotion and need. He cupped my breasts and squeezed, pinching my nipples so hard it bordered on pain. I threaded my fingers through his wet hair and pulled, wanting him even closer.

We were both panting, unable to get enough, when he released my mouth, his teeth tugging on my lip as we separated. "Bend." With his hand on my back, he eased me forward, folding me at the waist. "Hold on to the sides." My hands curled around the granite sides of the vanity, his hands curled around mine. "Look up." My eyes rose to catch the reflection staring back at me from the mirror. Brody was right: the level was perfect with the extra four inches from my shoes. My skin was flushed, my hair was disheveled and wild, and my eyes were full of blatant desire.

"Fucking beautiful."

He rubbed the length of himself along my wetness a few times before pushing inside. Once he made sure I was ready for him, he did exactly what he promised. Fucked me hard until I came just as hard. Then he seated himself deep inside of me and released with a carnal roar.

A few minutes later, Brody scooped me up and carried me to bed, slipping in behind me. I snuggled back against him, and his body molded around mine. "Mmm . . . I could get used to this kind of welcome home."

"That's good, baby. Because I threw out the vibrator in your end table drawer."

I froze, unsure if he was kidding or not.

Brody chuckled and pulled me closer. "Relax, I'm joking. But good to know one is in there. I'd like to use it on you sometime. Better yet, I think I'd like to watch you use it on yourself."

"You have a one-track mind."

"I do. All Delilah's pussy. All the time."

I elbowed him, and we both laughed. It felt good to have Brody in my bed. We talked for more than an hour in the dark, catching up on the last few days. It felt so . . . normal. Domestic. Natural. *Right*.

It was almost midnight when we settled, and I began to feel sleepy. "Brody?"

"Hmm?" He kissed my shoulder.

"You're spooning me? Brody Easton spoons?"

"Only you, baby. But don't be surprised if you get woken up by my fork later. There's an ass I plan to take still. I'm far from done with you."

I inhaled deeply and smiled, realizing I was far from done with him, too.

Over the next week, we spent every night together. Some nights I made him dinner while we argued over sports; other nights we ate out of take out containers sitting on the living room floor while we learned about each other—favorite music, favorite movies, foods we both disliked. Thanks to Brody's interesting question choices, we also knew what costumes we wore for Halloween at age eight and what animal we'd choose if we could be turned into one (Brody would be a lion. I'd be a dolphin). But I ended every day wrapped in Brody's arms.

Mr. CUM had been pissed that I hadn't brought the locker room story to WMBC. There was no denying he was right when he reamed into me on how my personal relationship with Brody had influenced my judgment on reporting a story. Although two days later he calmed when he realized there was a way to exploit that personal relationship. Brody agreed to an exclusive interview if his team made playoffs. That got me off the hot seat with my boss—for now.

One morning, Brody left early for his first practice after his suspension. My red throw pillows were strewn all over the living room floor from when we'd gone at it on the couch the night before. I picked up the two monogrammed red pillows, then the brown rectangular one I'd had since high school. Tracing my fingers along the script that spelled out *LOVE*, I briefly thought about the boy who'd given it to me so many years ago. I felt guilty for starting to let Drew go, but it was a decision I knew needed to be made. Too many years of my life had passed in a blur since the accident. This was the first time I didn't want to stand by and watch more pass. I wanted to live them.

After a long shower, I got myself ready for work. I was sitting on the edge of my bed, zipping up my knee-high leather boots, when the small framed picture of Drew that sat on my nightstand caught my eye. Brody had never said a word about it, even though it was impossible for him to have missed it. I looked down at the first boy I fell in love with and closed my eyes, thinking of all of the good memories. Up until now, I had always thought of Drew as just my love, not my *first* love. Realizing that he may have been my first but would likely not be my last was a monumental moment for me. I stood, holding the photo, then did something I never expected to do—I packed the photo into a box inside my closet. Drew would always have a piece of my heart, but there was finally room for someone else.

Brody

CHAPTER 20

After practice, I swung by my place and grabbed the wooden checkers set I'd bought for Marlene's birthday. It wasn't the exact one she used to have—this one was nicer—but it looked similar. On my way, I stopped at the florist and picked her up a bunch of colorful flowers.

"Morning, ya old bastard." I smiled at Grouper.

He scrunched up his forehead and looked at me funny. "What the hell are you so happy about, dipshit?"

"What's not to be happy about? I'm damn good looking, got a weapon for an arm, and you work for me, not the other way around. Life is fucking stupendous."

He shook his head. "Must be contagious. Haven't seen Marlene in this cheery a mood in years either."

"She should be. Eighty-one today. You didn't look that good when you were her age."

Grouper grumbled something.

"Where is the birthday girl? Day room?"

"I think her visitor took her back to her room a little while ago."

"Visitor?"

"The one who was here a few days ago is back again. Brought Marlene a present, too."

"What are you talking about? No one visits Marlene, except me."

Grouper shrugged. "Thought you knew. Pretty girl with the biggest blue eyes I've ever seen. They wouldn't have let her past security if she wasn't on the approved list."

The hair on the back of my neck stood up. *The biggest big blue eyes I've ever seen.* I tore ass toward Marlene's room. By the time I reached the door, my heart was beating like it was the first week of practice and I'd just run five miles in full pads.

Hearing her voice, I froze. Willow had moved from the Deep South to New York when she was ten, but she always kept a hint of her accent. The way she strung her words together was almost lyrical. It was something I'd always loved about her. I could lie with my head in her lap for hours, listening to her babble about all the things she wanted to see someday. But in that moment, as I stood on the other side of the door, the sound was worse than nails scraping down a blackboard.

I should have taken a moment to tamp down the anger boiling up within me, but I didn't. I pushed the door open. Willow was sitting on Marlene's bed, her back to me. "What the fuck are you doing here?"

At the sound of my voice, her head whipped around. Her naturally doe-eyed blues grew even wider.

Neither of us said a word. My chest burned. Swallowing acid would have been less painful than what looking at her again did to me after all these years.

Grouper must have heard me or sensed that something wasn't right, because he was suddenly beside me. He took one look at my face, then at Willow, and squeezed between me and the doorway to get inside of the room.

"Okay, Birthday Girl. It's time for physical therapy." It was only one o'clock; physical therapy wasn't until four. Luckily, most days, Marlene had no sense of time. Grouper maneuvered her wheelchair over and immediately began sitting her up in the bed. He wasn't in bad shape, but I knew from experience it wasn't easy getting her in and out of the chair. Typically a nurse and a porter did it together.

Ignoring the self-preservation that was keeping me standing in the hallway, I walked to the bed and lifted Marlene, setting her gently into her chair. She looked up at me. "Brody. I didn't hear you come in. Did you come with Willow?"

I responded with a lie on autopilot, the same way I had been for years. "We came in separate cars today."

She nodded. Grouper unlatched the lock on the chair and began to turn her toward the door. "Wait!" She held up her hand. "I need my teeth."

I kissed Marlene's forehead. "You have them in."

She did the usual check, raising her hand and tapping her nail on her front tooth. What was it with those things? She never trusted that I was telling the truth about her teeth, yet she happily accepted the thousands of lies I'd been feeding her about her granddaughter for years. Sometimes we believe things not because we know they are true, but because the lies are easier to accept.

Grouper nodded to me as he wheeled Marlene from the room, clicking the door closed behind him.

I stared out the window for a long time. There was so much I wanted to yell at Willow, yet it was all knotted up in my throat, clogging the words. Eventually, she was the one who spoke.

"How have you been?" she asked in a soft voice.

I let out a sardonic laugh. "Just fucking great." *This shit* was not happening. I turned to face her, leveling a death stare. "What do you want here, Willow?"

"What do you mean? I came to see my grandmother."

"It's been four goddamn years. Why now?"

She looked down at her wringing hands. "I missed her."

"Bullshit. What do you need? Money?" I took my wallet out of my pocket and pulled the wad of cash from it, throwing at her on the bed. "I'll save you the trouble of stealing it. Take it. And fucking leave. We're fine without you."

"You've been coming to see her every week all these years. I saw it on the visitor sign-in sheet."

"Someone had to."

She looked up at me. There were tears in her eyes. I had to look away. I was too fucking angry to let her manipulate me again. "I should have been here. Thank you for taking care of her for me."

"I didn't do it for you." The air in the room was making it difficult to breathe. The windows didn't open, and my lungs constricted, the pressure in my chest making it feel like it was about to explode. I needed to get the hell out of this place. Without bothering to say goodbye, I left the flowers and the gift I'd brought for Marlene's birthday on the bed and headed to the door.

Her voice stopped me as I reached for the door handle. I didn't turn around when she spoke.

"I've been clean for eleven months."

"Good luck to you, Willow." I never turned back.

Willow
CHAPTER 21

"You knew it wasn't going to be easy."

I pulled the last tissue out of the box that Dr. Kaplan kept on the glass coffee table between us. "Sorry."

"I'm well stocked. Don't worry about it." She gave me the same encouraging smile I'd grown to become dependent on over the last year. "Take a minute. Then tell me about the day. Start with your grandmother. Did she recognize you?"

I dried my eyes and wadded up the tissue in my palm. "She did. I was really nervous that she wouldn't. My legs were shaking when I walked in the first time."

"Understandable. It's been a long time."

"She knew me. She knew who I was. But she didn't seem to know how much time had passed. It was like she just picked a page from our history book, and everything continued from there."

Dr. Kaplan nodded. "Stage five, most likely. Moderate cognitive decline. I'm glad that she has progressed slowly; we talked about how some cases can move twice as fast as others."

"I know. It's selfish of me, but it made me happy that she could recognize me still."

"It's not selfish. Selfish people tend to be good only to themselves.

I think we can both agree that isn't the case. What you're more likely feeling is regret."

"I suppose."

"The thing with regret is, you can only regret the past. So for you, that's healthy. Regret the past. Use it. Make a new future. Visit her often. The more the regret is pushed into the past, the easier it will be."

"I am. I visited her every day this week."

"That's good. And how about the other regret that you need to deal with?"

"Brody?"

"Of course."

We'd spent the better part of a year talking about the man—who else would she be referring to? "I saw him. It didn't go very well."

She nodded and waited for me to continue.

"He hates me. I can't blame him. He assumed I was back because I needed something."

"Your history runs deep. You're going to have to earn back his trust."

"I'm not so sure he'll give me that chance."

"There's only one way to find out. Perhaps once he sees that you're genuinely clean this time, that you have a job, and you are planning on staying in Marlene's life, he'll come around."

I took a deep breath and exhaled audibly. "I know. It's not going to happen overnight. He can't even believe I'm sober, how can I expect him to believe that I've gone to bed and woken up thinking of him every day for the last four years?"

Delilah
CHAPTER 22

"Is everything okay?" Brody pushed spicy Thai chicken and fettuccini around the plate with his fork. Tuesday night, he'd said he wasn't feeling well and canceled coming by. And the last few days, he'd been quiet. Tonight his mood was something that resembled sullen. "Do you not like the pasta?"

"Yeah. I'm good. Sorry, babe. The pasta is delicious. Just tired."

The rest of the evening was pretty much the same. I felt like I was dragging questions out of him. Normally, I was good with quiet. I'd never been a person who felt the need to talk all the time to be comfortable. The thing was, the quiet wasn't comfortable tonight.

Later, I tried different subjects. Nothing seemed to interest him enough to talk. Brody was also having an after-dinner drink, something that was similarly out of character for him. He poured a stiff rum and Coke and sat down on the couch, staring into his glass as he swirled the liquid.

"What did you ever end up buying when you went shopping the other day?"

He sipped his drink and looked at me with a creased brow. "Hmm?"

"The family friend you were shopping for last weekend. You were in a gadget store when I called you, and you said you were shopping for a friend's birthday. Remember?"

Brody looked around the room before taking a sizeable gulp. Placing his drink on the table, he lifted a knee and turned to face me. "I got her a wooden checkers board. She lives in a nursing home and has a thing for game shows. She watches them on TV all day and likes to play board games."

"Oh. That's nice of you. Is she a friend of your dad?"

He looked me straight in the eyes this time. "She's Willow's grandmother, Marlene."

There was more to this story. And I wasn't sure I wanted to know the rest.

"After Willow disappeared, Marlene started to get confused a lot. She had no one but a drug addict for a daughter and a drug addict for a granddaughter. The woman spent her whole life seeing the good in people, and yet when her time came, when she needed that good to show for her, the two of them were nowhere to be found." Brody had one arm slung over the back of the couch, I reached up and took his hand and squeezed.

"My dad and I took turns looking in on her for a while after I got back from college. But then my dad eventually retired to Arizona, and I'd be traveling four days some weeks with the team. It just wasn't safe for Marlene to be alone anymore. So I moved her out of her place and into a private nursing home about three years ago."

"Wow. And you still keep in touch with her?"

"Haven't missed a Tuesday since the day I moved her in. Promised her she'd see my smiling face every week." Brody guffawed. "There's been some pretty shitty losses on Monday that didn't have my face smiling on Tuesday, but I haven't skipped a visit anyway."

"That's amazing, Brody. Not many people would do that for someone else. Especially not someone who isn't even their own family."

"She's always been like family to me. I was young when my mother died. Marlene tried to help me and my dad out whenever she could. Plus, someone had to be there for her. Willow sure as shit wasn't."

I'd been curious to ask about her since the night he told me about what happened in college, but the opportunity had never presented itself. Until now. "What happened to Willow? You mentioned she disappeared after the night with Colin."

"She was gone for a long time after that. Didn't resurface until my first year playing in the pros. That was probably her longest sober period since we were teens. Things were good for a while. Until they weren't."

"That doesn't sound good."

"It wasn't. She disappeared again one night. I searched for days. Went to all the usual hangouts I'd pull her ass out of when she was using. Missed half my practices, and when I did show up, it was a fucking waste of everyone's time. I had no focus. Halfway through the regular season, police knocked on Marlene's door one night. There were a few homeless camps down near the East River—mostly it's drug addicts who have checked out of life in general. A police boat was patrolling one morning, found her floating face-down."

"Oh my God."

"She'd been without oxygen for almost three minutes and was blue from the water temperature. Marlene and I spent two days at the hospital. She crashed twice, and they brought her back. They didn't know if she would have brain damage if she woke up."

"That's awful."

"If it were you or me, we would have died or been on a feeding tube drooling for the rest of our lives. But not Willow. Ten days later, she walked out of the hospital like nothing had happened."

"Wow."

"I thought maybe the whole thing had scared her sober. And for a while, I think it did. Until December third, four years ago."

"What happened then?"

"Nothing. It was the last time I ever saw her." Brody paused, lifted his glass from the table, and swallowed back the remainder of his drink. "Until this Tuesday."

Sleep was nearly impossible that night. There were so many things going through my mind. Things that I made a mental mountain out of because of my own insecurities. Like, for example, the fact that Brody kissed me good night and left it at that. I knew it wasn't normal for couples to have sex every time they spent the night together. Eventually, there would be nights when we would just need some sleep. We'd settle into a routine and some of the newness would wear off. It was normal. It happened in every relationship. But the fact that it happened on *that night* had me thinking the worst.

Around two in the morning, I decided to stop obsessing and roll over and go to bed. The small light on my bedside nightstand was on, so I reached over to turn it off. My eyes fell to the place where the framed picture of Drew used to be. The irony hit me then. After all these years, I'd finally decided to try and put my past behind me. Right at the same time Brody's decided to come back into his life.

The next few weeks everything seemed to resume to normal. The distance I'd felt for a few days when Willow returned was gone, and Brody returned to his usual cocky-charming self. He even came to Fit Factory with me one Thursday morning. We'd slept at his place, and there was one only a few blocks away.

On the walk over, he held my hand. For a guy who wasn't looking for more than a fun night only six weeks ago, he'd fallen into boyfriend mode like a pro.

"So what kind of girly shit are we doing at this place, anyway?"

I'd explained the rotational gym program I belonged to. He stopped on the sidewalk before I could answer. "It's not that Zumba crap, is it?"

"No, it's not Zumba day. But Zumba isn't crap. It's actually hard work. I leave there soaked—that means it was a good workout."

He returned to walking. "You were soaked this morning, and considering I had you pinned to the wall and did all the work, I don't think you got such good exercise."

"You're a pig, you know that?"

Brody dropped my hand and grabbed a handful of my ass right there on the street. "What's that say about you? You got it bad for a pig."

I rolled my eyes. But he was totally right. *I had it bad.*

A block away from the gym, Brody pointed across the street. "That's where Marlene lives. Broadhollow Manor."

I'd walked past the building before. From the outside, it looked more like a ritzy apartment complex than the terrible visual that came to mind when the words *nursing home* were spoken. "That looks more like luxury condos than a nursing home."

"It's a nice place. They keep it clean, and everyone is well taken care of. You should see some of the dumps that I went to see before finding Broadhollow. The places that the state will pay for are one step up from a shelter. I could have bought a luxury condo for cheaper than what the last few years cost me. But it's worth it. I'd never be able to sleep at night knowing she was in a hole in the wall, and I had bank just sitting around."

Even though this morning he had cooked me breakfast naked after delivering a delicious orgasm up against the bedroom wall, that last statement made me fall a little harder for the man. *My pig.*

Arriving at the gym, he opened the door for me to enter first. Before passing through, I stopped, stretched up on my toes and kissed him on the cheek.

"What was that for?"

"For being you."

He walked in behind me and swatted my ass as he whispered in my ear. "My girl likes dirty pigs."

The woman at the reception desk was on her cell phone as I signed in. When she hung up, I asked her about a guest pass. She didn't bother to look up from her phone.

"My membership has a few guest passes. I don't have one with me today. I was hoping it would be okay, and you could just look up that I haven't used any yet."

She huffed in annoyance, her attention having to be refocused from her cell to the computer that was *actually part of her job*. "Name?"

"Delilah Maddox."

Her nails clicked away. "Guest name?"

"Um. Brody."

She halted her clacking. "Last name?"

"Easton."

Well, that got her attention. Her head whipped up. "You're . . . "

"Delilah's guest." Brody filled in the blank when she trailed off.

"Oh my God. You're really Brody Easton. I *love* you! I'm a huge Steel fan."

"Thank you."

She propped both elbows on the counter, cupping her smiling face in her hands. Forget whiplash, this woman had bitchlash; she'd gone from bitch to entranced so fast.

"So what brings you here to our little gym?"

"Exercise," Brody responded flatly.

She giggled like he'd just said the funniest thing. "This class won't be exercise to someone like you."

My response was snippy because . . . well . . . because she was a bitch who had just insulted my exercise, the place she worked and . . . she was busy ogling my boyfriend. "That's okay. He exercised at home this morning. Wall lunges."

She nodded. "Interesting. Never tried those. Maybe you can show me how later?"

I plastered on a fake smile. "I don't think so. But could we get that guest pass?"

"Oh. Okay. Sure. No problem." She motioned to the entrance behind the desk. "Go right ahead. This one's on me. He doesn't need a pass."

The class was nearly full when we got there, so we took a spot in the back, dropping our gym bags next to us to claim real estate.

"You're cute when you're jealous."

"I wasn't jealous."

He raised an eyebrow and smirked. "Were too."

"I'm not the jealous type."

"Really?"

"Yes."

"You're full of shit."

"I am not."

"Care to put your money where your mouth is?"

"You want to bet that you can make me jealous?"

"Yep."

I extended my hand. "You're on. Loser gives the other a massage."

Brody shook my hand and winked. "Okay. But you won't be massaging my back."

"Whatever. But this contest goes both ways."

Brody looked around the room. It was almost entirely filled with women. "You're going to flirt with some of the women in here? I'm pretty sure this is the best contest I will ever win, and we haven't even started to play yet."

The bitchy woman from the front desk came in. "Alex is running five minutes late. So why don't we get you warmed up? Anyone want to volunteer to help me stretch out the class up front?"

Brody's hand shot up faster than a geek's in science class. Bitch looked pleased.

"Mr. Easton. What a treat. Ladies, we have none other than Super Bowl MVP Brody Easton in the class today! And he's going to come up here and show us how it's done." No one had really noticed us in the back of the room, but that changed instantly. Women turned around and gawked. Brody gloated and headed to the front of the class.

I had completely forgotten what an arrogant showman he could be. Shades of the first time I met him in the locker room were back as he stood next to the instructor, working his stretches. At one point, he smiled at me, then tugged his T-shirt over his head. His gym shorts were hanging low on his narrow waist, and every ripped muscle was on full display. *Especially that V.* The same one I'd recently discovered we both liked when I traced its path with my tongue.

I looked around the room. I definitely wasn't the only one drooling. I swear I smelled the pheromone soup wafting through the air. I would never admit it, but I didn't love the way these women were looking at Brody. Yet . . . it wasn't an immature jealousy. There was a comforting feeling to realize that I knew he wasn't really interested in them. The entire class might have been transfixed, but the man at the head of the class was only doing it to try to get a rise out of me.

After a few minutes of the Brody show, Alex walked in. He taught classes in the location I usually went to, so we were friendly. Perhaps even friendlier than my confident-to-win-the-bet boyfriend might like. I inwardly smirked, knowing it would only take a sentence or two after class to win our bet. I could practically feel my muscles relaxing under Brody's massaging rub already.

After class was over, the women circled Brody asking for autographs. He gloated, thinking he was getting a rise out of me, but truly I found the entire thing amusing and was pretty damn proud that jealousy hadn't reared its ugly head. When the crowd thinned, we headed to the door . . . but not before I stopped to talk to the instructor.

"Hey, Alex."

"Pretzel. Nice surprise seeing you in this location today." Alex's typical flirtatious banter was muted. He glanced at Brody.

"This is Brody Easton. An old family friend."

Brody squinted at me as he shook Alex's hand. That little bit of information, indirect confirmation that the man standing next to me wasn't my boyfriend, was all it took to relax Alex. "Nice to meet you, Brody. You two go way back, huh?"

"Apparently so."

"Tell me, was our little Pretzel always this smokin' hot?"

The air chilled instantly. Brody glared at Alex, who didn't even seem to notice since he went right on adding gunpowder to the cannon.

"Your downward-facing dog still needs to open up a little. Why don't you stick around a few minutes and let me help you stretch into it?"

"That sounds like a good idea." I turned to Brody and cheerily stoked the fire I smelled burning. "Why don't you go on to the locker room and Alex can help me with my positioning? I'll catch up with you out front."

Brody tried so hard, but Alex's dirty leer was too much to handle.

"Fuck this." His hand possessively gripped my waist. "You win. Let's get the hell out of here."

Alex looked confused as Brody quickly steered me toward the locker room. "Very cute," he growled.

"I thought so."

Leaving the gym, I taunted Brody about my win. "I would have thought you'd be stiff competition. Guess not."

"I'll give you stiff . . . " He took my hand.

"I wouldn't have pegged you for the jealous type."

"Me either," he grumbled.

"I have to grab a quick shower and head to the station. We have a late-morning planning meeting. They're adding a few last-minute interviews with some of the Eagles players before this weekend's game."

"Meeting with the enemy. You trying to kill me? First Yogi-Asshole and now spending time with the division rivalry. I think I need a little extra attention tonight. I'm feeling neglected."

"Oh, are you now?"

"Yep. I think I need you to show me how special I am."

"And what exactly would that entail?"

"I'll think of something. When I do, I'll be sure to text you the details while you're in the middle of your meeting." The man's wicked tongue translated well even in texting.

We turned the corner, heading down the block where Marlene lived. Brody was telling me about his schedule for the rest of the week when he suddenly went quiet. It took me a moment to catch up. "Brody?"

He was staring across the street.

"Everything okay?"

The streets of New York were bustling. At first, I didn't notice anything. But then I saw her. A woman had stopped outside of Marlene's building and was staring in our direction. People came and went, but she just stood there, fixated on us.

She was absolutely gorgeous. Model-waif thin with long blond hair and eyes so big, I noticed them across a busy street. My heart sank. I knew the answer but asked anyway. "Do you know that woman across the street?"

Brody turned his head face-forward and kept walking. "Yes. That's Willow."

And just like that, the confidence I'd felt earlier—the feeling of empowerment—turned into fear and vulnerability. And, yes, even a little jealousy.

Willow
CHAPTER 23

"That pretty face should never have an upside-down smile." My grandmother was losing her memory, lived in a nursing home, and had addicts for her sole surviving kin, and yet here she was, trying to cheer me up.

I forced a smile. "Sorry."

"You and Brody have a fight?"

Brody had apparently not filled Grams in on the last few years. I wasn't sure why or what that meant, but I went along with it. "No. We're good." I took Grandma's hand and squeezed.

"Good. That boy is a keeper. They don't make 'em like him too often anymore. Reminds me of my Carl in some ways."

"Really?" It was the first time Grams had spoken of Pop Pop. I had no idea if she remembered he was gone or not. Her memory was so random and selective.

"Yep. That boy is loyal. He fell hard for you and never got back up. Same way my Carl did for me."

She was right about one thing—Brody was loyal. Probably the most loyal person I'd ever come across in my entire life. But even the most loyal person had their breaking point. Seeing him on the street today reminded me of that. I hadn't expected him to be waiting around for me all these years. Not after everything I'd done to him. But what I saw today had been hard to see anyway. He'd looked *happy*. Holding a woman's hand in public. I should have been happy for him. But what I *should* do and what I *actually* did had never been the same.

I spent another two hours with Grams. She enjoyed the company and, honestly, I loved being around her. She was my root, made me feel grounded when I otherwise would spin out of control.

After *The Price Is Right* ended, I stopped in the ladies' room in the hallway and cleaned up, knowing I'd have to head straight to work or risk being late. I pulled my hair back into a ponytail and brushed on a little mascara and lip gloss. When I returned to Grams' room to say goodbye, a man was sitting in the chair next to her. He looked familiar, but I couldn't place why at first. "Hello."

The man stood and nodded. "I was just doing my daily visit with Marlene. I didn't realize she had company."

My jacket was draped over another chair, so I lifted it and began to pull it on. "Stay. Please. I was just about to leave. I have to get to work anyway." I smiled. "I'm Willow. Marlene's granddaughter."

"I didn't realize Marlene had a granddaughter. It's nice to meet you, Willow. I'm Grouper. Your grandmother likes to whip me at checkers a few times a week."

"Ah. Yes, game shark. She looks innocent, but she's a closet swindler."

Grouper looked to Marlene and shook his head. "You sound just like Brody."

"You know Brody?"

"Of course. Comes here every week like clockwork. Good man. Just don't ever let him know I said that." He winked.

"Does he ever bring his girlfriend?"

"Girlfriend? Oh, you mean the reporter. No. He comes alone. Tuesdays. Usually about ten."

I walked over to Grams and gave her a hug. Her shoulders were so much thinner than I remembered. My larger-than-life grandmother felt tiny, almost fragile. "I have to get going to work, or I'll be late."

"Okay, dear. Will you come back with Brody?"

"You know what? I will. I'll be back on Tuesday. It was nice to meet you, Mr. Grouper."

"Nope, no mister. Just Grouper. Like the fish."

"Oh. Okay. Well, it was nice to meet you, Grouper. And thank you for visiting with Grams."

"My pleasure. Let's hope the Steel win this Sunday, so we get a happy Brody here on Tuesday."

I smiled, refraining from saying what I was thinking. *I wouldn't count on Brody being happy on Tuesday, even if he wins.*

***

Monday was my only day off. Restaurant hours were hard on keeping up with any TV programs, so I had stopped bothering recording most things a long time ago. On the rare occasion that I remembered to set up something to record, it was even rarer that I actually watched whatever it was that I'd recorded. Except today. I sat on the edge of the couch during the last two minutes of the Steel versus Eagles game as Brody and the offensive line moved down the field. They were down by six and sitting on the thirty-yard line on fourth down.

Mindlessly, I tapped my foot on the floor as Brody drew back, and the ball went sailing in the air. *Come on, Brody. Come on.* I held my breath until the spiraling ball fell into the wide receiver's hands. Being on edge, anxious for the win as Brody stood on the field, reminded me of sitting on the old metal bleachers in high school, so many years ago. My best friend, Anna, used to steady my leg. *Quit playing the snare drum with your foot, you're shaking the whole bleacher.* God, those days really were a lifetime ago.

After the game, I decided to make cupcakes. I used to love to bake, although it had been a really long time since I'd had anyone to bake for. My apartment was small, with a galley kitchen that was tinier than most closets and a crappy stove, so baking wasn't something I'd thought to do since I moved in. But today I made Gram and Brody's favorite. The same red velvet cake with cream cheese frosting that I used to bake after Brody won a game back in high school.

On my way to my afternoon appointment with Dr. Kaplan, I knocked on my neighbor's door across the hall, two cupcakes in hand. Waiting as I listened for the triple set of locks to clank open, I looked around the dim third floor of my building. This place was really seedy, and that was saying something coming from the places I'd spent time in over the years. But New York City was expensive, and it was the only place I was able to afford at the moment.

Eventually, the door cracked open a tiny bit, the flimsy top lock chain still securely attached. I kneeled down to the little girl's eye level. "Hi, Abby. I made cupcakes. I thought maybe you and your mom would like some."

She nodded quickly with wide eyes. The door shut and then reopened without the chain. Abby reached for the plate. *Shit. I know that look.*

"Is your mom home?" The poor little thing was starving. She didn't even bother to lick the icing off the top or taste it before shoveling half the cupcake into her mouth with one bite.

Abby nodded her head while chewing. She was probably five or six, but she was tiny for even that. I'd gotten to know her and her mom over the last few months. Her mother was in recovery, like me. But I had a bad feeling that something might have changed over the weekend. The two guys I'd seen coming out of their place definitely screamed that the wagon had tipped, and Mom had fallen off.

I didn't want to scare Abby by prying too hard. "How about Mom? Can I give her the other cupcake?"

"She's sleeping."

It was four in the afternoon. "Is anyone else home?"

Abby shook her head.

"Can I come inside for a second, Abby?"

She nodded.

Who else would this sweet little thing let in?

I walked through their apartment and found Lena sprawled across her bed. I checked that she was breathing. A few beer cans were littered around the sparse room, but there were no signs of drug paraphernalia, at least.

"Lena?"

She groaned in response and rolled over.

By the time I returned to the kitchen, Abby was already halfway through cupcake number two. Curiosity had me opening the refrigerator. *Damn.* It was emptier than mine. *Way emptier.* An expired carton of milk, some ketchup, a jar of pickles—with only the juice left—and a Tupperware with something moldy inside. The kitchen cabinets didn't fare much better.

"I'll be right back, okay? Lock the door . . . wait for me to knock."

Abby spoke with her mouth full. "Okay."

My apartment wasn't exactly stocked with a gourmet feast, but I could make sure Abby had a full belly. I made a quick peanut butter-and-jelly sandwich and grabbed the half-empty carton of milk from my refrigerator before going back.

"Have you ever tried peanut butter?" The last thing she or her mother needed was for me to load Abby full of something that she was allergic to.

"I used to bring it to school for lunch sometimes. But I have to sit at a different table from Danny Mendez. He's allergic."

That made me feel better. I poured a glass of milk and watched her eat before leaving.

But the time I arrived at Dr. Kaplan's office, it was five after four. She looked at her watch. "You're late today."

I plopped down in my usual spot. "Sorry. I had to take care of something."

She took a notebook, stood from behind her desk, and moved to her usual chair across from me. Flipping to a new page, she wrote the date down before setting the notebook on her lap and giving me her full attention.

"So, what did you have to take care of?"

"I'm not using again, if that's what you're asking."

"I didn't say that you were."

"No. But I felt it in your tone."

"It was just a simple question, Willow. Let's not get started on the wrong foot today."

Maybe I had jumped to a conclusion she wasn't hinting at. "I had to make my neighbor a sandwich."

"Oh? Is she sick?"

"No. She's five years old. Her mother was sleeping, and I stopped over with cupcakes and realized she was starving."

"Her mother was sleeping in the middle of the day?"

"Yeah. I thought the same thing. I'm hoping for Abby's sake I'm wrong. Her mother has been clean for four months."

Dr. Kaplan nodded and wrote something in her book.

"What could you possibly have written down? That I made a kid a peanut butter-and-jelly sandwich?"

"Actually, I noted you befriended a little girl who has a similar home life to yours growing up."

"Oh." *I hadn't thought of it that way.*

"So . . . how was your week? Did you visit Marlene?"

"I did."

"And how is that going?"

"Good. Her disease sort of lets me pick up life with her at various spots. She doesn't seem to realize how long I was gone or remember all of the terrible things I've done to her."

More nodding. "And work?"

"It's good. My feet are killing me. But the money is good. I'm hoping to save up enough to move to a better neighborhood eventually. I'd like to be closer to my grandmother. It takes more than forty-five minutes on a good day to get to her from uptown."

"Have you been out socially?"

"No. But that cute guy in the suit asked me out the other day."

"At the restaurant. The one who asked you out a few weeks ago?"

"He came in with some friends again."

"And did you agree to go out with him?"

"No."

"Why not? You said yourself that you thought he was handsome and seemed like a nice guy."

"I'm not ready yet."

"Because of Brody?"

"How am I supposed to start dating when I still love another man?"

"People do it all the time. You need to move on, Willow."

"I know. I'm just not ready."

"When will you be ready?"

I shrugged. "I don't know. I'm seeing him tomorrow, though."

"You are?" Dr. Kaplan sounded surprised.

"Don't get excited. He doesn't know yet."

Her forehead creased.

"He visits Marlene every Tuesday. I've been avoiding going on that day so I wouldn't see him."

"But now you're going?"

"Yes."

"What changed?"

"I'm not sure." That was a lie. Dr. Kaplan already knew all about my past, but I was embarrassed to admit how selfish I continued to be. Seeing Brody with his girlfriend *had* changed things. I needed to see for myself that there was no hope for us. Or I'd never be able to move on.

Brody

CHAPTER 24

"Salmon." I nodded. Grouper had set up yellow caution cones barricading the section of the floor he was mopping in the main lobby. Snatching two of them, I jogged down the hall and set them four feet apart. "No touchdown pass, then the ball goes to my favorite nurse, Shannon." I winked at Shannon, who shook her head while smiling. "Shannon wears scrubs with little football players on them on Sundays. Did you wear those this Sunday, Shannon?"

She chuckled. "Sure did. Had my matching dangling football earrings on, too."

"See that? I'm thinking I shouldn't even give you the chance to win this ball, old man. You got football earrings?"

"Just throw the ball already, damn it." Grouper dropped the mop and jogged toward the cones.

For half a second, I considered pitching the ball over his head so he'd miss, then I remembered he'd probably spent Sunday playing checkers with Marlene while he rooted for my obnoxious ass. So I lobbed the ball for an easy catch instead.

"I still got it." He fist-pumped as he walked back.

"Yeah, you got it, all right. Hemorrhoids, arthritis . . . "

"Don't remind me. Got those, too. Your day will come. And I can't wait to see that pretty-boy face get some good age spots on it."

I chuckled. "Marlene in her room or the day room?"

"I think she's in her suite. Pretty little granddaughter of hers is keeping her company again this morning. I'm not going to have to referee anything in there, am I?"

Between the win on Sunday that moved us into first place and spending Monday night inside of Delilah celebrating, I'd thought nothing could ruin my mood. Fuck if I hadn't been wrong.

I contemplated turning around and leaving. But it was Tuesday, the day I'd been spending here for years. Years when *she* hadn't even give a shit whether her grandmother was alive. I was done letting her interfere with my life anymore.

At least this time, I was prepared to see her. Or at least I *thought* I was.

Willow turned around when the door opened, and my heart stopped beating. I hated her so much.

I hated her.

So damn much.

Yet when my heart started beating again, I couldn't stop it from racing.

"Hi." She smiled hesitantly, and those big eyes looked up from under long lashes.

I hate you.

I also hated that she was still as beautiful as ever.

I lifted my chin in her direction as my only response and walked over to Marlene. "How's my favorite lady today?" I kissed her on the forehead.

"Brody. You're just in time. Get a pad and paper."

I furrowed my brow.

"*Wheel of Fortune* is about to start," Willow explained. "Remember how the three of us used to—"

I looked her right in those big eyes. "I know when her shows are on. And *we're* not doing this."

Her bright face faltered. It should have made me feel better, but instead it did the opposite.

"You don't want to play?" Marlene asked.

"I'm going to sit this one out." Marlene looked disappointed, but the moment Pat Sajak came on TV, her face lit back up. If only we all had something that made everything okay, even if only for a few minutes. I stole a fleeting glance at Willow. She used to be my Pat Sajak.

When the first puzzle came on TV, the two of them fell right back into a time warp. Back in the day, the three of us would sit on the long plastic-covered couch in Marlene's living room. We'd write down our letter picks before the contestants called out theirs and keep track of how much we'd win if they guessed our letter. What Marlene didn't know was that Willow and I had secretly played for sexual favors. Whoever earned the most at the end of the show got whatever they were in the mood for that night. Most nights I let Willow win, just so I could hear her tell me what she wanted me to do to her.

The visuals came flooding back.

Willow at sixteen, looking up at me as I hovered over her. Her lips swollen from hours of kissing.

I hate you.

Her sitting up, her hair a wild mess, as she pulled off a white T-shirt. No bra underneath. My thumb tugging on her bottom lip, which she sucked between her teeth nervously.

I hate you.

At the sound of my chair abruptly skidding across the tile floor, Willow jumped. "Bathroom" was all I offered.

Refusing to concede my time with Marlene out of principle, I stayed for a while more, quietly sitting and trying to avoid any real interaction with Willow. When it was time for lunch, I helped Marlene into her wheelchair and brought her down to the dining room.

"I have to get going. Practice this afternoon."

"You two work too much." Marlene's usual lunch table was waiting for her. I made sure she was comfortable and said my goodbyes before heading back to her suite to grab my jacket.

I heard the door creak open, but I didn't turn around as I slipped on my coat.

"I made cupcakes," Willow said softly. "Red velvet with cream cheese frosting."

I stared out the window. "Not hungry."

She took two steps toward me and stopped. I could see her reflection in the window. "Do you want me to avoid certain days?"

"Do whatever you want. Makes no difference to me."

She nodded. "I saw the game yesterday. You know, you still do the same little celebration in the end zone that you did in ninth grade on the field at Kennedy High School."

I hated that she *thought* she knew so much about me.

I hated *her*.

She didn't know anything about me anymore. I made sure she knew it before I walked out the door. "I celebrated inside my girlfriend that night, not in the end zone."

Delilah
CHAPTER 25

The only time I didn't mind my boss popping into my office was when Indie was around. Mostly because Mr. CUM literally tripped over things when he came near her. Today, it was the garbage can just outside of my door.

Indie had spotted him coming down the hall and leaned over my desk like a barfly trying to attract attention in a pool hall full of horny cowboys. Her already tight skirt looked ready to bust at the seams as she wiggled her ass suggestively.

"Nice to see you, Charlie." She stayed bent over my desk and looked back over her shoulder to speak to him. No one called Charles Ulysses Macy "Charlie." Except Indie.

"Indie." He cleared his throat. "You're looking well."

She smirked. "You're looking at my good angle."

I interrupted before he could respond. "What can I do for you, Mr. Macy?"

"Yes... Um. We need you to cut a sixty-second spot for the playoffs."

"Really?" The sixty-second spots were always done by the big-name reporters and well-known faces.

"We need the female draw, so we're making the spots two reporters—one of each will be a woman."

"So you're basically using her for her body?" Indie stood and folded her arms over her chest.

"Um . . . no. We . . . "

"Relax, Chuck." She rested a hand on his arm. "I was just a little jealous. No one has used my body in a while."

Poor Charles had to adjust the growing bulge Indie was inciting. I actually came to the pig's rescue. "I'm happy to have the opportunity."

"Good. You'll drive down with Michael after the game on Sunday. Do a spot with Mara in Miami on Monday."

"Michael?"

"Langley. That's who you're shooting your spots with."

It took me ten more minutes to get Mr. CUM out of my office. When he was gone, I scolded Indie. "Why do you insist on doing that?"

She tossed a pen up in the air and caught it. "I mentally give myself two points for making him hard. It's a little game I play."

"Gross."

"I know. Do you think he's jerking off in the men's room? I get five points if he comes out and there's a little wet spot on his pants from post-ejaculation drip."

"Seriously, you might be more disgusting than him."

"Serves him right. He deserves to be treated like meat since that's how he treats others."

"But he *likes* it."

"He likes it while I'm playing with him, not while he's stuck playing with himself."

I caught the pen she was continually tossing in the air. "I have to be away an extra day now. Thought I only needed one on-air outfit. I need to get to the dry cleaner's before they close. Which means I'm out for yoga tonight."

"No yoga?" She pouted.

I began packing up my desk for the day. "Nope. I'll just have to work out with Brody tonight," I teased.

"Rough life. You're going to get laid by your gorgeous quarterback boyfriend tonight, then fly off for a romantic night away with Michael Langley."

"It won't be romantic."

"The way that man looks at you, my guess is it won't be from lack of him trying."

e ———————————————— *e*

Brody and I had dinner plans at his hotel tonight. I texted him that I was going to be late, but by the time I finished running my errands for the trip tomorrow, I was even later than I had planned. When I arrived at the Regency, Brody was sitting at the bar inside Silver Ivy. Siselee, the batting-eyelash waitress, was sitting across from him at the table, wearing her uniform.

"Hi." Neither of them had noticed me walk up.

Hearing my voice, Brody swung in my direction, knocking a glass clear across the table as he turned. It fell to the floor and shattered. All eyes in the bar took notice. "There she is!" he said loudly. When I came within his reach, he wrapped one arm around my waist and tugged me toward him. A busboy immediately ran over and began to clean up the mess.

"Our guy's had a little too much to drink," Siselee said.

Our guy?

"He had a bad day," she continued. Her high-and-mighty tone was irritating, and I fought the urge to put her in her place. Instead, I spoke to Brody.

"Hey. You okay?" He was definitely drunk. In his attempt to open his eyes wider, he actually tilted his head back. As if tipping his head back might help the lids snap open.

He smiled and snuggled into me—head first into my chest, of course. "I'm great. Now that you're here."

"Did you eat anything?"

"Nope. I was waiting for you."

"Sorry. I didn't think I'd be this late."

"That's okay. Siselee kept me company."

I bet she did.

Once the busboy had cleaned up the mess, Siselee was back with a tumbler filled with a clear liquid.

"I hope that's water."

"I brought him a fresh drink."

"I don't think he needs it."

"Sure, I do."

Siselee looked at me with a patronizing I-told-you-so face. "It's Tuesday."

"I'm well aware of that."

"It's the only day he allows himself to have a few drinks."

"Yes. But from the looks of things, I think we've skipped past a few and landed on overserved."

"He had a bad day."

"You know what, I think we're going to get something to eat in the restaurant instead of eating in the bar."

As I led Brody to the hostess station, the extent of his drunkenness became that much more apparent. His arm dangled around my shoulders, and he was actually leaning on me a little. "How about if we skip the restaurant and order room service?" I said.

"How about if we skip room service, and I eat you?"

"Even a perv when you're drunk, I see." I chuckled.

Upstairs in Brody's suite, I ordered a light dinner for two. Although I wasn't too sure that Brody would be awake by the time the food came.

He was fumbling with the buttons on his shirt, so I helped him undress while he sat on the bed.

"While you're down there . . . " Brody snickered when I kneeled down to untie his shoes.

"I think you might be too inebriated for even that." I slipped off his second shoe and rested my hands on his knees.

Brody slid my hand from his knee to between his legs, cupping my fingers around his hard-on. "I could see right down your shirt while you untied my shoes. I'm not so drunk that I couldn't take 'em off. I just liked the view."

I laughed. "Why don't you shower before dinner comes? Might sober you up a bit more."

"Are you taking one with me?"

"Not this time."

"All right. But I'm not taking care of myself while I'm in there. I'm saving that for you when I'm out."

"I would expect nothing less."

The food I ordered arrived just before Brody finished in the bathroom. He came out wearing a towel wrapped around his waist—just like the first time I met him.

Two months ago, I would never have guessed that all of Brody Easton's cocky arrogance only camouflaged his insecurities. Turns out, we weren't so different after all. For the last seven years since Drew died, everyone had been telling me that I was avoiding real relationships because I was afraid to get hurt again. I didn't see it . . . until I saw my own actions reflected back at me from Brody. We might have had different methods, but we were doing the same thing—protecting our hearts from loss again. You couldn't get hurt if you didn't let anyone in.

I set up our dinners at the dining room table. "Were you just bored waiting for me? Or did you really have a bad day?"

"Maybe a little of both." He scrubbed his hands over his face and sat at the table.

"Did you have a bad practice today?"

"Not too bad." He lifted the silver cover off his dinner and looked at the Caesar salad I'd ordered him. "Tomorrow is going to suck with the hangover I'm already starting to feel coming on."

"You don't usually have more than one or two. Is everything okay?"

Brody rubbed the back of his neck. "Marlene had a visitor when I went to see her this morning."

I suddenly lost my appetite. "Oh?"

"Willow. She thinks she can just walk back into our life and everything is going to be okay."

Something about the phrase *walk back into our life* made me feel even more uneasy. "Did you two have a fight?"

"No."

I nodded. We ate in silence for a few minutes.

"Just a lot of bad memories."

I had no idea how to respond to that, so I didn't. The air was thick, and it was difficult to swallow as we danced around other topics over dinner.

After dinner, Brody lay in bed while I brushed my teeth in the master bath with the door open. "I'm not going to be flying back with you Sunday night. The station is sending me to Miami after the game."

"Oh yeah? Who you heading to interview?"

"Payton Mara."

I finished brushing, pulled off the headband I wore while I washed my face, and was about to flick off the bathroom light when I noticed one of Brody's jerseys hanging on the back of the door. It was a practice jersey, but his name was emblazoned on the back. My fingers brushed over each letter in the dark. *E-a-s-t-o-n.* I was totally falling for him. There was no way to stop it at this point. I just had to hope that when this fall was over, Brody was there to catch me.

Knowing why his head was where it was tonight, I had two choices. I could get into bed, snuggle up next to him, and wonder if he was thinking of her while we drifted off to sleep. Or . . . I could chase away those bad memories and leave no room for him to be thinking of anyone but me.

If I'm going to fall, I might as well free fall and enjoy the ride down.

Stripping off my T-shirt and sweats, as well as my underwear, I slipped the practice jersey over my head. It skimmed down to my ass, barely covering me. *Perfect.*

Brody was staring blankly at the TV, so I walked to the dresser it was mounted above and set down my folded clothes *with a bend that revealed my entire bare ass.*

"*Fuck,* I love that. My name across your back and that perfect round ass."

I turned around and tilted my head coyly. "Thought you were sleepy?"

"I'd have to be dead to fall asleep with you looking like that." His voice dropped lower. "Turn back around."

"You just want to look at your own name," I teased, but I turned around anyway. The bed creaked as he got up.

"I'd brand my name across that ass if I could."

Crude, but the sentiment made me swoon a bit nonetheless.

His footsteps vibrated on the floor as he walked to me. Warm breath tickled my neck when he leaned down and spoke into my ear. "Bend over. I want to use you." He rubbed my shoulders. "I'm a little drunk and want to forget anything else exists for a while. Except me, inside you. Where everything feels right. You good with that, babe?"

I swallowed and nodded. It was exactly what I wanted. No room for anything except the two of us. *At least for tonight.*

CHAPTER 26

Sunday afternoon, I had just turned off the game when there was a knock on my door so light I wasn't even sure that it was a knock until the second rap came.

"Who is it?"

"It's me. Abby Little from across the hall."

As I unbolted the double set of locks, it struck me as funny that she felt compelled to use her last name. As if "Abby from across the hall" wouldn't be enough to identify her. Or even just "Abby."

"Hey there."

"Can I come in?"

I glanced over her head to the shut apartment door behind her. "Sure. Does your mom know you're here?"

"She's got company. She told me to come see if you were home."

That didn't sound good. "Is one of your aunts or uncles over?" I didn't even know if she had any.

"No. It's the tired guy."

"What tired guy?"

"The one who makes Mommy tired."

Coming down off a high would do that to you. My apartment was pretty lame—other than the TV, there wasn't much for a five-year-old to do. I honestly wasn't even sure what a five-year-old *did do.* "Do you have homework?"

"No."

I didn't have a kitchen table, only a single lonely stool that was counter height. I lifted Abby up and sat her on it. "Want a snack?"

She licked her lips and nodded. God, this kid was so easy to please. I supposed we appreciated the simple things in life when we were deprived of basics. Having an addict for a mother, those basic things often included food, medical care, and attention of any kind. I pulled a box of Reese's Peanut Butter Puffs from my cabinet and showed Abby. "Cereal okay?"

She nodded fast and gave me a big smile. Every time my mother dumped me at Grams' house, Grams always cooked up a feast. Up until that moment, I hadn't thought anything of it. I guess I just figured that she was my grandma—grandmas cook. But seeing Abby walk in made me realize for the first time that Marlene had probably known I was hungry, too. There was so much about my grandmother I'd taken for granted.

After Abby's belly was full, I washed her bowl and considered the situation. *What would Marlene do?* She would have asked me what I wanted to do.

"What do you want to do this afternoon, Abby?"

"Can we go to the park?"

"Sure. But we better go tell your mom and get your coat first."

The familiar smell of burnt plastic hit me when I opened the door to their apartment. "Lena?"

She didn't answer. But the smell of crack told me what she was doing. "Stay here a minute, okay, Abby?"

I left Abby in the kitchen and walked to the bedroom. "Lena?" I called again.

Nothing.

I knocked on the door, not realizing it wasn't fully closed. "Lena?" The impact inched it open. Enough so that I got a look at what was inside. Lena was on her knees, her head bobbing up and down while the loser crackhead who had been coming around held a fistful of her hair in one hand and a crack pipe to his lips with the other.

I froze. And not because seeing a woman giving a blowjob was shocking. Privacy and humility hadn't exactly been rampant in the abandoned houses I'd spent time living in with other junkies. No, I froze because of the crack pipe. I wanted a hit almost as much as I hated the shit.

The loser caught me staring and sneered. My watching was doing it for him. He took another long hit from the pipe, fisted Lena's hair harder and thrust his hips, so she had no choice but to take him deep into her throat as he came.

I wanted to vomit.

I wanted a hit of that pipe.

I needed to get the hell out of there.

I grabbed the first small jacket I could find in the closet and rushed Abby toward the door. *It could have been her watching that.*

"We can go?"

I was already opening the door to get the hell out of that apartment. "Mommy said it's fine."

Abby and I took the subway downtown. There was no way I was taking her to a park in our drug-infested neighborhood. That experience wouldn't be good for either of us. I also needed to get far away from temptation. So I took her to a small park I walked by every day, not far from where Grams lived.

We spent an hour in the park. I sat on a bench and watched Abby play with a little girl about her age. At one point, she ran over to me and asked if she could take a juice box from the little girl's mother. At least she was smart enough to ask permission before taking things from strangers—even moms in the park. That was a good sign, since God knew who she might be around with her mother falling back into drugs.

It was starting to get dark, and both of us clearly weren't ready to go back uptown. So on a whim, even though I'd already visited Marlene earlier today, I decided to take this little toothy, grinning girl to visit my grandmother. We headed toward Broadhollow Manor together.

The nurse stopped me at sign-in. "She's not doing that well this evening."

"What do you mean? I saw her earlier, and she was fine."

"I don't want to get you nervous. It could be nothing. But she's a little lethargic. More out of it than usual."

"Did a doctor see her?"

"Yes. And we're watching her for any signs of change. This sometimes happens with Alzheimer's patients, you should know. They have good days and bad days. It's difficult at times to know if a bad day is just a normal bad day or something we should be concerned with."

"Can I see her?"

"Of course. I didn't mean to scare you. I just wanted to warn you. She's had a good few weeks, but she does have bad days sometimes. This could just be one of them. We have a call into Brody but haven't reached him yet. Just to keep him apprised."

"I think he's away at a game." It stung that they would call to alert Brody, but not think of me. But I deserved it. "Is it okay to bring Abby? She's my friend's daughter, and we were around the corner at the park, so I thought I'd drop in again."

"Sure. Marlene was sleeping when we last checked in. But if she wakes up while you're in there, she just might be a little more confused than usual."

I explained to Abby on the walk down the hall that we were going to visit my grandmother, who sometimes got confused, but I didn't want to scare her, so I left it at that. Cautiously, Abby and I entered Marlene's room.

I breathed a sigh of relief when I found her sleeping peacefully. She didn't wake up during the hour we sat there, but the nurses came in every fifteen minutes and checked her vitals and told us everything was fine. Eventually, Abby started to yawn. It was almost eight and probably close to her bedtime. So I said goodnight and left my cell phone number at the nursing station, asking them to call me if anything changed. Even though the nurse said they would, I didn't put it past them to clear it with Brody first.

After we got back to our apartment building, I tucked Abby in at my place and told her to lock the door so I could go check out what was going on next door. The door to her apartment was unlocked—in this crappy neighborhood. That alone was enough to tell me there was no way I was sending Abby back to sleep there tonight.

Inside, I was relieved to find Lena sleeping alone in her bed. There was drug paraphernalia all over the place. On the way out, I grabbed a cell phone that was on the kitchen counter, hoping to find it unlocked and to see if there was anyone who could take Abby until things with her mother turned around. I knew from experience this wasn't going to be a one-night thing.

Abby told me her grandmother's name, and I went into the other room to call her. It definitely wasn't the first time the woman had gotten a call about her daughter. There was no shock in her voice at all.

Sophie, Abby's grandmother, only lived a few blocks over, so when she agreed to take Abby, I offered to bring Abby by. There was no reason she needed to see her daughter's place the way it was.

The chilly November air felt good as I walked back toward my apartment. Sophie lived in a decent building, and she and her husband had invited me in for coffee. I'd stayed until I saw Abby was comfortable at their place. I couldn't stop thinking about how Abby seemed so unaffected by being shuttled all over. Craziness had already become her norm. She just didn't know that her life was crazy . . . yet.

A few blocks from my house, my phone buzzed in my pocket. A local number was flashing on my screen when I dug it out.

"Hello?"

"Ms. Garner?"

"Yes."

"This is Shannon. I'm a nurse at Broadhollow Manor."

I stopped on the street. "Is everything okay?"

"We just called an ambulance. Your grandmother's stats are declining. Everything may be fine, but—"

"I'm on my way."

Delilah
CHAPTER 27

Whatever fear had taken up residence inside of me was slowly beginning to dissipate. Three nights of sharing a suite with Brody in sunny Florida had given me back my confidence in us. I still hadn't given up the room that WMBC paid for, not wanting anyone to ask any questions. Although, at this point, it was common knowledge that Brody and I were a couple. Some of my male colleagues who held a grudge because I was promoted over them had taken to making snide remarks whenever I walked in the room, alluding to how women reporters secured their interviews. I hated it, but not enough to stop dating Brody.

After the game against Tampa, then locker room interviews Sunday afternoon, Brody and the team got ready to head to the airport while I was meeting Michael Langley to drive down to Miami. The team was loading their bags on the bus outside of the hotel when Michael pulled up in a shiny red Jaguar convertible, the top already down.

Brody and I had talked about who I was traveling with, so it wasn't a surprise to him. But that didn't mean he was happy about it, by any stretch of the word. He wasn't angry, really. I would say it was more of an alpha-possessive-caveman-style jealousy thing he had going on. Strangely enough, I sort of liked it.

After stowing his bags under the bus, Brody returned to say goodbye. Michael waved but stood by his car a few feet away, waiting.

"Can you take off on Friday?"

"I think so."

"Offensive line is off on Friday. I want to take you upstate. Show you my cabin."

"You want to show me your cabin?"

"Yeah. And my cock. I always want to show you my cock. But I want to show it to you in my cabin Thursday night."

"How can I refuse such a tempting offer?" I laughed.

"You can't." Brody wrapped one arm tight around my waist and pulled me close. "We'll leave Thursday after you get off work."

"Okay."

He moved closer, our noses almost touching, but I could see the glint in his eyes. "You know I need to show him that you're mine."

"Are you going to lift your leg and pee on me like a fire hydrant?"

"My sweet girl's into some kinky shit. But I'm game if you are."

I nudged his chest with my elbow.

"Seriously. Have a safe trip. And tell fuckwad to keep his eyes and hands on the road, or he'll have me to deal with."

"Yes, Tarzan." I playfully rolled my eyes.

"Come here, Jane." Brody's hand squeezed the back of my neck while his mouth devoured mine. I became completely lost in the kiss. The spectacle he was making as he leaned me back in a dramatic dip and kissed me like there was no tomorrow didn't even register with me. Until he lifted us from the dip and released my mouth and the entire team who had been watching from the bus began to applaud.

I wanted to kill him then, even though he had warned me. Before he loosened his grip, he surprised me by slipping something over my head. It was his jersey. He wasn't kidding about wanting to brand me.

"Take good care of her." He nodded to Michael as he opened my car door.

The first few minutes of the ride were uncomfortably quiet. Eventually, Michael spoke. "So. I guess I know why you didn't want to go out with me."

"Sorry. I probably should have told you. But when you first asked, we weren't dating yet, and I really was busy like I said. And then the next time, we still weren't dating when I said yes, but by the time we—"

"It's okay. You don't have to explain." He glanced at me, then back to the road. "I'm not gonna lie and say I'm not disappointed. But I won't make things uncomfortable."

My shoulders relaxed a little. "Thank you."

The three-hour drive was actually really relaxing. The warm Florida sun beat down on my head while the wind from the open top kept me nice and cool. Between starting my new position a few months ago, meeting Brody, and then worrying about the reappearance of his long-lost ex, I had been really stressed lately. "I've never been in a convertible. I love it. Did you rent this car?"

"No. I actually have a home down here. In Miami. I keep a car at the house."

"I didn't realize that. Is it far from the hotel?"

"Twenty minutes with traffic."

"Oh. I can take a cab from there, so you don't have to go out of your way."

"I don't mind. But you're welcome to stay at my place instead of the hotel."

My eyes flashed to him.

"Relax. I have a guesthouse. You're welcome to stay there. We don't even have to be in the same building."

"Thank you for the offer. But I'll just stay at the hotel."

Michael shrugged like it wasn't a big deal. He was so easygoing. Staying in his guesthouse probably shouldn't have been an issue. Yet somehow it felt wrong. The hotel was definitely a better idea.

Traffic slowed to a crawl once we hit the Miami strip, and my phone buzzed in my bag. I dug it out and read the text from Brody.

Brody: Sitting on plane. Delayed. What are you doing?

I decided to screw with him a bit.

Delilah: Having margaritas poolside and working on my tan. Good thing I tossed a bathing suit in my bag.

Brody: With Langley?

Delilah: Who else would I be with?

Brody: You're fucking with me, right?

Delilah: Guess you'll find out when you see my tan marks.

Brody: Your ass is going to have my hand marks when I see you.

Delilah: Hmm . . . I might like that.

Brody: Are you fucking with me?

Delilah: About the drinks and pool? Yes. The handmarks . . .

Brody: I'm getting wood on the plane next to a 325-pound linebacker.

Delilah: LOL

Brody: Just announced we're finally cleared for takeoff. Gotta power off. Wish you were coming home with me. Even after three days with you, I miss you as soon as I leave.

My heart swelled a little in my chest. The man quite literally charmed the pants off me, without even trying. I was crazy about him and finally learning to sit back, relax, and enjoy it.

Delilah: Me too.

e ——————————————— *e*

It was after midnight when my phone buzzed again. I had just fallen asleep. Brody's name flashed at me on the screen. I answered, smiling, grogginess in my voice. "Hey."

"I woke you?"

"It's okay. I must have just fallen asleep."

"I shouldn't have called so late. Sorry. I'll call you in the morning."

The tone of his voice made me sit up. I reached over and turned on the light. "What's the matter?"

"I picked up my messages when we landed. Broadhollow Manor called. They took Marlene in an ambulance to the hospital."

"What happened?"

"They're not sure. She was a little out of it during the day. Then she took a nap, which isn't like her, and never woke back up. Her vitals started slipping, so they called an ambulance."

"Oh God. I'm sorry. Are you heading there now?"

"Yeah. They took her to St. Luke's. I'm in a cab on my way."

Brody barked orders at the cabby for the next five minutes, telling him not to take certain streets. The stress level in his voice rose as he got closer. "I'm gonna jump out and walk the last few blocks. Traffic is at a standstill on Eighth Avenue. At fucking midnight." He pulled the phone away from his mouth and spoke to the driver. "Pull over, let me out here." I heard the car door shut and muffled words as he exited the cab.

"I'll get a flight first thing in the morning."

"You have interviews to do. Your dipshit boss is already up your ass because of me. Stay. I don't even know what's going on yet."

"But..."

"Get some sleep. I'll text you when I know more."

"Please do."

"Yeah. All right. I'm gonna run. The hospital is only another block away, and I probably should call Willow and let her know what's going on."

I stayed up for a few hours hoping to hear from Brody again, but he still hadn't texted before I fell asleep. I hated that I was so far away. I wanted to be there for him. Just sit by his side if he was going to hear bad news, to bring him comfort. And maybe, just maybe, there was a selfish part of me that wanted to make sure no one else was sitting in my seat offering him that comfort.

CHAPTER 28

The emergency rooms you see on television are a crock of shit. Doctors and nurses running down the hall with gurneys, one kneeling and performing CPR on a patient as others maneuver toward some big double doors that open on their own—*yeah, right.*

I looked around the depressing gray room, almost every seat taken as people waited. And waited. Three women dressed in blue uniforms sat behind thick plated-glass windows, chatting away and drinking coffee. Two security guards stood at the entrance door. It felt more like a prison waiting room than a hospital.

Two hours had passed with no updates. I walked to the reception window and waited, twisting my necklace nervously. The women continued to ignore me until one eventually looked up at me, annoyed.

"Can I help you?"

"My grandmother was brought in a few hours ago."

"Did we call her name?"

"No."

"We'll call her name when the doctor is done examining her and give you a status update."

The woman's eyes stared above me, a non-verbal *Next*.

I went back to my seat and finished picking the nail polish off my nails, then went to the ladies' room. I had been holding it in, not wanting to miss being called, but Mother Nature had grown impatient.

When I came back, Brody was at the reception counter speaking to the nurse. I wasn't surprised he'd shown up. The nursing home had told me they'd left him a message. Yet seeing him standing there still stopped me in my tracks for a second. Even though he'd made it clear he wanted nothing to do with me, I walked to the window and joined him. He nodded at me in acknowledgment and continued his conversation with the same miserable nurse who had just turned me away. Except now, Miss Miserable was *smiling*. And she apparently *could* get up from her chair.

"Let me go back and check for you. The system still shows her in triage, but it's been a few hours. I'm sure they can give me an update. Just give me a minute."

Brody turned to me while we waited. "You just get here?"

"No. I was in the ladies' room. I came in the ambulance with her about two hours ago."

He nodded. "I just tried to call you. What did they find out so far?"

"I have no idea. They took her in and haven't given me an update yet."

The nurse came back to the glass a few minutes later. She pointed to the right. "I'll buzz you in. Why don't you come back?"

I followed Brody, even though I hadn't been invited. The nurse led us to an empty examining room and told us to take a seat. A few minutes later, a doctor came in. He peeled off one glove and extended his hand to Brody first. "I'm Dr. Simon. You're Ms. Garner's grandson?"

"I'm her legal guardian. Willow is her granddaughter." The doctor shook my hand. Until that moment, I had no idea Brody was her legal guardian.

"Why don't we take a seat?"

I didn't like the sound of things so far. We both sat, my hands wringing as the doctor spoke.

"Mrs. Garner has suffered a stroke. There are many different causes of strokes. We believe hers was a brain hemorrhage produced by an artery in the brain bursting."

"Oh my God." My hands flew to my mouth.

"Is she okay? Can it be treated? Fixed?" Brody asked.

"She's having a CAT scan done now. That will tell us the location of the bleeding and the level of swelling. We'll know more after we pinpoint the extent of the damage and the size of the hematoma I suspect has formed. Right now, we're still working on stabilizing her blood pressure and breathing. We had to put her on a ventilator to help her breathe, and we're treating her with medicine in her IV to try to regulate her pressure."

"Then what? You perform surgery?"

The doctor looked at Brody, then at me, then back to Brody. "Mrs. Garner is very weak right now. I'm not ruling out anything. We will do everything we can to treat her. But right now, in the condition she's in, she wouldn't withstand cranial surgery."

If the gravity of the doctor's words hadn't told me how serious it was, I knew things were dire from Brody's actions. He reached over and covered my hands with his.

"She should be back from the CAT scan in a few minutes if you'd like to see her. Results should come back pretty quickly after that."

"We'd like to see her. Thank you."

The doctor stood. "I'm sorry I don't have better news. Why don't you stay in here, and I'll have a nurse grab you when she's back?"

The tiny room felt smaller with one less body. Brody ran his hands through his hair. "You okay?"

"I think so." My delivery was less than convincing. It was hard to sound believable when you didn't even believe your own words.

Two fingers slipped under my chin and tilted my head up. "Let's not think the worst. We're going to think positive. That's what Marlene would be doing."

I stared out the hospital window, watching the sun slowly rise on the horizon. So simple. So magnificent. Yet I'd spent years not even noticing it or paying any attention. Even in my darkest hours, I'd counted on the sun rising the next morning. Not unlike the two people sleeping in the room.

After a few minutes, I peeled my eyes away from the beauty outside and looked over at the rest of my world. The only things I'd ever known for sure in my life were that the sun would shine again and that these two would be there for me. Now nothing was certain except for that sunrise.

Grams was sleeping, a dozen tubes connected to her, the sound of the ventilator sucking the air out of her lungs and hissing new life in joined by the rhythmic beeping of her monitor. She'd made it through the night, which was more than the doctor initially thought would happen. Now it was a matter of time until they could repeat the CAT scan and see if the bleeding had stopped.

My watery eyes fell on the man sleeping next to my grandmother. Brody had finally dozed off an hour or so ago, sitting up in a padded chair. I told him he could go, head home and get some rest for at least a few hours, and I would stay. But he never even considered it. Grams had always been like family to him. After his mom died of cancer when he was only seven, Grams had filled the matriarchal void in his life. She was always there for him. And he, in turn, had been the only reliable person in her life after Pop Pop had died.

Women had always loved Brody. With his undeniable good looks, physique of the professional athlete that he is and stature as one of America's most admired quarterbacks, there wasn't much not to like. Add a heaping dose of confidence and the ability to make a woman feel like she was the only person in the room, and it was no wonder women literally chased after him. But the thing that makes him a man who was impossible to get over is exactly who he was right now. The most devoted person I've ever known. When the man loves, he loves hard, nothing stood in his way.

God, I would have given anything to have my old life back again. To turn back time so I could appreciate everything I had, rather than throw it all away. *I* deserved to be the one sitting in that bed, not Grams.

I spent the next hour mindlessly fiddling with my necklace, watching the two people I cared about most in the world, and falling in love with them all over again. When Brody's eyes fluttered open and found me sitting across the room, our gazes locked for a long moment. I saw the moment he gave in. He might hate me down deep, but he was letting go of his anger. For now at least.

"How is she?" he asked.

"The same."

"How long was I sleeping for?"

"Two hours, maybe."

"You sleep at all?"

"Not yet."

He stretched out in the chair, arms reaching up and neck going from side to side. "Why don't you go home? Get some sleep. I'll call you if anything changes."

"I want to stay."

It looked like he was going to say something but then changed his mind. Instead, he just nodded.

"Still drink sugar with some coffee in it?" He stood.

"I do. Still drink it black and disgusting?"

He chuckled. "I'll go find us some."

Things between Brody and I relaxed a lot more after that. We weren't best friends again, but I also didn't feel like he was shooting an imaginary bow and arrow, with my forehead as the target.

"How long has she been in Broadhollow Manor?"

"A little over three years."

I nodded. I had no idea how long it had been since I'd seen the two of them. Years of my life had been wasted and gone. The screwed-up thing was, now that I was sober, it felt like the world had stood still for me. I'd aged, but life had never progressed. It was as if I were picking up after pushing pause on my life for a long time. The thing was, my life had been the only thing paused. The world had gone on around me.

Brody and I made small talk while we kept vigil. It was better than the silent treatment, although there were so many meaningful things I needed to say that I still didn't have the courage to speak. When the nurse came in a few hours later and asked us to step out for a little while so she could wash Grams and take her vitals, Brody and I headed to the cafeteria to grab a bite to eat. We wandered into a gift shop first.

"You need anything?" He had a baseball cap in his hand.

"A toothbrush would be nice."

The woman at the counter recognized Brody when she rung us up. Walking out of the store, he pulled on the cap, bringing the bill low on his face.

"Disguise?"

"Sort of."

"Is it everything you thought it would be?"

"What?"

"Being famous." When we were teenagers, we used to spend hours dreaming of what being a famous football player would be like.

He glanced at me. "Nothing turned out the way I thought it would."

We ordered two egg sandwiches from the cafeteria and sat down to eat. Brody finished his in what seemed like three bites. I ate only half of mine.

"You're not going to eat that?"

I smiled. Brody always had a ridiculous appetite. Wherever we went, both of our plates were wiped clean, but it was usually because Brody devoured everything on his plate, then attacked mine.

"Nope. Help yourself."

He finished off my breakfast and guzzled his small black coffee.

"Do you remember when we went to that Oktoberfest during senior year, and you ate that guy's full plate of food because you thought it was mine?"

"Yeah. I almost got my ass kicked by Paul Bunyan in lederhosen. That was the biggest person I've ever seen wearing overalls in my life." We both laughed at the memory. We had snuck into a German festival, but only had twenty bucks between the two of us and were starving and unwilling to forego beer. So we each ordered an appetizer and the biggest mug of beer we could afford. Brody was off talking to some guys from the football team, and when he came back, I told him he could finish my appetizer while I headed to the bathroom. He proceeded to eat the entire fifteen-dollar meal that was on the table. Only it was on the table next to where my leftover appetizer had been. We had one large, pissed-off German guy to contend with when he realized that his meal was gone.

When we got back to Grams' room, the nurse was done, and a doctor came in a few minutes later. He told us that although her stats had stabilized from the medication, she wasn't trying to breathe on her own, and that wasn't a good sign. They would repeat the CAT scan in the early afternoon to determine the extent of the damage. Each doctor who stopped in felt compelled to warn us that things were not looking good. It was as if they were trying to prepare us for what the afternoon test would bring.

Brody and I were both quiet for a while after the doctors left.

"She has a health care proxy. I found the papers when I was cleaning out her things in the apartment. She and your grandfather had them drawn up years ago. I never tried to have a new one made, because my lawyer said her mental capacity would be an issue if we drew up any legal documents. So even though I'm her legal guardian now, her health care proxy was made when she was able to make her own decisions. And those decisions were her wishes."

"What does that mean?"

"It means her medical decisions get made by the person who she wanted to make those decisions, not me."

"And who is that?" The answer was obvious, but I hoped I was wrong.

"You."

Delilah
CHAPTER 29

I'd tried to reach Brody three times since the morning, but each call had gone straight to voicemail. I finally ended up sending him a text before Michael and I taped the spot with Payton Mara. When we were done, the text still didn't show as delivered. I was growing concerned for so many different reasons.

"Everything okay?" Michael asked on the way back to the airport.

"Sorry, yes," I lied. Well, sort of. "I just don't like to fly. I get nervous for hours before." It was the truth, but it wasn't what had me preoccupied today.

"I think our seats are next to each other. My hand is available for holding. And squeezing if you need."

I forced a smile. "Thank you. But usually I need more of a drool wiper than a hand-holder."

He glanced sidelong at me before his eyes returned to the road, so I explained, "I take a Xanax, it knocks me out pretty good. But it's either that, or my heart might crack a few ribs pounding so hard to get out of my chest."

"Ah. Drool wiping it is, then. Even though I was looking forward to an excuse to hold your hand." This trip had proven that Michael was the nice guy that I initially thought he was, not the bad guy Brody had warned me about. Although I was glad I hadn't gone out with him. Until Brody, I'd avoided anyone who might make my heart race. Letting anyone in other than Drew had felt like I was cheating. But somehow, Brody had wormed his way into my heart without my even seeing it happen.

Michael and I had just cleared security when my phone buzzed in my jacket pocket. Brody's name flashed on the screen.

"Hey. I've been trying to reach you all day. Is everything okay?"

"Sorry. I was in the hospital, and my phone was off. I just turned it back on." He sounded exhausted.

"It's fine. I was just getting worried. How's Marlene?"

"Not good. They're doing a repeat CAT scan now, so I'm heading to my place for a quick shower and change of clothes. She had a stroke."

"Oh God. I'm sorry."

"Thanks. They're keeping her alive with machines right now. But they're not giving us much hope that the second scan is going to come back better than the first scan. She has bleeding in the brain, and she's not strong enough to survive surgery."

"I don't know what to say. What can I do?"

"There's nothing anyone can do. The doctors are doing everything they can, and they're still not sure it will be enough."

"I'm at the airport in Miami. My flight should land about seven. Will you be there all night?"

"Yeah. I'm probably gonna stay again tonight. I have practice early tomorrow, and I already missed practice today. Not sure how things are gonna go, but I want to stay as long as I can. Coach will fine me, but he'll understand when I explain things in person."

"I'm available to bring up dinner or come sit with her so you can take a little break."

"Thank you. But I'm good for now, babe."

"I wish I would have had the chance to meet her before now. The way you talk about her, I know how much she means to you."

"Yeah. She's pretty great. More like family to me than most of my real family. They say blood is thicker than water, but that doesn't mean shit. Everyone needs water to live."

"That's a beautiful thought. You should tell her that, Brody. Even if her eyes aren't open. Maybe she can hear you."

"You know what? You're right. There's a lot of shit I probably should have said to her before now."

"I'm sure she knows how you feel, but getting the words out might help both of you."

"Thanks, babe."

"I hope it turns out okay."

"Me too."

Normally, I would take half a pill before getting on a short flight. Instead, I took a full one. Aside from my regular preflight jitters, I was anxious to get back home, wanting to be there to support Brody if he needed me. Unfortunately, I'd soon find out, that I wasn't the only one ready to console him.

Willow

CHAPTER 30

Lust. There's a reason that it's just a scramble of the letters that spell slut.

I was literally sitting on my beloved grandmother's deathbed, and yet my heartbeat accelerated the minute Brody walked back into the room. Dressed in a pair of jeans and a fitted thermal, he turned the identity-shielding bill of his cap backward, and I had to force my gaping mouth closed. With his backward baseball cap and hair sticking out all over, he looked just like the jock I fell for.

"Anything?"

I shook my head. "They only brought her back a few minutes ago. There was a backup in CAT scan. The nurse said results would be backed up, too."

He dug something from his pocket and extended his hand palm up, holding a swipe card of some kind. "Your turn."

My forehead creased.

"My place is only four blocks away. You said you live all the way uptown. I picked up a T-shirt and those yoga pants you women wear in the hotel gift shop and left them in the bathroom for you, in case you want to change."

"The hotel gift shop?"

"I live at the Regency Hotel."

"You do?"

"Yeah. During the season. I stay in the cabin the rest of the year."

"The cabin? You still have the cabin? Is it finished?"

He smiled. "I'm still working on it. But it's getting there."

The cabin upstate was the first major purchase Brody had made when he turned pro. The land was beautiful, but the place was a disaster. He'd wanted to rebuild it all himself. I'd only visited it once, but the memories had stayed with me. It was one of the last good weeks I'd had before I spiraled out of control this last time. We'd christened every room the week we were up there. One memory, in particular, replayed in my mind often. We had just made love in front of the fireplace that looked out at the lake, and we talked about spending the offseason there together, fixing the place up. He had told me he was going to build another fireplace in the bedroom because he loved the way my eyes looked in the fire's glow. Brody and I had a lot of memories, but that one, that time in front of the fireplace, I remember feeling utterly and completely loved.

"Go." He snapped me back to the present. "We're probably going to be here again tonight. Penthouse two."

"You sure you don't mind?"

"I wouldn't offer if I did. Go. I got it here for a while. Besides. Can't have you smelling up the place, can we? That's my job."

I'd never been in a penthouse before. But it basically looked like what I expected it to look like. Large, open, clean and fancy. What it didn't look like was Brody's home. Some binders with the Steel's logo rested on the end table in the living room. The dining room table held some mail and a folded jersey. But little else screamed that someone lived there for four months of the year.

I wandered into the master bedroom. The spacious walk-in closet was filled with clothes and shoes. One whole side was practice jerseys, football pants, sweatshirts and Under Armor. There had to be at least twenty pairs of sneakers and cleats lined up on that side of the closet. I opened a few of the built-in drawers—everything was folded neat and tidy. Brody had always been more of a *shove it in a drawer and make it fit* kind of guy. Someone else was definitely putting away his laundry. The absence of any women's clothing in the closet made me think that someone was a maid, rather than his girlfriend.

Behind a dividing wall was a large master bath with a double sink and an enormous tiled shower. No fancy shampoos and conditioners, no perfumes or makeup. No sign of a woman spending frequent nights here. Although there were enough water jets and space in that shower to have a small party. It made me wonder if Brody *entertained* often.

As I headed out of the master suite, I couldn't help myself. I was already overstepping boundaries by snooping, might as well jump in with both feet. I slid open the bedside table. Inside was a set of Beats headphones, an iPod, some business cards and a stack of folded papers. I moved some of the papers to the side, revealing a half-empty box of condoms and an almost empty bottle of lube. Well, that answered that question. I guess he did *entertain* often.

There was another, smaller bathroom in the hallway. That one had the clothes Brody mentioned purchasing from the gift shop. Feeling even dirtier than I'd felt when I first came in, I took a quick shower and mentally scolded myself for violating Brody's trust when he had been so kind to me. Again.

It was a full hour after I returned to the hospital when the doctor finally walked in. His face broke my heart before he even spoke. Brody had been sitting on the other side of Grams' bed and stood, so I did the same. I suddenly felt lightheaded, but I couldn't move to sit back down. My hand reached for my necklace. I had a nervous habit of playing with it whenever I was scared. Only, it was missing. So I wrapped my hand around my throat and waited.

"The results from the repeat scan are back." The doctor paused and took a deep breath. "And I wish I had better news." He looked at

Brody and then at me. "Your grandmother suffered a massive stroke that affected the blood flow through the main middle cerebral artery. The blood was basically pooling in one area, causing the other side of her brain to be completely deprived of blood."

"Was? Does that mean it's stopped?" I clung to the only potentially positive word that he spoke.

"It's slowed. But the damage is extensive. The areas that were deprived of blood are swelling. The brain is encased by the walls of the bony skull, and the swelling is causing severe intracranial pressure. This pressure prevents blood from flowing, causing more damage, which in turn causes more swelling. It's a vicious cycle."

"What can be done?" Brody asked.

"Well, the most effective way to treat massive brain swelling is a surgical procedure called a hemicraniectomy. We would remove a portion of the skull to allow the swelling to expand beyond the confines of the skull. But in your grandmother's case, it's highly unlikely that she would survive the procedure. As you know, we intubated to help her breathe when she came in. Unfortunately, her body isn't even trying to breathe on her own. And the reactiveness of her pupils has slowed. We'll continue to monitor her brain functions closely, but you need to prepare yourself for the worst. I'm sorry."

I think we were both numb. So many questions ran through my mind, yet when the doctor asked if I had any, I just stared at him like I didn't speak the language. Eventually, he turned to Brody. The two of them talked quietly for a few minutes. I heard the sound of different voices, but the words didn't register. It was a feeling I was all too familiar with, the consummate fog of a drug-induced haze. A craving that had finally begun to subside in the last few months came barreling back with a vengeance. My hands gripped the arms of the chair, so it didn't knock me over.

The doctor closed the door as he left, giving us privacy. "You okay?" Brody walked to me and kneeled down next to where I was sitting.

"No."

He covered one of my hands with his. "It's a lot to take in. I know."

A laugh came out, as bitter as it tasted. "You know what I'm sitting here thinking? After everything the doctor just said?" I looked Brody in the eye, and he held my stare until I continued. "That I want to get the hell out of here so I can go get high. My grandmother, who took me in and never gave up hope on me, is dying. And what do I want to do? Run away. As usual."

Brody looked down for a long time. I figured he was trying to swallow the hatred he had for me. But when he spoke, he surprised me. "It's normal. You're scared, so you want to run."

I scoffed, hating myself. "I must be scared a lot."

"You know what, Willow? I think you are scared a lot. I'm no shrink, but people have two choices when they're scared. To run or to fight. You lived a rough life before Marlene. Running was a survival instinct for you."

I stared at my lifeless grandmother. "I don't want to run now. It's the least I can do."

"So don't."

"You say that like it's easy."

"It's not. Nothing about this is easy."

I covered his hand with my other one and looked up at him. "Thank you."

"You're welcome. We'll get through this. Just fight with me."

Brody had missed practice yesterday, so he had no choice but to go today. He was gone about five hours. The look on his face when he walked back into Marlene's room was one of total relief.

"How is she?" he said.

"About the same."

He nodded. "And you?"

"I'm fighting."

Brody smiled and took off his jacket. "Glad to hear it."

"How was practice?"

"Got knocked on my ass plenty."

"Hard to focus?"

He ran his hand through his hair. "Yeah. My head wasn't in it today."

"I was thinking while you were gone. We should put her game shows on tomorrow. Maybe even play the way we used to play with her. Maybe she can hear us, and that would make her happy."

"That's a good idea. She'd like that. And I should call over to Broadhollow Manor, let them know what's going on. Grouper would probably want to stop by and visit."

"He seems like a nice guy."

"He is. Just don't let him know I said that."

I laughed. "Funny. He said the exact same thing about you."

Brody smiled. "I knew the old bastard loved me."

Hours later, the doctor came back in. He told us to go get some sleep and come back in the morning. Tomorrow they would rerun the scan, and then we would likely have some big decisions to make. I couldn't even think about tomorrow yet. Around midnight, we decided to go home for a few hours.

"Come on. I'll give you a ride. My car is in the lot across the street since I came straight from practice."

I wasn't even going to pretend to put up an argument. The last two days had caught up with me, and lifting my arm to open a door felt like an effort.

Brody's car was a Range Rover with an interior of supple leather and wood. "This is much better than the Bronco," I teased, referring to the 1981 red-and-white-striped jalopy he driven throughout high school and college.

He smiled "Just a little."

"Although that Bronco held a lot of good memories." I glanced into the backseat of his fancy new car, thinking of the endless hours we had spent fooling around in the wide back seat. Brody caught my glance, and our eyes met for a brief second. Neither of us said another word the rest of the way uptown, except when I needed to give directions.

Pulling up to my apartment, I was a little embarrassed. The building was in a bad neighborhood—proof of that was hanging out right at the front door. Two guys who screamed "drug dealers" watched as we pulled to the curb and stopped.

"This is where you live?"

"Yeah. It's what I can afford. I'm hoping to move soon, though."

Brody started to say something, then stopped.

"Thank you for the ride. For everything."

"You're welcome."

I made it halfway to the door when Brody called after me. "Willow?"

He jogged to catch up to me. "Stay at the hotel I'm staying at. At least tonight. I'll get you a room."

"That's sweet of you. But I'm fine. Really, I am."

"I wasn't worried about you." He lied right through his teeth. "It would help me sleep better tonight. Knowing you weren't . . . " He looked around, his thoughts evident without having to voice them.

"I'll get my stuff."

Delilah
CHAPTER 31

I set my alarm for six, even though I hadn't really decided if I was going to go or not. After a quick shower, I grabbed my phone from the charger and scanned our texts from last night again.

Brody: Not good.

Delilah: I'm sorry. Anything I can do?

Brody: A naked picture might help . . .

Delilah: LOL. Glad to see you sound more like yourself now. This afternoon when we spoke, there wasn't one sexual innuendo. I was worried.

Brody: Me too.

Delilah: You staying at the hospital tonight?

I remembered typing that last text and then editing out one word. The initial text read: *You staying at the hospital tonight alone?* But immediately afterward I felt selfish and was glad I hadn't sent it. He was going through a horrible time, and my jealousy had no place.

Brody: No. Heading back to Regency soon. I'll be back for visiting hours in the morning at nine.

Delilah: OK. Hope you get some sleep.

Brody: Call me in the morning. I'll set an alarm for seven thirty so you can talk dirty to me before I shower.

My mind was busy debating whether I should or shouldn't as I dried my hair and got my clothes ready. Slipping on an expensive bra and panty set that I'd splurged on last week, I realized my head was bullshitting itself. Who was I kidding? I'd shaved my legs and donned new sexy underwear. I had already mentally decided I was surprising Brody with an in-person wake-up call, even before I admitted it to myself.

Luckily for me, the uniformed elevator operator remembered seeing me with Brody. So when I explained with a blush that I wanted to surprise my boyfriend, he slipped the key into the slot with a sly grin. It was a good thing, because I had completely forgotten access to the penthouse floor required a special key.

There was really no reason for me to be nervous, yet there I was, standing in front of Brody's suite, a bag of his favorite pumpkin spice muffins in one hand and coffees in a cardboard carrier in the other, and I was anxious about knocking unannounced.

I took a deep breath, raised my knuckles and rapped on the door marked *PH2*.

No response.

Pulling out my phone, I checked the time—seven thirty-three. Maybe he was sleeping still, or in the shower . . . or had decided to leave early.

I knocked one more time. The second time louder than the first.

I had just started to turn away when I heard the sound of feet walking toward the door.

Brody answered, wearing only tight black boxer briefs. He had a toothbrush in his mouth, and his hair was a sexy mess. His foaming mouth turned to a smile.

I held up the bag of muffins. "I brought you breakfast."

His eyes swept me from head to toe, making me feel deliciously violated. "You certainly did."

I was very glad I'd changed my outfit four times and decided on something a bit on the sexy side.

He stepped aside, holding his arm out for me to enter. "Ladies first."

I handed him the coffees as I passed. "Ladies first is just the Brody Easton way of saying, 'Let me check out your ass.'"

"You know it." He chuckled and disappeared into the bathroom, coming back after he had finished his teeth.

"I thought maybe you could use a happy wake-up call and something to eat."

Brody took the bag from my hand and tossed it over his shoulder before wrapping his arms around my waist and tugging me close. "That's perfect. I'm fucking starving."

"What are you doing?" He walked me backward until the backs of my knees hit the couch.

"I'm going to eat." He gave me a gentle but firm shove so I fell back, landing on the couch. Looking up at him, my eyes stared at his beautiful face, but I was quickly distracted. Trailing down his broad shoulders, across his muscular pecs and abs, my gaze landed on his glorious carved V. That indentation could seriously make me forget my name.

"You look hungry, too." He smirked, catching me ogling him.

"God, you wake up looking like that. Your body really is ridiculously incredible."

He rubbed his bulging erection through his tight underwear. Watching him touch himself made me clench my thighs together. "I'm glad you like it. But I want to see more of yours. Pull up that skirt."

I hesitated for a brief second. I'd only just walked in the door, and daylight was shining in through the living room windows. But I'd come here hoping to bring him some happiness in the midst of a couple of tough days. Plus . . . look at that V.

I reached down to the bottom of my skirt and gathered it, letting it bunch around my hips. I would look like a wrinkled mess at the office later, but I knew when Brody was done with me, I wasn't going to care in the slightest.

"These are in the way." He reached down, and with one quick tug tore off my brand new panties.

Before I could retort that I would have taken them off, he dropped to his knees and buried his face between my legs.

Oh God.

He devoured me. Licking and sucking, his hands gripping my hips to hold me in place when I started to wiggle around.

I need to move.

But the more I bucked, the harder he held me down and the more aggressive his tongue lashed out at me. It was frustrating—I needed to gyrate my hips to meet his rhythm. Realizing I wasn't going to get anywhere pinned by his strength, I dug my fingers into his hair, attempting to take some control back.

He chuckled when I pulled his hair to move his head slightly up, but took the hint and shifted his focus to my aching clit. Alternating between fluttering and sucking, he brought me to orgasm. I had been inside of his apartment less than ten minutes.

He carried me to his bed after that, and we had sex.

Good sex.

No. *Great sex.*

The kind where he searched my face as he glided in and out of my body with smooth strokes and then, when my eyes fluttered open, our gazes met and he smiled down at me. Breathless and beautiful.

Afterward, he pushed the hair off my face as we both lay on our sides facing each other. "Thank you for giving me that."

I grinned. "Thank *you* for giving me *that.*"

He laughed. "You know what I meant. For letting me get lost in you for a little while. And not complaining when I basically attacked you as you walked through the door."

Complain? Was he crazy? "I can think of worse ways to be greeted."

He kissed my lips gently. "Today is going to suck."

I propped my head up on my elbow to listen.

"They're warming us up to the idea of removing all the tubes and letting her go peacefully. I just know it."

"I'm so sorry. That's such a hard decision for you to make."

"I'm not the one who's going to need to make it."

"I thought you were her legal guardian."

"I am. But she signed a health care proxy years ago. Before she started to show any signs of dementia."

"Oh. Who makes her health care decisions then?"

"Willow."

That only made sense. "Has she been handling things okay?"

"She's upset. But holding her own right now. I'm not sure she would ever come back from this one if she disappeared on Marlene now."

I nodded. "How long has she been clean?"

"She says eleven months."

"Do you believe her?"

"I think so. She seems more like the Willow I knew than she has in a long time."

An uneasy feeling settled in. The Willow he knew was the Willow he fell in love with. If Drew wasn't gone and walked back into my life tomorrow, what would I do with a second chance?

We stayed in bed for a little while longer. I pushed whatever immature jealousy I had aside.

"Tell me about her."

"Marlene? She's tough as nails and soft at the same time. She did nice things for people, but never wanted anyone to know she did them."

"My father used to say altruism was spelled wrong, it was spelled a-n-o-n-y-m-o-u-s."

"That's how Marlene lived. When Willow was on one of her binges, she used to frequent this squatters' den in Bushwick. It was a real hellhole—no heat or running water—yet a handful of addicts actually called it home. One snowy January, Marlene insisted on coming with me to look for Willow. When we went inside, the place was freezing. Most of the people who were passed out had newspapers piled on top of them for warmth. We took Willow home, and a few days later I was back there to drag her ass out again. Only I went without telling Marlene the second time. When I walked inside, everyone had a coat on—they were all wearing Marlene's coats. She had went back the next day without telling me and gave away all her coats."

"Wow. She sounds like a beautiful person."

"She is. It killed her to go to those places, too. She had to watch her granddaughter follow in her daughter's footsteps. I'm glad she got to see Willow sober for a few weeks before this happened."

"I am, too."

We talked about Marlene until I was going to be late for work. "I need to wash up and get to the office."

"Take a shower with me."

"I'm already running late, and you wanted to get to the hospital when visiting hours started. Showering together is definitely not a good idea."

"You're probably right."

"I'm just going to throw my hair up and jump in the shower to wash off. I'll use the guest bathroom."

Brody pouted. "I like you with my scent all over you."

I took a quick shower and was just about to step out when something shiny near the drain caught my eye. At first, I thought it was a coin, but when I bent over to pick it up, I realized it was a necklace caught around the grate.

I untangled it, and when I lifted it, a pendant fell to the floor. A pendant in the shape of the letter W.

I was already dressed when Brody got out of the shower in the master bath. "You're done quickly." He snickered. "And that wasn't the first time today."

I was inwardly freaking out but somehow managed to deliver my words calmly. Holding out my palm, I offered the necklace. "This was in the shower. It almost washed down, but the clasp was caught on the drain cover."

He furrowed his brow and picked the necklace up, the W dangling between us. *Symbolic*. His eyes closed for a moment and then rose to look at me.

"It must be Willow's."

I held his stare but said nothing.

"She showered here yesterday. She must have dropped it."

"She was here?"

"Yes. But by herself. I came home and took a shower, then when I went back to the hospital, I gave her my key and told her to use my place to shower. She lives all the way uptown, and we wanted to be there when the doctors came around."

I nodded. Then I walked to my purse and fished out my phone, checking it quickly for no reason other than that I needed to focus on something else. Brody just stood there and watched me. When I put on my coat and remained quiet, he spoke again.

"Are you upset with me for doing that?"

"Should I be?"

He ran his fingers through his hair. "I really didn't think about it. It just seemed like the right thing to do. But now that we're standing here, I'm thinking maybe it wasn't."

"How would you feel if I let Michael Langley shower at my house?"

Brody's jaw clenched.

"And didn't mention it to you."

"Point taken."

"I have to get to work."

Brody reached out and stopped me from passing, pulling me in close for a hug. "I'm sorry," he whispered in my ear. "Forgive me. I should have thought about it more than I did. I don't want you mad at me."

I pulled my head back to look him in the eyes. "Nothing else happened? She was here alone, showering?"

"Nothing. I swear."

I thought about it for a minute. "Okay."

He blew out a long breath of air. "Thank God. I don't think I could handle you being mad at me today."

I forced a smile, remembering what the last few days had been like for him. With or without Willow in the picture, the man loved Marlene. It couldn't be easy. "I'm not mad. Text me from the hospital. Let me know what the doctors say this morning."

"Thanks, babe."

In truth, I wasn't lying. I really wasn't mad. Nervous, jealous, scared—maybe. Strangely, I was dating a former player who'd never tried to hide that relationships weren't his forte, yet I believed him when he said nothing else had happened. What worried me was that he was opening his heart to Willow again, more than his home.

Stepping out of the elevator, I bumped straight into a man who was waiting to enter, never even seeing him until my foot was on top of his. He fumbled before catching the coffee he was holding, but not before a splash of it hit his crisp white dress shirt. I apologized profusely and attempted to make it the rest of the way out of the lobby unscathed. I almost made it, too. Until my collision with the glass turnstile exit—my face actually smacked into the bright yellow *Out of Order* sign with the big arrow pointing to another door. *That* accident wasn't my fault—I was paying attention as I walked. The problem was that my attention was on the beautiful woman sitting in the lobby, staring at me—and not on the electric door that wasn't working.

Willow.

Brody

CHAPTER 32

Football players were supposed to be tough. Ten three-hundred-and-fifty-pound men piled on, kicking and scratching, elbowing and clawing, to get at the lone guy holding a scrap of leather. I'd been the guy on the bottom of the pile a hundred times. We got back up, brushed the dirt from our eyelashes, discreetly straightened a dislocated thumb, and jumped back into the action for another round.

But tough had its limits. Even a diamond, if you hit it at the exact right place, the spot where it was flawed and weak, would sometimes shatter. Marlene was my weak spot.

Willow cried while the doctor spoke. She didn't make it past *no functional brain activity*. Silent tears fell as he continued on about our choices, one worse than the other. But I held strong. Even thanked him before he left, saying he would come back later that afternoon to discuss our decision. When I closed the door behind him, there was just enough time to catch Willow before she fell.

She crumpled in my arms, her shoulders shaking, body trembling, sobs racking her body. The croak in her howl revealed her physical pain. I held tighter.

Hours later, she was better—patched back up as best as I could. Hell, she'd even laughed a few times in the last hour as we played *Wheel of Fortune*, one of us on either side of Marlene as we wrote down our guesses.

The last puzzle had most definitely been a mood changer.

Category: Thing.

_UCK _E IN THE A_ _ TONIGHT.

Really?

Only one of us had gotten LUCK BE IN THE AIR TONIGHT. And it definitely wasn't me.

After a good laugh, Willow went down to the cafeteria to grab us some lunch. An aide came in and changed Marlene's pillows and refreshed the pink plastic pitcher with new water. She straightened up a bit and nodded before she left.

Busying myself, I noticed she had left the bedside drawer open just a little, so I walked over to shut it. But for some reason, I opened it first. Inside was only one thing—Marlene's powder-blue denture case. They had taken her teeth out when they put the breathing tube down her throat. I stared at it—I had no idea why, it was certainly a random enough thing to set me off, but seeing that case made me lose it. I bawled like a bitch.

It had been years since I cried.

When I heard the door open behind me, I was still standing in front of the open drawer. I shut it, leaned down, kissed Marlene on the forehead and went to the bathroom without turning around for Willow to see my face.

This morning with Delilah felt like days ago. Between emotions running high and a day of marathon game shows, I hadn't texted her an update all day. I dug my phone out of my pocket and powered it on.

Brody: Still at the hospital. Leaving soon for practice. Coming back here tonight after. Doctors are going to turn off the ventilator at nine.

Delilah: That's good, right?

Brody: No.

Delilah: Oh God. I'm sorry. I thought you meant there was an improvement.

Brody: It's what she would have wanted.

Delilah: I'm glad you know that, and I hope that brings you some peace.

Brody: Breakfast tomorrow, maybe?

Our texts were flowing fast, but there was a long pause before her next response.

Delilah: I actually have a breakfast meeting I can't miss. Lunch, maybe?

Brody: OK.

Delilah: Call me whenever you need tonight. The time doesn't matter. I'll be thinking of you.

That night, Willow and I took turns saying goodbye to Marlene before the doctor came in. I don't remember saying goodbye to my mother—I was too young when she died. But I imagined it felt an awful lot like saying those last words to Marlene did.

I looked down at her frail body. "There are so many things you taught me over the years. To never give up. To love someone worth loving, flaws and all. Hell, I can say someone isn't all there in their head a thousand and one ways because of you. But you also taught me the one thing I need most right now: When life knocks you down, stop and look around for one thing that's good, because there is always something. Then cling to that good." I kissed her forehead one last time and covered her hand with mine. "Here's the good I'm holding on to today. I'm lucky to have known someone who was so hard to say goodbye to."

I couldn't possibly have hidden my tears from anyone that time.

Not long after we said our goodbyes, the doctor removed the breathing and feeding tubes and turned off all of the monitors. I didn't know what I'd expected, but she simply stopped breathing.

Marlene Elizabeth Garner died at 1:03 a.m.

Willow
CHAPTER 33

Life is filled with a series of tethers. Imaginary threads that connect us to people from the moment we're cut from our mother's cord. I'd spent the first twenty-five years of my life trying to cut those threads and fly high, out of reach. It wasn't until eleven months ago that I woke up one morning and realized those tethers weren't chains that were keeping me down. They were lifelines, and my threads were so frayed, there were virtually no lines left to my life. Last night—or maybe it was actually today, I wasn't even sure anymore since one day had blurred into the next—the strongest thread that had ever existed in my life was cut away.

Brody handled all of the plans. Tonight we would have a small service at my grandmother's church. Tomorrow we would drive to the cemetery and lay her to rest. And then . . . I didn't know what came after that. I only knew I didn't want to lose Brody again.

I dressed in a simple black dress. It was a summer dress and the air outside had the chill of late fall, but a sweater was going to have to make do since I didn't have money for shopping. Brody knocked on my door right on time. I had told him I would meet him downstairs, explained that parking was difficult to find. But the reality was, I hadn't wanted him to see where I was living.

"You didn't have to come up."

I hadn't put my heels on yet, so he was almost a foot taller than me. I saw him look over my head and scan my apartment. I knew what he was doing, and I certainly couldn't blame him.

I opened the door wide and stepped aside. "No drugs. I'm clean."

"I wasn't . . . "

I arched my eyebrow as if to say *yes you were,* and he confessed with a grin. "All right, maybe I was."

He came inside.

"Let me give you a tour." I twirled a circle with my arms extended. You could tour my entire studio apartment, except the bathroom, in one pivot. "Tour over. So how do you like it?"

"I like it. It's . . . warm."

"It's not really. You better keep your jacket on."

"It's yours, right?"

"You're really taking this *find one good thing* to heart, aren't you?" I teased.

"I am."

"Just give me one minute, I'm searching for my black heels." My apartment was small, but the ceilings were high. Typical for Manhattan. There was little surface space left, so they built up.

One wall in the living room had built-in storage that started at about seven feet. I hopped up on the small ratty love seat that served as my living room furniture and stood on the back, balancing as I opened different compartments.

"What are you doing? You're going to fall." Brody walked over and reached up to my waist, steadying me as I searched through the storage cupboards. He moved with me, making sure I didn't fall as I walked the length of the couch top, inspecting and closing different doors. When I reached the last one, I found the shoes shoved into the top corner and had to stand on my tippy toes to reach them.

"Got 'em," I waved the shoes in the air like I'd just won a prize.

Brody lowered me back to the ground as if he were lifting a carton of empty milk. When he took his hands away, I longed for them. *God, I miss his touch.*

Turning to face him, it was easy to slip back into a comfortable place. I wrapped my hand around his bicep and squeezed. "Thanks for the lift. Big muscles. Have you been working out?"

He chuckled. "Get your shoes on, wiseass."

That one unexpected moment, something so completely insignificant as Brody helping me reach my shoes and then joking around, made me feel more like my old self than I had in years.

"Bring an overnight bag. I want you to stay at the hotel again tonight, and tomorrow night, too."

"I'm fine here, Brody. I appreciate it, though."

"Can you just do it for me?"

The man had no idea what I would be willing to do for him. I nodded and threw the clothes I'd picked out for the service in an overnight bag.

On the way out, I heard voices coming from my neighbor's apartment. Lena and Abby's apartment. "Can you just give me a minute?"

I listened before knocking. Brody stood behind me.

The familiar sound of rusted locks clanked and then Abby opened the door. Her face lit up, and she ran to hug my legs, catching me by surprise. "Can we go to the park again?"

I smiled at the little ball of energy. "Not today. I'm going somewhere with my friend. This is Brody."

She looked at Brody, found zero that interested her, and returned her attention to me. "When you're done?"

"I'm actually going to be busy for a few days." I looked into her apartment. "Is your mom here?"

"No. Grandma brought me to get more clothes."

With that, Sophie appeared. "Didn't I tell you not to open the door?" she scolded

"It was only Willow."

Sophie put her hands on her hips. "And how did you know it was Willow? Did you ask who it was, Abby?"

Abby looked at me, then back to her grandmother. "No." She sulked. "I forgot again."

Her grandmother tried to hide a smile. "We'll work on it." She turned her attention to me. "Hi, Willow. Don't you look pretty."

"Thank you. I heard voices and wanted to see if everything was okay."

Her eyes pointed to her granddaughter. "Everything is good. Abby is probably going to stay with me for a while." I read between the lines. She was *probably* going to stay with her because she had no idea where the hell her daughter had disappeared to. The situation brought me back twenty years. Thankfully, Abby had Sophie like I'd had Marlene.

"Well, aren't you lucky, Abby? I used to spend a lot of time with my grandmother, too. Her house was one of my favorite places in the world to go when I was your age."

Sophie smiled. "We're going to have a great time, aren't we, Abby?"

Abby and I were lucky. I shuddered to think of what life was like for the girls who didn't have a Sophie or a Marlene. "We have to get going. But you have my number. If there is anything I can do to help—"

Abby interrupted, jumping up and down. "Like take me to the park."

I chuckled. "Yes. Like take Abby to the park. Just give me a call. I work nights, so I have time during the days."

Sophie thanked us for stopping by and then Brody and I headed to the car. "What was that all about?"

"Abby's mom was sober for a few months. She went off the wagon a few days ago. I found her partying with a dealer while Abby was home, so I took her to the park to get her out of there. When things got worse, I called her grandmother and brought her there."

Brody nodded. "I don't think this is a great place for you to be."

A group of thug-looking teenagers were circling his fancy car when we walked up. I looked at Brody. "I can't imagine what would make you say that."

He walked right up to the scary-looking teens. "What's up, guys?"

"Shit, man. You're Brody fucking Easton."

"I am." He extended his hand, and their demeanors went from street thug to sports-idolizing little boys immediately.

"You guys watching my car for me?"

"Those are some nice-looking rims you got there. We didn't know this sweet piece belonged to you."

Brody opened my car door and waited until I got in. I couldn't hear what he was saying, but he talked to the man-boys for another minute before shaking hands again and getting in.

"Making friends?"

"Making *you* friends. Told them to keep an eye on you."

"I'm capable of taking care of myself."

"You don't belong in this neighborhood."

"No. *You* don't belong in this neighborhood. I fit in perfectly fine. I think you're forgetting who I am."

He started the car and put it into gear. "You're right," he mumbled under his breath, "I need to remember that."

I expected perhaps a nurse or two to show up to the church. I was not prepared for hundreds of people who attended Marlene's service. Not a single person was there because of me. The large church was packed with friends and teammates of Brody's. I don't know why I was surprised; everyone loved the man. He introduced me to a few people, and the first chance I got, I excused myself to go sit in a pew. Right before the service was about to start, Brody walked to the front row to join me. His hand was meshed with his girlfriend's, and there was another woman with them.

Luckily, the priest began to speak, forcing any uncomfortable introductions to wait. The service was simple, and I thought I had gotten through it without falling apart. Until the priest asked if anyone would like to get up and say a few words, and Brody stood.

He talked about how his mother had died when he was seven, and his dad had never remarried. The one grandmother he had lived a country away, and he had no real experience with girls. That got a good chuckle from the audience. Then he told a story I had never heard.

"After my mom's burial, everyone came back to our house. I don't remember too much, but I remember people were sitting around talking and laughing. I didn't get how they could be smiling when my mother had just been buried. So I went outside to stew a bit, and my neighbor, Marlene, found me out front on the stoop. She sat down next to me and tried to get me to talk, but I wasn't much in the mood. After a while, she told me to follow her, and we went back to her house next door.

"She took me into the kitchen and started asking me to grab things for her. Vanilla, milk, flour. She'd point to the cabinet where they were, and I'd get them out. Eventually, we started to talk while she made cookies. When we were done, I remember sitting down at her kitchen table with a big glass of milk and a tower of oatmeal-raisin cookies in front of me. She explained that there were going to be days in life that would be very hard, and the best way to get through them was to find one good thing to focus on. My mom had just died, and it was pretty impossible to find good in anything, but Marlene was so nice to me, I didn't want to disappoint her. So, before I left to go back to my house, I thanked her and told her that the one good thing for me was her making me cookies that day.

"I've never told anyone this, and Marlene and I never discussed it, but for the next twenty odd years, I'd often discover a batch of oatmeal-raisin cookies left where I could find them. In fifth grade, when I flipped over my bicycle handlebars trying to do a wheelie and broke my arm, warm oatmeal raisin cookies kept me company that night. In eighth grade, when I threw an interception that lost the playoff game against our biggest rival, there was a Tupperware full of cookies on my doorstep. Senior year, when I didn't get into my first pick of colleges, cookies. Five years ago, when my dad retired to Arizona and we packed the last of his things in the moving truck, cookies in the front seat of my unlocked car after I hugged my dad goodbye.

"This morning, on my way here, I stopped off at the bakery around the corner from where I grew up. It was Marlene's favorite bakery. I bought a bag full of oatmeal-raisin cookies. For more than twenty years, she kept up making me those cookies, and every time it would bring me a smile. But this morning, as I ate one, it just wasn't the same. You know why? Because it was never the cookies. It was the lady who took the time to recognize I might not have anything to smile about, and made sure to give me a reason. *She* was my reason.

"Marlene is survived by her daughter, Amanda, and her granddaughter, Willow. She may not have been my blood, but she was there through all my sweat and tears—so she's my family, too. I know Marlene wouldn't want any of us to cry today. She'd want us all to find that one good thing and hang on to it until things get better. But to truly honor the life of Marlene Garner, the next time you see someone having a bad day, make them a batch of oatmeal-raisin cookies in her honor. It could mean more than you'll ever know."

I was overwhelmed with emotions when Brody was done. When he returned to his seat between Delilah and me, he saw me crying and leaned down to whisper, "Find that one good thing that this brings, Willow. It's what she'd want you to do."

My breaths stuttered as I looked up at him. I kept quiet, but all I could think was, *This brought me back to you.*

Delilah
CHAPTER 34

After the graveside service, I had to go back to my office, and Brody had to go to practice. Tomorrow morning, I was due to head up to Buffalo for the day for an interview, and I hadn't even started my research. This time of the year, right before playoffs began, the station spent a lot of time and money gathering interviews with prospective playoff teams. Depending on who actually made it in, a lot of them would be archived and never aired. Buffalo was a long shot for a last-minute wildcard slot in the playoffs.

My desk was a mess of papers when Indie interrupted. It was already almost eight, and I had more work to do before I called it a night, but her visit was a welcome distraction anyway. She plopped down on the visitor's chair in my office, a box in her hands.

"Come on in. I wasn't busy." I waved at the disaster that made me look busy. But the truth of the matter was, I couldn't really focus. The sadness in Brody's face, the way his voice broke as he spoke in church today, had deeply affected me. It was all I could think about.

"I made you something."

"You *made* me something?"

She looked around my office. "Is there an echo in here?"

"I'll probably regret it." I tossed my pen onto the desk and leaned back in my chair. "But let's see what you made."

Indie reached into the box. "This is you." She had constructed a stick figure of sorts. Binder clips had been snapped together in various ways to make two legs, two arms, and a body. The metal of two clips formed a neck and attached a stapler remover that acted as a head. The way the staple remover had its mouth open, with sharp prongs, made the figure look more like a roaring dinosaur with sharp teeth.

"I think you have too much time on your hands."

"I've had two hours a day to fill since you haven't been around to hang out with the last few days." She reached into her box again and pulled out another creation. "This is Brody." The carefully created clip art looked just like the one of me, only a full head taller.

"We look like we could be related." I arched an eyebrow.

She ignored me and took another creation out of the box. This one was easy to identify: it was a snake sculpted out of paperclips. The body coiled around, and again, a staple remover was attached as the head. At least the fangs and open mouth seemed a little more realistic on a snake. She placed it on my desk with the other two.

"Why do you have three staple removers?"

"I don't. I came into your office while you were in Mr. CUM's meeting and stole the one out of your top right drawer. I saw Fred Nagel was in the meeting, too, so I stopped by his office on my way back and swiped one from him. By the way, why does his office smell like ass?"

I laughed for the first time in days. "I didn't know it smelled."

"You mean you haven't sniffed the entire floor yet?"

"Shut up."

Indie rearranged her figure art on my desk, moving the snake between Brody and me. "The snake's name is Willow."

"Why am I not surprised?" After the service yesterday, Indie had talked my ear off. While I was focused on Brody, Indie had been watching Willow. She was certain from the way that Willow gazed at Brody that the woman was using Brody's sympathy to get close to him again. I didn't know what her intentions were, but I couldn't stop thinking about how Brody felt about her. Seeing them standing together at the church had made everything I knew about their history so much more real.

Does he still love her?

What if he wanted to give things a second chance, now that she was clean?

"You need to get in there and put an end to the walk down memory lane."

"They just lost someone they love. They have a lot of history. If I can't trust him to mourn with her, then I can't trust him at all, and it's not meant to be."

Indie threw her hands up in the air. "That's crap. We don't leave everything up to fate, we fight for the shit we want."

"What if he still loves her?"

"Then you'll get hurt. I'll buy you ice cream, and we'll both gain five pounds sitting on your couch watching Nicholas Sparks movies for a month."

I thought about it for a moment. "Will it be Ben and Jerry's Cherry Garcia?"

"With chocolate sauce on top."

I took a deep breath. "He asked me to meet them for dinner tonight. They're having dinner with some people who worked at the nursing home where Marlene lived."

"And you said no?"

"I told him I had a lot to do before I left in the morning."

"Like what?"

"Research."

"On?"

"The team."

"You know every statistic for every team in the damn NFL. Whatever you think you need to learn, you don't."

She was probably right. I glanced at the time on my phone. "Dinner is probably half over already."

"Go bring him dessert."

Willow CHAPTER 35

Laughing over dinner with a man more than twice his age was the first time I saw the old Brody I knew. The sixteen-year-old boy who was filled with cocky arrogance, yet unlike most boys his age, had everything to back up that arrogance. Even more so today.

I watched as Brody swallowed a bit of his meal, mesmerized by the squareness of his jawline. The angles had become even more prominent over the years, turning a boy with some softness in his features to a man with hard, chiseled lines. The start of a five o'clock shadow ran along his tanned jaw, bringing a darker shade to his skin that made his pale green eyes appear even more startling.

He caught me staring and furrowed his brows, then gave me a hint of a smile that made me feel like we were the only two in on a secret before he went back to talking to Grouper.

I was quiet while we finished our meal. As the seconds ticked by, I became acutely aware that we had only hours left. After tonight, there was really no reason for us to see each other. Marlene had been the only thing that bound us together at this point. And she was gone. The thought created a physical ache in my chest.

"You okay?" After we had said goodbye to Grouper and Shannon, Brody and I walked to the elevator bank together.

I nodded.

He pushed the seven button for me and thirty-three for him. When we reached my floor, I stepped out, and Brody held one arm up against the top of the sliding doors, stopping them from closing. "I have practice at nine. Coach has been good about my missing and being late the last week. But if I'm not back on time tomorrow, he's gonna have my ass. I'll meet you for breakfast at seven and drop you on my way?"

Uptown wasn't on his way at all, but I agreed anyway. I'd take whatever I could get.

My hotel room was quiet. I'd always hated the quiet—it left nothing to drown out my thoughts. More so now that I was sober. That was the most difficult part of sobriety—the inability to escape my own thoughts.

Over the last few years, I'd thought of Brody almost daily. But over the last few weeks, I'd found myself constantly wondering what things would've been like for us if I had never disappeared that last time. If my life hadn't spiraled out of control. Would we still be together? Be married? My thoughts were always filled with *what if.*

I showered and flicked on the TV for company, burying myself under the covers in an attempt to get lost in a show. The first channel I landed on, a couple was in the throes of a passionate kiss. Brody was an amazing kisser. So dominant and controlling, he didn't kiss gently. There was always a rawness to the way his mouth consumed mine. I reached up and ran my fingers over my lips, letting my eyes flutter closed in memory.

What if . . .

I flipped the channel. FX was replaying a series that had wrapped up last year, *Sons of Anarchy,* an inside look at motorcycle gangs. It was filled with guns and violence. *Perfect.*

I watched for a few minutes. Then suddenly the scene of a group of leather-vest-wearing bikers in a clubhouse was over, and I was staring at the tattooed back of a naked blond man. The camera panned down to the man's taut ass as he furiously pumped inside of a woman. She moaned. *Brody was so good with that incredible body.* God, it had been a long time since a man had made me moan.

What if . . .

I flipped the channel again.

ESPN was showing highlights from last weekend's football games. The Philadelphia quarterback sailed the ball into the end zone and into the hands of a wide receiver. He pumped his fist and celebrated the game win. *Brody and I used to celebrate game wins in his bedroom.* I literally shook the thought from my head and clicked the remote.

What if . . .

I needed to clear my head of Brody. Flipping back to the hotel's information channel, I gave up on television and clicked on music. The screen displayed choices like Top 40, Classic Rock, Hip Hop, and Country. I picked Classic Rock. Bad Company's "Feel Like Making Love" streamed through the television.

God, I really did . . .

I listened to Paul Rodgers sing about golden dreams of yesterday for as long as I could. When I couldn't take it anymore, I flipped to Country Music. Alan Jackson's "Remember When" blared about remembering your first time.

Brody was my first.

The universe was completely out to get me.

Or . . .

Maybe it was a sign.

What if . . .

There were dozens of songs on my playlist that reminded me of Brody. I always skipped over them but never deleted any.

What if . . .

After tomorrow, there would be nothing keeping us connected.

I didn't want to spend a lifetime hitting skip.

Always wondering . . .

What if . . .

It was time I deleted them all and moved on, or let the songs play.

My life was filled with so many regrets. In that moment, I knew if I didn't at least try, it would be the decision I regretted the most. I ripped the covers back, got out of bed and dressed, my mind jumping all over the place. The chances of Brody still having any feelings other than disdain and hatred for me were practically nonexistent. But . . .

What if . . .

I had forgotten to give Brody his elevator key card back the other day. He wouldn't even know I was coming up to his suite until he opened the door. Not giving myself enough time to think about all the reasons I shouldn't, I took the elevator to the penthouse. I had no idea what I was going to say or do. I only knew it was my last chance, and I didn't want to live wondering *what if.*

Brody answered on the first knock. He was still wearing the slacks from his suit, but his dress shirt and belt were unbuttoned. *God, he's magnificent.*

"Willow?" I still hadn't said a word. "Everything okay?"

I shook my head, and we stared at each other for a long moment. "Can I come in?"

For a second, I thought he might turn me away. He closed his eyes, but when he reopened them, he stepped aside for me to enter.

Delilah
CHAPTER 36

Indie would have laughed at me. I stood in line at the late-night grocery down the street from the Regency with an assortment of pastries from the bakery counter that was just about to close. When she'd told me to bring Brody dessert, cannolis had been the furthest thing from her mind.

I knew I was totally stalling. After Drew, I'd never thought I would feel like this about another man. When Brody's name flashed on my screen, it made me smile. Seeing him in person made my heart beat faster. Sometimes I read a simple text from him a dozen times.

The thing was, with Drew, it was different. I could make a list of a million things I loved about him. I thought that was what true love was. Logical. Practical. Love was a list of tangible things that said he was the right guy.

But with Brody, I couldn't find the words to describe what I felt about him. I could probably make a list of a million reasons I should have stayed away. Yet I knew in my heart he was the one. My soul had picked him, not my mind.

The checkout line was flanked by racks of seasonal impulse buy items. Pink school erasers with turkeys stamped on them, small painted pumpkins, packs of NFL trading cards. I brought the eraser to my nose, the smell reminding me of elementary school. I tossed a few in my basket, along with a handful of trading card packages. By the time the cashier got to me, my stall had cost me thirty-three dollars.

The empty elevator made up for lost time. It sped up to Brody's floor so fast, my head felt a little lightheaded when I stepped off. A mixture of excitement and nervousness hit me as I raised my hand to the door.

My knock was light but echoed through the quiet hallway.

I waited. My heartbeat accelerated as the seconds passed.

Maybe he was sleeping already?

I knocked again. The second time louder.

Footsteps vibrated on the floor as they neared.

When the door swung open, I lifted the cannolis, dangling the bakery box by its red-and-white string. "Thought you might like some dessert?"

Brody was still dressed in the clothes he'd worn to the service. Well, actually, it looked as if he had just been interrupted from undressing. His white dress shirt was unbuttoned, the belt on his fitted slacks was hanging loose, and his feet were already bare. My first thought when I saw him was, *What a waste it was to buy cannolis when there are better things to eat.*

I smiled. But something in his eyes made my heart sink before he uttered a word.

He turned, glancing back into his hotel suite. When he faced me, his expression said everything. "I wasn't expecting you."

"Should I leave?"

"No. It's just . . . Willow came up a few minutes ago and—"

"Willow is in your hotel room with you?"

He dragged his hand through his hair. "It's not what it looks like. I swear."

"Then tell me. What is it?" I peered into Brody's suite and saw Willow standing in the living room. Her feet were bare, and she was watching us from a distance.

"She needed a friend. It's been a rough few days."

"And you were going to console her while you were half-dressed. . . in your hotel room?"

"That's not what I was going to do."

"Tell me then." I raised my voice. "What the fuck were you going to do?"

"Nothing. I just couldn't . . . I couldn't turn her away."

"Why not?"

Brody held my stare. "Because I couldn't."

I dropped the cannoli box and turned back to the elevator. The damn car had already disappeared. I pushed the button twenty times, desperate to get the hell out of there.

The door to Brody's suite slammed closed, and for a second, I thought he had gone back inside. But then he was behind me. He put his hand on my hip. "Don't go. Please. Nothing happened. I swear."

Thankfully, the elevator car came quickly. I stepped inside and turned to Brody. "I actually believe you. I don't think anything physical happened between the two of you. That's not why I need to go."

"Then why?"

"You need to figure that out on your own." We stared at each other as the doors slid closed.

I held the tears at bay until I hit the street. Then everything flooded all at once. The sadness. The disappointment. The heartbreak. I gasped for air, leaning against the outside of the hotel, bent over and holding my knees.

Brody must have taken the next elevator down because I saw him running out the door just as I climbed into a cab and sped away.

e ———————————————— *e*

The cab pulled to the curb outside of my apartment building, and then I decided I didn't want to go home.

"I changed my mind. Can you take me down to Chelsea—One Fifty-Five West Twenty-Second Street?"

"You're paying the fare from where I picked you up."

"Of course." I could have cared less if the fare was five hundred bucks; I just knew I didn't want to go home. It was almost ten, but Indie wouldn't care. Staring out the window at the street as we headed back into traffic, I didn't cry. It was as if my insides were hollowed out and even though I wanted to cry, wanted to get it out of my system, the tears couldn't fight their way through the vast emptiness to escape.

I walked into Indie's building in a fog. In the elevator, I stared at the button panel, unable to figure out what I was supposed to do. Luckily, an older gentleman walked in with a small dog on a leash and took charge.

"What floor?"

"Ummm. Seven." After I had said it, I wasn't even sure it was the right answer.

The hallway smelled like marijuana, confirming I had gotten off on the right floor. Indie's neighbor, Devin, was a pothead.

I knocked lightly, and she opened the door without asking who it was. A smile lit her face when she saw me standing there, but it quickly fell. "Oh, honey." She had no idea what had happened, yet she pulled me into her apartment by wrapping me in a hug. Tears threatened, but they still didn't come.

"Come on." She led me into the kitchen and flicked on the light. "Sit." She pointed to a chair, and I complied. Honestly, I'm glad it was Indie I turned to, because I was so lost, I would have taken orders from a complete stranger.

She opened the cabinets, pulled out bowls and proceeded to scoop two heaping servings of Ben and Jerry's. Placing one in front of me, she slid me a spoon and then sat across from me. "What happened?"

"Can we talk about something else? I don't know. The weather? Work? Global warming? Anything else."

She nodded and shoved a spoonful of ice cream into her mouth. "I'm thinking about sleeping with Devin."

"The pothead?"

"He fucks like a jackrabbit."

I almost cracked a smile. Almost. "How would you know that?"

"We share a bedroom wall."

"He takes ten minutes to spit out a sentence, he's always so damn mellow. How is that even possible?"

She shrugged. "You just interrupted a good session. You want to go listen?"

"Think I'll pass."

She was quiet for a few minutes. "You sure you don't want to talk about it?"

I stared into my half-empty bowl. "I really fell for him."

"I know you did."

"I put the framed picture of Drew inside my closet." Saying Drew's name felt like a tiny fissure in the wall I'd put up over the last hour.

"It was time, honey. Whatever happened with Brody, it was still time."

I nodded, my shoulders heavy. "That's the irony of it. I was finally taking steps forward, and he went backwards."

The first tear fell and then all hell broke loose. Once it started, I couldn't stop it. I sobbed like I hadn't in years. The cry felt so monumental—I wasn't just losing a boyfriend, I was losing Drew all over again, too. My heart had betrayed him for another man, and now I mourned for two losses.

Indie hugged me tight. "Let it all go, honey. Let it all go."

Delilah
CHAPTER 37

"Could you tell CUM that you need more work done on your laptop?" Indie craned her neck, following the handsome—and very young—IT guy as he walked from my office to the elevator bank.

I flipped open my computer, signed in, and checked that all of my files were intact. They were only updating my virus software, but last time I'd handed my laptop to anyone for maintenance, a week's worth of research had disappeared. I clicked on the Steel folder and pulled up my itinerary for tomorrow.

"You sure you don't mind doing this?"

"Are you crazy? I can't wait." Indie's cell phone buzzed. She looked down, smirked, and turned the phone to face me. The screen displayed a cartoon picture of a jackrabbit.

I downloaded last week's game statistics from the company database as she answered. "Devin, sweetie. Can you do me a favor?"

I half listened to one side of the conversation as Indie asked her neighbor to feed her fish.

"The food? Yes. It's in my bedroom. The small end table next to the bed." There was a pause and then, "That would be great. How about if I make you some dinner when I get back to thank you?"

She was smiling like a Cheshire cat when she hung up.

"What are you up to?"

"Nothing. Just being a friendly neighbor and asking Devin to feed my fish."

"And you keep the fish food in your bedroom drawer?"

She shrugged. "It's Manhattan. Storage is at a premium."

I squinted at my all-too-happy friend. "What else is in the drawer?"

She stood. "Why, whatever do you mean?"

"Did you or did you not just direct Pothead to go into your drawer that contains a vibrator and fish food?"

"No!"

My face called bullshit.

"It doesn't have a vibrator in it. Moved that to my underwear drawer."

She walked to my office door. "It has black lace lingerie, fur handcuffs, condoms, and flavored lotion. Leave at ten tomorrow?"

"Yes. And Indie?"

"Hmmm."

"Thank you for doing this."

I'd barely slept last night. The thought of having to go into the Steel locker room tomorrow and pretend that everything was fine made me feel like vomiting.

I wasn't sure what I thought would happen after I ran out of the Regency four days ago, but it certainly wasn't what happened. *Nothing.* Nothing had happened. I had never been the kind of girl who wanted to be chased, but some sort of attempt at contact would have made me feel better. It made me wonder if Brody had just gone back into his suite and moved on.

But then I'd seen a picture of him walking into practice the other day. His eyes had been dark and sunken, his head hung down in defeat. Against my better judgment, I called the press photo up on my computer. He looked like he'd singlehandedly just lost the Super Bowl.

It was all I could do to stop myself from calling him every time I saw it. And apparently I was into self-inflicted pain—because I had made a point of looking at the photo an awful lot over the last few days.

A piece of me felt guilty for running away from him after he had just laid to rest a woman he cared for deeply. It had been two years since my dad died, and the agony of the loss was still fresh some days. But then I remembered that Brody wasn't alone. He had *Willow* to console him. I needed to force myself to remember that every time I got the urge to call him. And what if I called, and she answered the phone?

"You ready, Thelma?" Indie popped her head into my office.

"You bet, Louise."

The drive to Maryland was five hours, although it actually went by quicker than I had expected. Indie was one hell of a road-trip companion. Not only did she stock us up on road-trip essentials— Pringles, trail mix, and Cheez-Its—but she somehow managed to keep my mind off of all things Brody Easton, for at least a few hours of the drive.

Our hotel was near the stadium. The corporate travel office had booked a block of rooms, knowing the city was going to be a madhouse during the days leading up to the first playoff games. I wanted to switch to anywhere the Steel weren't staying, but the city was booked solid. As we neared the stadium, Indie broached the subject.

"It's going to be impossible to avoid him. I scouted the nearest ice-cream shops. There's a Baskin Robbins one block to the east and a Scoops about four blocks to the west."

"Thanks." I chuckled.

"Can I ask you something?"

"Of course."

"You have to promise not to get pissed at me."

I didn't like the sound of that. "Okay . . . "

"You believed Brody that he didn't cheat on you, but you don't believe that he is over Willow?"

It didn't make sense, but for some reason, that *was* what I believed. "Yes."

"Have you wondered why you believe him about one thing, but not the other?"

Even though I had pretty much done nothing but think about everything that had happened the last few days, if I was being honest, I actually hadn't questioned why I would trust him about one thing, yet not the other. "I guess it's because I feel like he can control his desires, but he can't control his heart."

"But how do you know his heart still loves her?"

The question seemed ridiculous to me. "He loved her and lost her. Why wouldn't he still love her?"

Indie reached over and took my hand. "Sweetie. Are you talking about Brody and Willow or are you talking about you and Drew?"

e ──────────────── *e*

Michael and Indie chatted away during dinner. There were six of us from WMBC having a business meeting at the hotel's steakhouse, although we really hadn't talked much business at all. I tried in earnest to enjoy myself, but a perpetual state of glum followed me around like a shadow I couldn't outrun.

"What's your thinking on it, Delilah?" Marvin Clapman was the head of the station's engineering division. He was one of the few remaining employees who'd been there since the station was founded forty years ago. Having worked his way up from equipment repairman, he was now responsible for everything from the microphones working to the feed making it to the television in the viewer's living room. And he was staring at me expectantly, waiting for an answer.

"Um, I'm sorry, could you repeat the question?"

His eyes narrowed. "The Pro Bowl. Is it better for the station that they keep it during the bi-week between playoffs and the Super Bowl?

Or should it come after, so the players from the two teams in the Bowl that were selected can go?"

"Oh. I think it's better for the station that it stays in the bi-week. People want something to watch during that off week, so the advertising is prime. But it's better for the players for it to be after."

Luckily, Aileen Fisher, one of Marvin's department heads, jumped into the conversation, so I was off the hot seat. I tipped my head back as I downed the last of my wine and looked through the bottom of the glass. There was a commotion near the front of the restaurant. My stomach sank at seeing familiar faces. Familiar *player* faces.

The entire restaurant paused their dinner to watch the hostess seat them. Even if they weren't famous football players, the sight would still have caused a hush. Six extraordinary large men dressed in suits, one louder than the other. I breathed an enormous sigh of relief at not finding Brody amongst the crowd. Until I saw that the party of six was being seated at a table for eight, with two empty chairs.

If I was distracted before, I was totally useless as I stared at the door, waiting to see who would fill the vacant seats. Indie was sitting diagonally across from me, and her eyes took in my panic.

I knew the minute he walked in the door. I had been looking down at my cell phone in my lap, desperately trying anything to keep distracted, when a faint murmur began. The sound grew as the men made their way into the restaurant. Brody was with the offensive-line coach.

He didn't see me at first, but I couldn't look away. He looked sad, tired even, his normally cocky smile nowhere to be found. It opened a crack in me, and I was suddenly nervous that a wave of emotions would smash that crack open wide, and I wouldn't be able to control myself sitting in the restaurant.

Halfway to his table, he stopped. I watched his eyes roam the room, searching for something. Since the day I'd met Brody, I'd felt him before I could see him. It seemed impossible, so I thought it was just my crazy romantic heart playing tricks on me. But when his eyes landed on mine, I knew I wasn't crazy. He had felt me in the room and searched for me.

Our gazes locked. The impact of seeing the hurt in his dimmed green eyes was like a direct blow to the chest. I felt as though someone had kicked my chest open with a steel-toed boot and reached in and gripped my heart in their hand.

We stayed that way for a few seconds, yet it felt like so much longer. Then, somehow, his eyes managed to hold mine while they swept over the table. His jaw tightened at finding Michael Langley sitting next to me. I saw the shutters go up on the window of pain in his eyes, right before he turned his head and walked to his table.

"What the hell just happened?" Marvin said. The entire table had been watching the exchange go down. With his head buried in equipment, Marvin was quite possibly the only person at the station who didn't know about my relationship with Brody.

Indie kicked Marvin under the table and answered for me. "Just some baller making goo-goo eyes at a pretty girl."

The waitress appeared from nowhere. "Are you ready to order your main course?"

"I'll have an apple martini."

"Okay. And for dinner?"

"I'm not hungry."

Indie mumbled, "Shit," under her breath. Rightly so. I wasn't much of a drinker. And the last time I drank martinis, I was in bed for two days. I couldn't even remember half the night. At the time, I'd thought it was the scariest thing ever and never wanted to get that drunk again. But right then, I wanted whatever it would take to make me forget. And fast.

During my first martini, I stole fleeting glances at Brody.

During my second martini, I glared at him like he had just kicked my dog.

After my third martini, I could barely hold back tears.

He never looked my way all night.

Indie saw my face and wrapped up dinner as quickly as possible. When we stood to leave, I couldn't hold the tears back any longer. They came so fast, they blurred my vision. When I wiped them away, the only thing that was clear was Brody staring at me from the other side of the restaurant.

        ℮ ——————————————— *℮*

I nosedived into the bed. Indie tried to get me to undress, but I was dead weight. She only succeeded in rolling me over and tugging my jacket off. She slipped off my shoes. "You okay?"

I nodded and pulled my knees up, wrapping my arms around them. At least the crying had stopped.

"I'm going to wash my face and brush my teeth. You need anything?"

I shook my head. Alcohol made me mute.

She was tying her hair into a knot on top of her head when there was a soft knock at the door. She went to the door, sighed loudly and walked back to me. "It's Brody. I'll get rid of him. Stay here."

I nodded, doubting if I could get up even if I wanted to.

"Is she okay?" Brody's voice was low.

"She's fine. Just needs a good night's sleep."

"I want to see her."

"I don't think that's a good idea."

"You seem like a good friend. But just so you know ahead of time, I'm going to lift you up and deposit you outside this door if you don't move out of my way."

"Brody . . . " Indie warned.

I stumbled from the bed. "Let him in. It's fine. I'm drunken not so much."

Indie shook her head. "Drunken not so much, huh?"

I waved her off with my hand. "He's used to it. Dealing with plastered women. Right, Beaston?" (My attempt at Brody Easton obviously had failed.) "Maybe that's what I should have done. Smoked some heroin and then he'd fall deeply in love."

Brody's jaw flexed.

I turned to Indie, wrinkling my nose. "Do you even smoke heroin?"

Indie shrugged; she looked very uncomfortable standing between us. She turned to me, cupped my face in her hands and held my eyes. "Do you want me to stay?"

I covered her hands with mine. "I'm fine."

She searched my face, then nodded. Walking straight up to the hulking, brooding man standing in the doorway, she jabbed her finger into his chest. "I'll be back in fifteen minutes. If you hurt her any more . . . so help me God. I'll blow the first guy from housekeeping with a set of passkeys, sneak into your room while you're sleeping, and when you wake up, you'll think Lorena Bobbitt had visited."

She grabbed her running shoes from the closet and disappeared after one more menacing look.

Then it was just a slightly drunk me and Brody.

"Can we sit down?"

"Why? You're not staying long."

Brody clenched his teeth so hard, I thought he might crack a pearly white. "Because you're swaying back and forth. Thought it might be better if you sat your ass down."

I turned back to the room. *Not* because he wanted me to sit, but because the room began to spin. I sat on the edge of the bed. Brody stood in front of me.

I looked up. Even in my intoxicated state, I could see my future with just a glimpse into his green eyes. I was suddenly terrified. My eyes darted around the room. The dresser, the TV, the other bed . . . anywhere but at the man standing right in front of me.

He kneeled down. "Delilah?"

"You should leave. There's nothing to talk about."

"Bullshit."

"Nothing happened."

I stared at my hands for a moment. "It doesn't matter."

"Fuck if it doesn't."

I waited and then dragged my eyes up to his. "Do you love her?"

He closed his eyes and took a deep breath before reopening them. "Yeah. But not like you think. We have a lot of history. I just don't want to see her hurting herself anymore."

When I looked away again, he put two fingers under my chin and lifted so our eyes met. "I love you, Delilah."

"You can't love two women at the same time."

"You can. You just don't love them the same. If you fall in love with someone else, the other person you still love was never meant to be yours forever."

His words eviscerated what was left of my fragile heart.

I couldn't do that to Drew. I just couldn't.

Brody covered my hands with his. "Do you love me?"

I didn't answer.

"Delilah?"

I couldn't love him. I still loved Drew.

I was terrified, as I looked into his eyes, that he could see through my lie. "No. I don't."

CHAPTER 38

"You look like shit."

Every time I blinked my eyes, my head throbbed harder. I attempted to lift my aching skull from the pillow but had to put it back down again. It was nearly four in the morning when we finally went to sleep. I'd cried so much, I was certain the headache was caused partly by dehydration.

"What time is it?" My voice was a groan littered with cracks.

"Time for you to get your sorry ass out of bed."

I pulled the cover up over my head. "I liked you better when you felt sorry for me and sat up handing me tissues from the box." After Brody had left, Indie held me for hours while I cried. I cried right through intoxicated and straight into a hangover.

"You have to be at the pregame at one, and it's going to take you an hour to get the swelling under your eyes down. I ordered you breakfast. Dry toast, a pot of coffee, orange juice and a side order of ice for that face."

I pulled the blanket down enough to poke one eye out. "Where are you going?" She was tying her shoes.

"For a run."

"Ugh." I pulled the cover back over my head.

"There's two Motrin on the table next to you and water. Suck it down and stay in bed until room service knocks."

"Yes, Mommy."

She chuckled. "Be back in an hour. Don't fall back asleep."

e ——————————————— e

At least I look way better than I feel. I stared at my reflection in the shiny metal-and-glass door in the hallway leading to the locker room. The Steel had won 21-14, with Brody running in the winning touchdown with thirty seconds left in the game. He deserved to be happy. The last week had been awful, to say the least. A lesser player might not have been able to focus and play the way he had. I was proud of him, but also extremely anxious to walk into that locker room.

Playoff games had triple the number of reporters. Everyone needed a sound bite for the news tonight, and most wanted more. The lines to speak to the players would be an hour long. We had three reporters going in today, not just me. Nick approached with Michael Langley at his side. "You ready?" Nick had flown in this morning, and I doubted he knew that Brody and I broke up.

"Yes." I picked up my bag and started to follow, but Michael stopped me, putting his hand on my arm.

"You okay?"

I forced a smile. "I'm ready. Don't worry."

"That's not what I asked. Are *you* okay?"

I took a breath. "I will be. Thank you."

He nodded.

We waited in line forever and worked out our attack plan of player interviews. Michael claimed Brody and a defensive lineman who'd recovered a fumble. Indie had mentioned seeing Michael at the gym this morning, and I had a feeling that she had filled him in a little— enough to make sure I didn't have to interview Brody. I was grateful for the reprieve. I picked two of the less exciting players, careful to also stay away from Colin, who happened to have had the best game of his career. It meant the lines for my interviews would be the shortest.

I tried to avoid stealing glances at Brody, but my eyes didn't follow my brain's direction. He was wearing his signature towel wrapped around his waist, but his cocky smile was nowhere to be found. At one point, Nick, Michael and I were standing in the open center of the locker room, and my eyes locked with Brody's. He was between interviews and waiting for Angie Snow and her cameraman to finish setting up to film. A pang of jealousy hit me. Angie was gorgeous—young, blonde, curvy and very touchy-feely. She said something to him and reached out to touch his arm, and I had to look away. But like a bad car accident, I went back for more gore.

Brody's eyes flitted back and forth between Angie and me as he spoke to her while her cameraman tinkered with his equipment. I was so preoccupied with watching the two of them, I didn't realize Michael had asked me a question and was waiting for a response.

"Delilah?"

"Hmmm?" I turned to Michael.

He furrowed his brow. Then leaned into me and whispered, "We can handle this if you need to take a break."

I assured him I was fine and just a little overwhelmed by the craziness of my first playoff locker room trip. When Michael had leaned down to me, his hand had gone to the small of my back. I hadn't even realized it was still there until I saw the look on Brody's face. His eyes were burning into where Michael was touching me. He looked furious, about to blow. I must have looked like a deer in the headlights when his eyes lifted to meet mine.

Angie's cameraman said something, and Brody's attention was forced back to the impending interview. Just as the light flashed on Brody and the cameraman lifted his camera into position, Brody glanced over at me one more time. It was the exact same minute Michael leaned in again to say something. I grimaced as I watched Brody's face shift from angry to an evil smile.

He turned his focus back to Angie, and she shot her first question off. His response played out in slow motion for me. He grinned wide, then his hand slowly went to the knot at his towel, and he gave it a little tug. It fell to the ground. I didn't stick around to watch the rest—I already knew what came next. And my guess was that Angie wouldn't put up half the fight that I had.

Delilah
CHAPTER 39

January 15th—Drew would have been twenty-six today. This was the first year that I wouldn't be spending his birthday with his family. Mr. Martin had retired a few months back and had finally convinced Mrs. Martin to move to Atlanta, where Drew's sister already lived. I was happy for them, but when they packed, it meant they had to pack up Drew's things. Even last year, six years after Drew died, his room had been untouched when I went over to celebrate his birthday.

The car ride out to the cemetery was long. I was alone with my thoughts and tried to recall memories of the good times Drew and I shared. Homecoming, senior year in high school. I smiled. Some of the guys from the team had booked a few hotel rooms, and we all went back after the game.

That first time Brody kissed me in his hotel room, it hit me so hard, I wouldn't have been able to stand if he wasn't holding me so tight.

I forced Brody from my head. Again. It was becoming a full-time job lately. A plane from the nearby airport was flying low overhead in front of me. I remembered back to when Drew and I flew to Alabama to meet the football coach of the college he was planning on attending. It was my first flight, and my nerves were on edge. Drew had held my hand and calmed me by telling dirty jokes.

Brody took my breath away on the plane with a kiss and tried to stick his hand up my skirt under the blanket.

I switched on the radio station. It only jumbled my mind more.

Pulling up to the cemetery, my phone buzzed, so I put it on speakerphone and sat in my car to talk.

"Hi, Mrs. Martin."

"How many times do I have to tell you to call me Jana, dear?"

I smiled. "Hi, Jana."

"That's better. How are you, sweetheart?"

"I'm good. How are things in Atlanta?"

"Hot."

I looked at the temperature on the dashboard. *Thirty-five.* "Wish I could say the same."

We talked for a while about the move and how they were settling into Atlanta life. Then she surprised me. "How are things between you and that handsome quarterback going?"

The fight between Brody and Colin had brought my relationship with Brody into the news. I'd wondered if it had made its way to Atlanta. "Um . . . we're not . . . "

"Oh. I'm sorry, honey. I just thought . . . well, I saw some pictures of the two of you, and the way you looked at him . . . I just thought maybe you had found someone."

"The way I looked at him?"

"You looked happy. I thought I saw the way you looked at Drew in your eyes. I was hopeful."

I didn't know what to say. "It didn't work out."

She was quiet for a long time. I thought maybe we'd been disconnected. "Mrs. Martin? Jana?"

"I'm here."

"Oh. I thought I lost you for a minute."

"Sweetheart, I could be totally out of line, but I'm going to say this anyway. Do you remember a few weeks before the draft when you broke up with Drew? Because you wanted him to be able to focus on school and football, and he didn't want to leave you behind?"

"Yes."

"You cared about him so much, you wanted him to succeed and be happy, even if it meant you didn't get to be with him."

"I remember. I told him I didn't want to go out with him anymore. He was pissed for about ten minutes, then stormed back in, realizing what I was doing. He could always see right through me."

"Well, he felt the same way about you, you know."

"I know." There had never been any doubt in my mind that Drew loved me.

"But do you understand what I'm saying? Drew would want you to meet someone. He would want you to move on. Be happy. Fall in love. Have a family someday."

"Of course he would. I just haven't met anyone who could replace Drew."

"That's what I worry about, Delilah. No one has to replace Drew. He'll always have a place in your heart. But you can love two men at the same time. You just love them differently."

It wasn't lost on me that Brody had basically said the same thing.

"Thanks, Jana."

"Don't be afraid to love again, dear."

I spent a long time that afternoon sitting beside Drew's grave. Unlike other times I came to visit, my time wasn't spent crying. Instead, I thought about what Jana had said. Was I afraid to love again? Light snow started falling before I left. Unlike most New Yorkers, I loved the winter. Hot chocolate, bright lights, warm sweaters, snow, and football.

I leaned my head back, opened my mouth, and stretched my arms wide to catch the flakes as they came down. After a few minutes, I wished Drew a Happy Birthday and headed back to my car. Reaching the sidewalk, a hundred feet from the warm confines of my Jetta, I slipped on that pretty white snow I'd just been enjoying. I wiped out, landing on my ass with both feet up in the air. For some reason, I went hysterical laughing. An elderly man walking by with his wife stopped to help me up, but I waved them off, unable to speak through my fit of laughter.

I sat there alone on the sidewalk, the snow frosting my hair white, and cackled until my laugh turned into a cry. The cry turned into a sob before I finally got up. My teeth were chattering, my lips were swollen from the bite of winter, and my body trembled. I was a mess . . . but for some reason, everything seemed to be clear all of a sudden. It wasn't that I was afraid to fall in love. I was pretty sure I had done that already. I was afraid that if something happened again, I wouldn't be able to get back up.

Brody

CHAPTER 40

"Ready to go, you damn cripple?" Grouper took his time getting up, his bones creaking as he lifted himself from a chair in the dining hall.

He wagged his bony finger at me. "You should be so lucky to be in as fine a shape as I'm in when you get to be the ripe old age of sixty."

"Sixty? Who you kidding? You have age spots older than sixty."

Grouper grumbled something under his breath. He lifted a box off the table. "This is the last of Marlene's things. There's a nice little gold cross necklace in there and some old coins—not sure if they have any value or not. Everything else is pretty much paperwork. We donated everything to Phoenix House like you asked. They were pretty excited to get all those clothes. More than half of 'em had the tags on still. You sure did spoil her."

"She deserved it." I took the box from Grouper and waved goodbye to Shannon at the nurses' station as we walked to the front door.

"That place said you'd be surprised at how many of their patients aren't young kids anymore. Drug and alcohol rehabs are more than thirty percent women over the age of fifty." He shook his head. "Would never have guessed."

I didn't know the statistics, but I knew Marlene would want her stuff to go to a place where people were trying to get help. "Thanks for taking care of that for me."

"You gonna bring the cross to Willow?"

"I'll mail it to her. She moved upstate yesterday. Her roommate from rehab bought a place up near Saratoga, and Willow needed to get out of the city. Place she was living had too much temptation for a recovering addict. It was easier to score drugs from her neighborhood than it was to buy milk. Marlene left her a nice little chunk of change, so I'm hoping it starts her on a new life."

He nodded. "That's good. Marlene would be happy about that."

We picked up Grouper III and one of his buddies on the way to Media Day. The two of them were wearing Easton jerseys and didn't shut the hell up in the back of my car the entire way to the stadium. Their excitement was contagious.

"They always that loud?" My eyes slanted toward Grouper.

He nodded. "The Good Lord made old people go deaf for a reason."

Even arriving at Media Day four hours before the start, the place was mobbed. More than two thousand members of the media from all over the world and four thousand fans were expected to attend the day's event, which was the unofficial kickoff to the Super Bowl next week. If today turned out to be anything like previous years, the crowd on the field would resemble more of a circus than a news event. Crazy fans dressed as superheroes, women with painted bodies, and questions that were often off the wall.

The league had set up extra security and a valet, with a roped-off parking area for each team. I navigated the signs to the Steel entrance. "Once we get inside, keep a close watch on those two. The fans can get pretty rowdy."

Grouper smiled. "Such a big softie under all that hard ass. Do your teammates know what a wussy you really are?"

"Bite me, Flounder."

The valet sped off with my car, hitting the gas with a lead foot, and the four of us walked to the entrance through wooden police barricades. Both sides were lined with fans who had probably camped out all night. I hoisted Grouper the third onto my shoulders and walked to the crowd lined up three deep to sign autographs.

A kid about fourteen or fifteen had half his body leaning over the wooden barricade. I took his first, scribbling my name, then held the pad and pen up to my passenger. "You want both our autographs, right?"

The kid nodded, even though he had no idea who the boy on my shoulders was.

"You sign too, little fish."

"I don't know how to write my name in script."

"Just fake it. That's what I do. Scribble a lot."

Guppy balanced the pad on top of my head and did as I told him. The crowd got a kick out of it. We signed for fifteen minutes and then went inside before I got fined for being late to the pre-event team meeting.

I handed Grouper and the guppies VIP badges to wear around their necks and fan admission tickets. "Back here at six?"

"You got it, boss."

"Boss? Now you're talking." I grinned at Grouper. "I like it."

Fifteen minutes before the event was to start, I stood alone in a luxury box high above the swarm of people on the arena floor. I looked out through the glass window and sipped from my water bottle. Both sides of the arena were lined with booths set up for each of the starting players to sit in. Microphones dangled from wires high above the ground, and I knew from experience that crowds of reporters would soon be yelling their questions and shoving even more microphones in our faces.

This week was the pinnacle of what every player worked for—making it to the Super Bowl. Yet I hadn't felt like celebrating with the rest of the team after our meeting. Instead, I'd ducked into the first private area I could find so that I could take a few minutes to look for her. It had been ten long days since I'd seen her face, and I would take whatever glimpse I could get. Now I knew what a fan felt like stalking a player.

Part of me was still pissed at her for saying she didn't love me. But a bigger part of me didn't believe it was true. Her eyes had said something different than her lying lips. After my anger had subsided, I'd replayed the last few months over and over in my head. A wounded chick playing a mix tape that her ex made her before he dumped her had nothing on me. The only good thing was, every time I was exhausted at practice, I thought of that douchebag Langley with his hand on my girl's back, and I suddenly had a fresh burst of energy. Angry energy, but it worked at my job.

Finding her in the crowd of thousands took less than a minute. I guzzled the last of my water bottle, following her with my eyes. She was wearing a black dress, a fitted red blazer, and had on high-heeled black leather boots that came up to meet the hem of her dress. Sexy as all fuck, while showing barely any skin.

Suddenly she stopped walking and looked up, scanning the arena as if searching for something. When her eyes found mine, even across half a stadium, it was all the sign I needed. This shit *was not* over. And I was going to find out once and for all why she was pretending it was.

Delilah
CHAPTER 41

I'd thought about calling Brody dozens of times over the last week. Even called up his contact on my phone on more than one occasion, but each time I only ended up staring at his name. What would I say? There wasn't much that I remembered clearly from that last night in the hotel room, but the way he looked when I told him I didn't love him back was burned into my memory. It was the one thing I didn't want to remember, and yet the only thing that kept haunting me.

You know that feeling you get when someone is watching you? Well, multiply the intensity of that times a thousand, and that's what made me look up. I felt it in my bones, in the acceleration of my heartbeat, in the sheen of sweat that broke out on my skin. The question was definitely not *Is Brody looking at me?* The only question was *Where is he watching from?* It didn't take me long to find out, and I couldn't look away, even when I should have. When he turned away without looking back again, it was like pouring salt on an open wound that refused to heal.

Staring up at an empty luxury box, I paid no attention as I walked. The mass of people swarmed in all different directions, and I smacked straight into the back of another reporter. It had to be Angie Snow of all people.

"Delilah Maddox." Her smile was sugary sweet, but the intonation in her tone was false.

"Angie. How are you?" There were very few women in the world of men's professional sports. It wasn't like we had a club or anything, yet we all knew each other's names and faces. I'd met Angie at an event a few years back. We were both covering college games still.

"I'm good. A little disappointed, though."

"Disappointed?"

"Easton. You're a lucky girl. I thought you were done with him, and he was back on the market. I didn't realize you were still together."

I'd had my nails done that morning. The thought of getting them shaved into sharp points next time suddenly popped into my head. "We're not together anymore."

"Oh. Good to know." She smiled, and I folded my fingers into my hand, digging my nails into my skin. "Well. Good luck today." The blonde bombshell flipped her hair and turned to walk away.

"Wait. Angie. What made you think we were still together?"

"Well, usually when a cowboy shows me his horse, he lets me take a ride on it."

I cringed. "And Brody didn't?"

"Wrapped the towel back around his waist after he intentionally let it fall. And after my interview, when I suggested he give me a private viewing of what was under the towel again—alone at my place that night—he blew me off."

I breathed a little. "Oh. I'm sure that doesn't happen often."

One of her perfectly plucked and dyed eyebrows arched. "Often? It *never* happens."

I felt Brody come up behind me before I heard his voice. Angie's eyes rose above my head as he took my elbow into his hand. "Excuse us a minute, Andy, would you?"

"It's Angie."

The next thing I knew, I was being steered out of the arena and into the hall. Brody kept moving, clutching me tightly to his side as if I might run if given the opportunity. When we got to the entrance to the men's locker room, it was being guarded by Henry Inez.

"Hi." It came out just as nervous as the first time we'd met, maybe more so.

He nodded. "Dam. Mr. Easton."

Brody scrunched up his brow. "I need to use the locker room for a few minutes."

"Not supposed to let anyone in. Even players."

I sensed Brody's anxiety. "We won't be but a few minutes. It's just impossible to escape all the reporters. They can be pretty annoying," I joked.

Henry stepped aside, shaking his head. "A few minutes. That's it. We rotate when the interviews start inside."

"Thanks, Henry." Brody wasted no time pushing the door open. But I stopped. "How's Larissa's arm doing?"

The security guard smiled. "Cast comes off tomorrow. It's a good thing, too. She's threatening to take a saw to it herself to get back on the court."

"That's great."

Brody tugged at my arm, pulling me into the locker room. Inside, I glared at him. "That was rude. I was talking."

"We only have a few minutes."

I folded my arms over my chest.

He grinned. "But it never took me that long to get you off."

"Brody . . ."

His eyes darkened as he moved to me. With every step he took, I retreated, until my back hit a tiled wall. He lowered his face to mine, our mouths inches apart. "I think you lied."

"About what?" I had the immense urge to lean forward and press my lips to his.

He shifted and leaned toward my neck, running his nose along the vein that pulsed with my heartbeat. It was beating out of control, and my breath was joining in on the race. "About how you feel about me.

I think you lied." He moved to my ear, his voice raw. "I think you feel everything I feel."

I said nothing, but the hitch of my breath spoke volumes.

"I bet if I slipped my hand into your panties right now, you'd be as wet as I am hard."

"Brody . . . "

He pulled back a few inches and cupped my face with both hands. "And it's not just your body that has a reaction to mine. I think you feel it . . . " He slid one hand from my chin, down my neck, and stopped when his palm covered my heart. "Here. I think you feel it here, too."

My heart was pounding under his hand.

"What are you afraid of, Delilah?"

He stared into my eyes, so open and vulnerable, and like a coward, I closed mine. Neither of us moved for a long time.

The door to the locker room creaked open. "Easton. Interviews are starting, and the shift is changing. Time's up," Henry yelled, and then the door closed again.

I opened my eyes. My words were barely audible. "I'm sorry."

He pushed my hair back, and his thumb stroked my cheek. His smile was real, but sad. "There's nothing to be sorry about. You'll figure it out."

He let go of me and took a few steps toward the door before turning around. The cocky smile I hated to love was back now. "Oh, and Delilah? Now it's your turn. You'll come around. But when you do, I think I'll make you beg for another chance."

Brody

CHAPTER 42

I felt like a twelve-year-old boy again. In two days, I would play in the motherfucking Super Bowl, there would be an arena half full of women wearing my name on their backs, and here I was jerking myself off in the shower. To say I was frustrated was an understatement.

When I'd told Delilah last week that the ball was in her court, I hadn't been thinking of how often I would see her. Super Bowl week was a media frenzy, and I saw her beautiful face every day. After our locker room understanding, something changed—the anger and hard feelings between us were gone. We were friendly even. Which made it exceedingly harder to keep my hands to myself.

Last night, she'd been at the practice field for a coach's interview. I'd waited around like a damn puppy just to walk her to her car after she was done. When we got to her Volkswagen, she stood with her back against the door, and I knew if I had leaned in and claimed her mouth, she wouldn't have objected. I was more certain than ever that she wanted me; what I needed now was for *her* to be certain it was what she wanted. She needed to push past whatever was holding her back and make the decision to be with me. So I'd intentionally brought up Marlene and how Grouper had cleaned out the last of her things before I brought him and the guppies to Media Day. I casually mentioned that I'd mailed Marlene's cross to Willow, who now lived upstate. She had said that she believed nothing happened between Willow and me, but I needed her to know that Willow wouldn't be part of our lives going forward.

That night at the hotel, after Marlene's service, Willow and I had a long talk. She admitted she had come to my suite hoping for us to get back together. As much as I hated that I hurt Delilah, the conversation between the two of us needed to happen. I needed to say goodbye to her once and for all, and she needed to hear me tell her to move on. It was a long time coming for both of us. While I wished her luck, there was no connection holding us together anymore. And I was good with that. Whatever crack of the door that I had left open for Willow, it was finally shut once and for all.

I had offered to pick Delilah up to drive her to the stadium today for the final press conference since we were both attending, and I was shocked as shit when she agreed. She'd told me to text her when I arrived so I wouldn't have to park, but a car ride to the stadium wasn't enough time with her. So I showed up an hour before our planned departure time and rang the buzzer, pretending that she had gotten the times mixed up.

"I'm sorry. I thought you said eleven."

I did. "Nope. Ten."

When she opened the door, it was obvious she had just gotten out of the shower. Her hair was wet, and she was dressed in a pair of logoed Steel sweats and a pink ribbed tank top—sans bra.

"Nice sweats." *Nice tits.* The damn things were saluting me.

She stepped aside for me to enter. "I'm not ready. But I'm fast. I can get done quick."

I quirked an eyebrow. *Good thing I took care of myself not an hour ago.*

Delilah chuckled. "Such a perv." She waved toward the living room. "Make yourself comfortable."

I watched the sway of her hips until she was out of sight, and then made myself at home. The entire place smelled like her perfume. I sat down on the couch with the remote and flicked on the TV. Every station was talking about the upcoming game. Athletes were superstitious—I didn't like to know the odds before a game, so I hit the off button and looked around. The end table held a photo album that I'd never seen before. Not thinking twice, I grabbed it and started to flip through.

It was page after page of Delilah and some guy, who I could only assume was Drew. He was in a football uniform in half the pictures, and apparently Delilah didn't have to grow into her looks as many women did—she was smokin' hot at every age. Most of the photos looked like they were from high school, but some looked like they might have been from college. The two of them were arm-in-arm in most pictures. Smiling, laughing. A pang of jealousy reared from within when I flipped to one of them kissing. It was probably eight years old, and the poor guy had been dead for almost as many years. God, I was an asshole.

I put the book back on the coffee table and closed my eyes for a few minutes to clear my head. I smelled her come back into the room.

"Do you want something to drink?" She was smiling, and then suddenly her face dropped. I followed her line of sight to the photo album. She walked to the coffee table and picked it up, storing it in the console beneath the TV.

"No, thank you," I said.

She scrunched her face.

"You asked me if I wanted something to drink. I'm good."

"Oh. Yeah. Right." She paused and looked around the room. "I'll just be a few more minutes."

When she disappeared, I stared at the cabinet that Delilah had just put away the photo album in. *Young love. Loss. Football.* It was like a light bulb had turned on for the first time. My head fell back against the couch. How had I not figured it out before? Had I been hit one too many times in the fucking head at practice? I smacked myself in the skull and groaned. *Jesus Christ, Brody. It's so obvious.*

I stood and paced back and forth for a few minutes, trying to gather my thoughts before walking into the bedroom.

"Hey." I leaned against the doorframe and waited for her to come out of her closet.

She came out wearing a navy skirt and a white shirt, with a set of pearls that caught around one breast and hung down to her waist. Classy, yet sexy. Although I preferred the pink tank top without the bra as long as it was just the two of us. "Am I taking too long?" She was carrying a pair of navy heels in her hand.

"No. Can we sit?"

"In here?"

"I just want to talk a minute."

She hesitated but then walked to the bed and sat down on the edge. I kneeled, balancing myself on one knee, and took the shoes from her hand, slipping on one at a time. She looked down at me, confused. "Thank you."

"Anytime." There was so much I wanted to say, yet I wasn't quite sure of the words.

"Everything okay?" she asked

"Other than I'm a dumb fuck? Yeah, everything is fine."

"I don't understand."

"Can I ask you something?"

"Sure."

"And you'll answer?"

"I'll try."

"Why aren't we together anymore?"

She closed her eyes. When she opened them again, her eyes were sad. "I don't know how to explain it."

"Try. I'll listen."

"Well. That night when I came to your suite and Willow was there, I was upset. Jealous even. I hated the thought of another woman near you. But when you told me nothing happened, I believed you. I never doubted you would keep to your word and be faithful."

"But you still think I have feelings for her. The same kind of feelings I have for you."

She looked away. "I don't know what I think."

"Look at me, Delilah."

Tears welled in her eyes.

"You wanna know what I think? I think you loved Drew the same way I loved Willow. And when you lost him, it hurt for a really long time. So much so that you were afraid to do it again." I wiped a lone tear from her cheek. "This whole time I thought you were afraid to fall in love with *me*, that I was the problem.

"It's not you."

"I know that now. You're just afraid to fall."

"I'm sorry."

"Don't be sorry. This makes my job much easier."

"Easier? How?"

"Changing me was going to be a lot of work, but proving to you that if you'll take a chance on me, I'll be there to catch you won't be as hard. Let's face it, I'm an asshole. It ain't easy to change an asshole."

She laughed through her tears. "I think I just need time."

"I'll be right here waiting."

She wrapped her arms around my neck and hugged me for a long time. It wasn't the outcome I had hoped for, but at least I knew I was on the right track.

Delilah
CHAPTER 43

Two weeks after the Steel won the Super Bowl, life had finally begun to calm down. Brody had lived up to his promise—being there for me and letting me take my time. The only time he'd even attempted to touch me was right after he'd won the game. Everyone was celebrating on the field, and he'd managed to find me. He picked me up, swung me around in the air, and then planted a fat kiss on my lips. We both spent the next seven days in a craze. Between media coverage, the team parade, and dozens of interviews, I was surprised he even found time to see me. But he did. Every single day he made time for me. There were no grand gestures or attempts to move things along, either—he just showed me every day that he'd be there for me. How could a girl not fall the rest of the way when she knows she can count on the man she adores to catch her when she does?

The buzzer sounded right on time at three o'clock. I'd asked Brody if he would mind doing a short interview this afternoon down at the station. He'd said yes without hesitation, even though I knew he was pretty much at his limit of cameras in his face. I also knew that he wouldn't listen to me when I told him to text me when he got to my apartment. He always came up. I wasn't sure if it was him being a gentleman or him hoping I would have a moment of weakness, and he wouldn't have to be a gentleman anymore. Knowing Brody, it was fifty-fifty.

I opened the door, and there stood the most delicious man I'd ever laid eyes on. He had on a navy wool peacoat, with a navy-and-light-green plaid scarf that brought out the golden specks in his green eyes. The morning after the Super Bowl, he'd called me saying he had to drag his ass out of bed to shave before the day full of interviews. I'd mentioned I liked him better with a few days of scrub. Since then, I noticed scrub had become a permanent fixture.

"You running late?"

"No. You're early." I was wrapped in a fuzzy bathrobe and had my hair up in a ponytail.

He looked at his watch. "You said three."

"No, I said four." I took a play from his book. Did he really think I would believe I constantly got the pickup time wrong? He thought he needed to be sly to spend an extra hour in my apartment. But today, I was the one being sly.

I rolled my eyes and stepped aside. "You seriously have an issue with time."

"I could swear you said three." *That's because I did.*

"Well. You know the drill. Make yourself comfortable. I'm just going to take a quick shower." I disappeared into the bathroom, and my quick shower turned into a marathon grooming session. I shaved every last hair from the waist down, except for a thin line between my legs. Afterward, I rubbed moisturizer on the entire surface of my body and brushed out my damp hair. Initially, I thought I would traipse into the living room buck naked, and he would figure the rest out. But I decided to do things Brody-style. I wrapped a plush, dry towel around my body and prepared to cross a line there would be no coming back from.

"Change of plans," I yelled from the bedroom as I primped myself in the full-length mirror. "Would you mind if we did the interview here?"

"Sure. Whatever you want."

Brody was watching TV, his back to me, when I walked into the room. I took a deep breath, rounded the couch and stood in front of him. He was slouched down but perked up the minute he saw me standing wrapped in a towel.

"Think I can ask you a few questions, Mr. Easton?" I spoke into my hairbrush.

He furrowed his brow but played along.

"How does it feel to be a two-time Super Bowl MVP?"

"It feels pretty damn good. But I've been asked that question about a thousand times, Ms. Maddox. Don't you have any original questions?" The first time he'd asked me that, I wanted to kick his ass. This time, I loved that he remembered our early encounter.

I arched an eyebrow. "I do have an original question, actually." Nonchalantly, I reached up and tugged at the knot of the towel wrapped around my body. It fell to the floor. "If I told you I loved you more than anything in this world, would you give me another chance?"

Brody stood. His response was serious, and he spoke directly into my eyes. "I'd give you every fucking chance I own to be with you again."

We collided, closing the distance between us. Brody kissed me long and hard, wrapping his thick arms so tight around me, it was hard to breathe. But nothing had ever felt better. He lifted me up into the air and cradled me against his chest. Before I realized what he was doing, he was carrying me into the bedroom. "I hope that's the only interview I really have to do. Please tell me we don't have to go to your office to do another one."

"The only thing you have to do for the next few days is *me*."

He set me down next to the bed and began stripping out of his clothes. He shook his head as his eyes caressed my body. "So you finally admit you love me, but I can't make love to you yet."

"Why not?"

"Because I need to fuck you hard and come inside you in a way that makes me feel like an animal right now."

266

"I want that, too. God, I want that, too."

He lifted me, guiding my legs to wrap around his waist, and turned us toward the wall. "We'll save the bed for making love. But I'm going to take you up against that wall right now."

He kissed me until my lips bruised, and I gasped for air. The restraint he had been clinging to finally snapped, and the way he stared at me like I was his next meal was the most raw and sexually arousing thing I ever saw in my life. My back securely pinned against the wall, Brody's hand slid from my ass to my opening, and he dipped two fingers inside. "Jesus, you're soaked."

He gripped my hips and thrust inside of me. My eyes fluttered closed; it felt so good to be filled by him, so right.

"Delilah, open your eyes."

He pumped into me harder as his gaze held mine. "Tell me. Tell me again."

"I love you."

He whispered over my mouth. "Again."

My body began to build toward climax. My breathing became more labored, and my words turned hoarse. "I love you, Brody Easton. I do."

He told me he loved me over and over again as he thrust deeper and deeper. "I fucking love you," he groaned as he came inside of me.

We stayed up against that wall for a long time with our foreheads pressed together. A moment of utter clarity struck me as we looked into each other's eyes, our chests rising and falling in unison. For the last seven years, I had been searching for peace. I had thought peace was a place where there was no turbulence or fear. Where there were no highs and lows and where happiness was found in the calm at the center. But at that moment, I finally realized peace wasn't about avoiding things. It was about making the choice to live life with all its chaos around you, and in the midst of it all, having calm in your heart.

Brody Easton, the man who'd entered my life like a storm, had turned out to be my calm. How was that for irony?

Delilah

EPILOGUE

I left the house while Brody was still sleeping so I could sneak in a doctor's appointment before heading to the office.

I hadn't expected them to do a sonogram today. My blood sugar had been a little high with my first pregnancy, so they were keeping a close watch. Brody was a nervous wreck about anything that could indicate a problem for the baby or me, so I'd stopped in for my urine test alone so as to not cause him stress on today of all days. It was our anniversary. Or anniversa*ries*, to be exact.

"Your sugar looks good, Delilah. Since you're here, why don't we also do a quick sonogram? Check your fluid level."

That was new with this pregnancy. Oligohydramnios—low levels of amniotic fluid. Mine wasn't a cause for alarm, but just like my glucose levels, the doctor wanted to keep an eye on it. "Sure." I felt bad for having a sonogram without Brody—the man teared up every time he looked at the screen, even when it was early, and the fetus only looked like a big ol' tadpole.

I changed into a gown, and the doctor came into the testing room. After squirting cold gel across my growing belly, he began to swirl his magic wand around. I heard the strong heartbeat the minute he switched on the sound. After a few minutes, the doctor told me the fluid level had increased, and everything looked good so far. He focused on one area in particular. "Do you want to know the sex today?"

"Really? I thought it was too early."

"Sometimes it is. But this little one isn't shy and is exposing itself to me right at this moment."

e —————————————————————— *e*

I'd only worked part time since our baby was born last year. Two days a week kept my foot in the door and also gave me an excuse to travel with my husband for away games. I patted my belly. Things would get more difficult once this little one arrived.

"Stop feeling yourself up." Indie planted herself in the guest chair in my office and turned the tape dispenser toward her. She unrolled a long strip of tape and stuck it to her face from ear to ear, pushing up her nose to resemble a pig's.

"That's attractive."

A few minutes later, Mr. CUM walked in and did a double take at Indie's face. She just smiled like there was nothing wrong. It made him flustered. "Preseason starts next week. Can I count on you to get that husband of yours in for an interview?"

There was nothing the man denied me. "I'll see if he's up for it."

When Mr. CUM disappeared, Indie raised an eyebrow. "If he's up for it? That man would eat shit for you. Literally."

"Such a lovely analogy." I began to pack up my desk. "I can't let Mr. CUM think my job is that easy now, can I?

Indie's phone buzzed, and her face lit up. I knew who it was without having to ask. A few months ago, she'd met her own baller at the barbecue Brody and I had thrown at our new home in Larchmont. The two of them had been inseparable ever since. It meant I got to spend more time with Indie, which I loved. They had even joined us upstate for the weekend two weeks ago at our newly finished cabin.

She looked up from her phone. "You leaving early?"

"Not early. On time for a change."

"What would possess you to do that? Having a studly husband at home with a baby and carrying around a second one yourself?" She *pfft* at me with a smile. "You have your priorities all screwed up."

"I have to stop and pick up something for Brody for our anniversaries on the way home, too."

"You two really sticking to the traditional present crap?"

We'd been married on the anniversary of the day we met, so we had two things to celebrate each year. "Yep. The first year is paper. Second is cotton."

"Sounds horrible. What did Brody get you? Cotton maternity bloomers and a napkin?"

I laughed. "No idea. We haven't exchanged gifts yet."

On the way home, I stopped at the store to pick up a last-minute gift. I had written Brody a love letter and bought him a cotton shirt that I thought would bring out the color of his eyes. But there had been a change of plans since this morning.

The house was unusually quiet when I walked in. Only Tank, our ridiculously large Neapolitan-mastiff, came to greet me at the door. "Alright, boy." He wagged his tail, and I had to catch the small table near the door he almost knocked over. "Calm down. Where are the crazy man and your sister?"

Dropping my leather laptop case and bag on the floor in the entryway, I slipped off my shoes and headed into the kitchen. It was empty, but there were three yellow sticky notes on the fridge and a small box on the island counter.

Phrase, the first note read in big letters. My husband had taken to watching game shows during the day in the offseason.

The second note read: *Hint (since you suck at games) What you are to me.*

Underneath, on a separate sticky note, he had drawn an arrow, and below it read: *Go to the couch already.*

270

Smiling, I walked to the living room. Brody had piled all the throw pillows on the tufted ottoman. I picked up each one and laid them out on the rug.

D was embroidered in script on a red throw pillow. I used to have a matching M, too, for Maddox. But Brody had thrown that out and replaced it with the next pillow the week after we got married: *E.*

M—This was one I'd never seen before. A new addition to our hodgepodge collection. It was a soft-pink pillow—stuffed with, of course, traditional anniversary cotton—and monogrammed with our daughter's first initial.

Y—Another new addition. Fluffy, pink and embroidered to match the new M. Both of our mothers' names were Yvonne, which was why we had picked it for our daughter's middle name.

B—For Brody. I had added the red embroidered pillow when we moved in together.

LOVE. The rectangular brown pillow Drew had given to me when we were just teenagers. The pillow was tattered and patched and even though it reminded me of him, it also served as a daily reminder of the incredible man I'd married. After Brody and I moved in together, I'd tucked the pillow away in the closet. It felt odd to display a gift another man had given me. One day I came home and found it on the couch. When Brody found me looking at it, he'd wrapped his arms around my waist and told me Drew had helped make me into the women he fell in love with and that the pillow didn't have to hide.

D-E-M-Y-B-LOVE

I rearranged each pillow to spell out the message Brody had left me until I solved the puzzle.

MY BELOVED

I seriously had the best husband in the world. The first time he told me that any man who bought me roses wasn't worth my time because I deserved something unique, I thought he was being verbose. But the man had backed up all of his words with actions since the day I met him. His gifts had always been as thoughtful and unique as he was.

If it was even possible, my heart swelled a little more in my chest as I set out to find my family upstairs. When I arrived at our bedroom door, I heard Brody talking to the baby; he hadn't heard me come up. I stepped back from the doorway and listened to him changing his daughter's diaper.

"You stink, you know, baby girl. Your mother, she always smells amazing. That's probably why you're going to have a little sister or brother barely a year younger than you."

I covered my mouth to stifle my giggle.

"What's with this powder? I can never get this stuff to come out." I heard him smack the plastic bottle a few times and then, "Shit." I pictured him fanning away a plume of white talc.

The tearing of the plastic tape sounded on one side and then the other. Marlene giggled.

"What do you think is so funny, huh? You're the one with no teeth."

The rocking chair creaked, and I knew he had sat with her on his lap. The two of them spent a lot of quality time in that chair lately. He liked to tell our daughter crazy stories when he thought no one was listening. "You know, you look a lot like the lady you were named after with those big pink gums."

"Da Da Da." Of course, she hadn't learned Ma Ma yet. My daughter was definitely a daddy's girl.

Brody started telling the baby some story about her namesake accidentally dropping her teeth down the garbage disposal, and I let the two of them have their time together and snuck back down the stairs. A little while later, Brody came down. His black shirt was half white with talcum powder. He pulled me into a kiss, then leaned down and kissed my belly. "Marlene just went down early. How long have you been home?"

I wrapped my arms around his neck. "Long enough to solve my *Wheel of Fortune* puzzle. I love it. Thank you. Do I win a prize?"

"A big one. I'll give you that later." He winked. "Did you open your box?"

"I didn't, actually. I wanted to give you your present first." I walked over to the bag I had left by the doorway and pulled out a simple white box wrapped with a red bow.

"I took the baby to the park half the day so she would pass out early." He shook the box. "I'm hoping there's a sexy teddy for you in here."

"It would have to be a maternity teddy at this point." My belly was definitely bigger earlier this time around. I rubbed at my bump. "I don't think maternity and sexy cotton teddy go together very well."

"You're nuts. I think you look hot as shit this way. Extra curves." His hands cupped into the universal gesture for large boobs. "Extra tits. I might keep you knocked up for years."

I smacked at his abs. *Hard as a rock.* I really was one lucky woman. "Open my present, perv."

Brody slipped off the bow and opened the box. He scratched his chin, then picked up the brown leather mitt. "You do know this is a baseball glove, right? I play football."

"Wiseass." I took the ball out of the box and handed it to him. "The center of the ball is made of cotton. For our two-year anniversary."

"Oh. Thanks, babe." He leaned over to kiss me, but I put my hand on his chest and stopped him.

"Try the glove on."

He pouted at my rejection but did as I asked. Slipping his fingers inside, he found my second present. After he had removed the rolled-up papers from the glove, he went to toss them on the table.

"Those aren't stuffing. That's your one-year paper anniversary present."

Brody's forehead crinkled as he unrolled the first of a series of sonogram prints. He looked down at the picture and then back up at me.

"What's this?"

"I had to stop in to do a urine test at the OB today. Just to check my blood sugar. My count was normal, but the doctor did a sonogram to check my fluid level."

"Everything okay?"

"Yep. But take a closer look at the picture."

He held them up to his face. "Is that—?"

"A penis."

Brody's eyes flared. He would never admit he wanted this baby to be a boy. In all honesty, he would be perfectly happy with a house full of healthy girls. But if he could pick the sex . . .

He surprised me by lifting me up and spinning me around. "A cock! My baby's got a cock!"

I laughed. "That's one way of putting it."

When he finally put me down, he spoke to my stomach. "Did you hear that, kid, you're going to be a man."

"Um . . . I think he's going to be a boy first."

My crazy husband picked me back up and spun me around again, this time yelling, "A boy, we're going to have a boy! A boy, we're going to have a boy!"

I laughed. When he put me down, he opened the sliding doors that led to the yard and screamed to whoever might hear him: "A boy. It's a damn boy!" He was so loud, the whole neighborhood probably knew now.

I loved that I could give him this gift. We were so blessed; there wasn't much more to ask for in life. We had found true love, had a healthy baby girl and a boy on the way, had friends we adored and jobs we loved. We were happy beyond our wildest dreams. Dreams that weren't even imaginable for either of us only five years ago.

When Brody stopped yelling, he walked to me and cupped my face in his hands, speaking softly. "I love you, Delilah Easton."

"How come you're whispering now?" I teased. "Don't you want the whole world to hear how much you love me?"

He kissed my lips. "Didn't you hear? I just told them."

THE END

Dear Readers,

Thank you so much for all of your amazing support! Please sign up for my newsletter so that we can stay in touch, and receive a SNEAK PEEK at Chapter 1 from your choice of three books!

Visit the link below to SIGN UP now!
https://app.mailerlite.com/webforms/landing/z0d7x2

(You will only receive 4-5 emails per year and never be sold or spammed!)

ACKNOWLEDGEMENTS

Thank you to all of the amazing bloggers that have dedicated their time to read my books. I am forever grateful for everything you do that allows new readers to find me every day. Your reviews, teasers, comments, shares and support are invaluable and mean so much to me.

A special note to some people I am incredibly thankful for—

To Penelope – Thank you for going above and beyond with this book. Editing, searching for images, the title...I'm pretty sure your name should be on the cover along with mine because of all the time you put into this one!

To Julie – For always being there when I need you. (Sometimes a dozen times a day.)

To Cheri – Thank you for the countless hours of searching for half naked men. And for finding the gorgeous body that graces the cover!

To Sommer – For another absolutely stunning cover design!

To Luna – For beautiful teasers and all of your kind support.

To all my readers—Thank you for allowing me to tell you my stories. Your continued support for my books has been nothing short of amazing. It is an honor to provide you with an escape for a few hours. I love your emails and reviews, so please keep them coming!

Much love,

Vi

Facebook: https://www.facebook.com/pages/Author-Vi-Keeland/435952616513958

Website: http://www.vikeeland.com

Twitter: https://twitter.com/ViKeeland

Instagram: http://instagram.com/Vi_Keeland/

Pinterest: http://www.pinterest.com/vikeeland/pins/

Goodreads: http://www.goodreads.com/author/show/6887119. Vi_Keeland

Amazon Author Page: http://www.amazon.com/Vi-Keeland/e/B00AZJ8TT0/

Mailing List Signup: http://eepurl.com/brAP09

Books from

VI KEELAND

Life on Stage series (2 standalone books)
Beat
Throb

MMA Fighter series (3 standalone books)
Worth the Fight
Worth the Chance
Worth Forgiving

The Cole Series (2 book serial)
Belong to You
Made for You

Standalone novels
Cocky Bastard (Co-written with Penelope Ward)
Left Behind (A Young Adult Novel)
First Thing I See

Lightning Source UK Ltd.
Milton Keynes UK
UKHW040730180222
398865UK00001B/26